Love & light,
   now & always!
Morwenna J. Holman
   September 2013.

WESTERDALE

Morwenna Holman currently lives in Morley, West Yorkshire, with a group of rescued cats who are the most precious part of her life. Being a committed vegan, she embraces Animal Rights philosophy and holds strong spiritual views which leave no room for money or materialism.

She has suffered from depression and anxiety all her life, but writing novels, poetry and children's stories helps this, as does walking with friends on the isolated Yorkshire moors. Being psychic and in touch with spirit enables her creativity to flow. But is also lucky enough to have a large circle of supportive friends.

WESTERDALE

Morwenna Holman

WESTERDALE

Olympia Publishers
London

www.olympiapublishers.com
OLYMPIA PAPERBACK EDITION

A CIP catalogue record for this title is
available from the British Library.

ISBN: 978-1-84897-315-2

(Olympia Publishers is part of Ashwell Publishing Ltd)

This is a work of fiction.
Names, characters, places and incidents originate from the writer's
imagination. Any resemblance to actual persons, living or dead, is purely
coincidental.

First Published in 2013

Olympia Publishers
60 Cannon Street
London
EC4N 6NP

Printed in Great Britain

CHAPTER 1

It was late afternoon and a premature darkness, caused chiefly by the advent of a great storm of wind and rain, came down suffocating the village of Scarshead, a remote settlement in the broad northern county of Stradshire. The year was 1825 and the month September, early enough to revel in the annual transformation of the usually satanic moorland that fell away from the narrow streets- mile upon mile of obtuse purple bells that emitted lustre from the swart earth.

The fierce gale, a constant aural roar to the few cottagers of Heldon moor, had, by slow degrees, bent every moveable object in its path into a southern slant, the scant line of fir trees gracing the horizon almost bent double beneath the colossal force. This was a region of grotesque deformity. Gnarled bushes flanked the lower part of the moor, beaten into knots by exposure to the rough weather, feeble chimney pots twisted gracelessly in the blow and even the people themselves became lined and worn scarce before they reached a score of years.

Down the main thoroughfare of the afore mentioned village walked a solitary figure clad in a long, thick coat of some coarse worsted material, carrying upon his back the untidy knotted bundle of goods that marked a traveller. His face was concealed beneath the brim of a broad, weather-beaten hat that drooped weakly at the edges where it was doused with rainwater, a great quantity of the liquid running as a ceaseless rill down the man's neck. This he appeared to regard as the least of his troubles for he peered about him sharply with small gimlet eyes that shone violet in the strange half-light and the expression upon his lips was half of scorn and half of amusement – one thin lip raised in hauteur. His coarse chin was covered with the rough stubble of an untended beard and his complexion could generally be noted as swarthy, reminding any casual observer of the Romany blood of gypsies. His gait belonged to the heavy tramp of the shepherd, labourer or bailiff – in short the lower working man, yet he seemed to emit in his journey a sense of pride somewhat above this definition – as though he looked upon everything only to criticize it. His steps were brisk and rough, he neither paused nor stopped and at last he tramped out of the thoroughfare and on, once more, to the narrow turnpike road that led straight into the heart of the moor.

Along this road he encountered an elderly man who leant upon a stick and kept his eyes low upon the ground in order to gain protection from the assailing wind. When the stranger observed his companion he shouldered his burden a little higher and cupping one hand to his mouth shouted above the fresh roar of the gale,

"Any work doing in this quarter?"

The old man, who was evidently surprised at being addressed by the grim figure, lifted his head and cupped one ear as though to explain he had not heard the stranger's question. At this the other raised his quivering lip and snarled again, "I said, any work doing in this quarter?"

The elder shook his head and gazed up at the vague outline of the village which was swiftly diminishing into the oblivion of night.

"I canna say," mumbled he, continuing on his way.

The stranger did likewise with not a backward glance. His first words had smacked of a rich, northern accent, while the latter had rung with the tensions of a genuinely bad temper. His steps fell into a regular beat once more as he carried on his way to a rough, beaten track among the heather and in a few moments he found himself amidst the silent desolation of the moors. He stopped, gazed skyward to where a small patch of eerie yellow sky shone through the darkness, and uttered a string of jumbled, scandalous curses which would have shocked any passer-by, had any been seen in this lonely spot at this time.

"Damn you!" cried the man in furious tones. "Why do you infiltrate my path with giant boulders which I have no hope of climbing past? Damn your inhuman, spiritless hands that made this dreary world breathe! By Jesu! Every day I live I'll damn your name and blight your earth until it is every bit of it as desolate as this black moorland on a winter's night!"

He spat forcibly, clamped his hat firmly down upon his head and pushing on his burden until it rested more comfortably on the point of his shoulder, he stamped briskly once again along the winding track.

Journeying onward for another two hours brought him into contact with no vague sign of settlement, nor any human presence; his sole companion being the roaring wind and the far-off weird shriek of a goatsucker, one or two other such birds whirring off at the jar of his approaching steps. Sky and earth were as oblivious darkness – no glint of moonlight pierced the clouds and apart from the eerie whine of the gale and the rustle of his footsteps a heavy oppressive silence fell. He continued in this vein for a considerable way, occupied with his own grim inner reflections that matched the drear discomfits of the scenery which fell around him, invisible and sinister in the night hues. Then, suddenly, his weary eyes spotted a solitary light; very faint, very distant, yet no elusive will'o' the wisp in his sight. Accordingly he stumbled on eagerly towards it and soon narrowed it down as the shine of a candle in an unshuttered window.

Presently the grim outline of a mansion rose up before him and his feet trod a hard, stony path which curved from the moorland to an elevated position, ending abruptly in a great hewn door over which hung a glass lantern, creaking piercingly in the soughing of the wind. The stranger stopped, half turned towards the light and observed dimly through the rain and misty windows the flitting of a shadow behind the candle flame which blew it almost horizontal. He raised one hand and banged loudly upon the door. For a moment silence, then far off the angry howl of a dog, a prolonged click and then the never-ceasing tempest of rain.

Suddenly the light was snatched from the window and the long inward scrape of blinds being drawn closely together reached the traveller's ears. He, however, seemed more than content to wait and he took a step forward as if to try another assail on the door. In the darkness his broad, sullen brow contracted, he set his lips together firmly; something in the line of a scowl and remained motionless. A full minute passed by. The stranger stood as silent as if hewn from a rough block of granite from the numerous crags that raised their great heads hereabouts. Then, slowly, he lifted one thick arm and banged again. The wind howled mournfully and rushed in upon him as he stood, inwardly brooding, his black eyes fixed upon the wooden barrier not ten inches from his grim face. Then he raised his narrow orbs and observed carelessly that the great door was falling inwards and presently a lighted candle – the very illumination from the windowsill – was thrust out at him, its flame sweeping his face and all but leaping onto his skin. With one practised clench he wrenched the arm of the hitherto invisible form, which yielded the light, and drew it out into the darkness. He raised the drooping candle to ascertain the nature of the figure he had arrested. The refulgence revealed a small, cowering woman of equal years to her captor – which was then about twenty – a slender, almost wasted body with huge nervous eyes that shone grey-blue in the flame. A little abashed at whose arm he twisted the stranger let go, drew off a fraction and re-directed the light onto the nearby house wall.

The young woman straightened herself swiftly and rubbed the lower portion of her left arm which the traveller had cruelly crushed.

"Were you wanting to see my father?" asked she at last in a hesitant tone when several minutes of tense silence had ensued.

"Yes," replied he, never taking his raven black eyes off her face."Is he within?"

"Yes," murmured she, lowering her own eyes demurely to the ground and backing away until she had reached the door handle. The traveller followed swiftly and grasping her arm once more thrust the half-spent candle into her hand. They mounted the single step inside the door and the young woman barred and locked the heavy barrier, concealing the key within the folds of her vermillion dress.

"You are quite dampened," noted the visitor, reaching out a hand and rubbing the doused material of her dress. She shook her head and gazed, almost apprehensively at the spot he had caressed.

"It is no matter," replied she.

Taking up the candle once more she strode briskly down the draughty hallway and over the bare stone passageway, until she paused beside a huge wooden door beneath which another light shone that paled her own expiring candle into insignificance. She turned the handle gently, opened the door, and ushered in the stranger who found himself in a great, lofty chamber covered lavishly with thick rugs of many colours, strangely shaped chairs and in one corner an immense fire that threw out an all-embracing warmth. Over the carved mantle piece gleamed two oil lamps, a third light flickering softly upon a table; in a small wooden chair near the fire sat an elderly man wrapped in an enormous thick horse blanket and sporting a ragged grey moustache. The woman now approached the figure softly, feeling every movement was closely watched by piercingly observant eyes, as cold and hard as the frozen snows of winter.

"Father," whispered she hesitantly. "Father, are you awake?"

"I am," replied he broadly, sitting up and grasping her hand. "What is it Elizabeth, dear?"

"Father, there is a-a-a gentleman to see you," she said, drawing away uneasily as the stranger approached the fireside.

"Good evening," commented he of the black eyes. "Tis a wild night out there, Mr....?"

"Drayton," said the old man.

"Yes, Mr Drayton, I am beholden to your cheerful fireside for searing my wet clothing. Yet I have not come for comfort – I am come to ask you if you know of some work hereabouts? I have enquired in the village six miles or so back but they are as communicative there as the rocks and stones I passed in the night!"

"Well," returned Mr Drayton seriously, transferring his gaze into the fire grate. "I am not ignorant of work that is begging....Yes..Aye. Remove your damp clothing. Elizabeth will take it. Now sit opposite me. I am not a well man, you must be patient. What is your name?"

"Grimshaw," the stranger replied, coolly fixing his cold orbs on the lovely form of the daughter." My name is Heaton Grimshaw."

And as he spoke he removed his thick coat and pulled the dripping hat from his head to reveal long, thick tresses of curled black hair that framed the almost unhealthy swarthiness of his skin. He handed his clothes to the girl, as he did so he put his arm around her waist and caressed her. Elizabeth drew off hurriedly and the stranger sat down immediately. Mr Drayton, who had not observed the intimate caress, continued the interrupted conversation.

"Well, Heaton, what can you do?"

"Ride as good as any man living, out shoot every gamekeeper in Stradshire and lift enough fish to feed the whole of England without even a rod!"

"Hmm...you are not untalented. What is your age?"

"Twenty."

"Oh you are still quite young!"

"Not at all," returned Heaton with a flash of fury in his dark eyes."I am as strong as any fully grown man, fleet of foot and able to fight any one who says otherwise."

"You are experienced with horses you say?"

"Aye, breaking and training, the lot, I grew up with them so to speak. I climb on any animal and can master it. Now I have said enough. Do you know of any work?"

"Aye, I do," replied Mr Drayton immediately. "You observe a sick man lying here, one who has precious few months to live; a man nevertheless with a horse dealer's yard which I planned to give away to my younger brother over at Garstang Hall in return for his assurance of enough money to end my existence in comfort. Now I am suddenly offered other plans. Do you catch my drift Heaton?"

"Aye."

"With yourself as my manager what need I to give everything up to Joseph's hands? No I have strength in me not to yield. Well, time must prove if you are suitable. Are you content Heaton?"

"Aye," responded the morose young gypsy. "Work is work to me. I am happier mastering something, feeling some less resistant spirit snapping under my will. Aye, I will stay!"

"Good, good, we are agreed. Clap your hand there Heaton and Elizabeth shall bring you some supper. My servant is usually in attendance, but her mother is ill and she was called away suddenly to Scarshead. I do not expect her back at all tonight."

There was a momentary silence, then Drayton bent down and picking up a small brass bell he commenced ringing it until his daughter reappeared.

"Yes, Father?" enquired she anxiously. "You do not feel ill do you?"

"No, no!" replied he. "Elizabeth, Mr Grimshaw is to stay with us. He is to be my manager. Perhaps at last our future is sealed! Warm the sheets in an empty room and bring us a full supper tray. You have walked far today, Heaton?"

"I'll not say where I came from," replied the addressed figure with taciturnity. "But 'tis not many miles."

The tray was brought and the sheets turned down for the guest. Mr Drayton retired almost immediately to bed, for it was obvious he bore the deep, ingrown pain of a long standing cancer that threatened to engulf his body. His daughter helped him tenderly, Heaton no more sorrowing for his sick employer as for the stars in the heaven. He gnawed his meat crudely and lavished great quantities of ale into his empty stomach. Then he sat, darkly brooding in his chair, his coal black eyes choosing frequently to rest on the fair features of she who sat sewing opposite. Now, by the keen lamplight, he could see the thick auburn locks of braided

hair and the countless ginger freckles that graced her otherwise
ivory skin. She kept her eyes fixed severely upon her work, but
he felt instinctively she lamented his presence and he furiously
flung stronger and stronger glances her way.

Eventually she gazed at the clock, folded up her work and
rose swiftly, blowing out the candle and taking the little lamp off
the table.

"Now Mr Grimshaw," murmured she, still avoiding his eyes.
"If you could follow me I shall show you the way to your room."

At this he rose and grasped her cruelly by the arm.

"Why don't you look at me?" snarled he, furiously twisting
her flesh mercilessly beneath his strong fingers."Why spend all
evening avoiding my glances? Am I not good enough for you to
fix your eyes upon?"

"Oh Mr Grimshaw," cried she, turning her face this way and
that, but ever avoiding his."Be kind, be merciful, let me go!"

"Mercy! That is a spent emotion in me. Do not snivel for
compassion – you do not deserve any! You are not so high and
mighty. Now look at me!"

Seeing that she still hesitated, he nipped up her skin between
his fingernails until her arm bled. Wincing from the pain, she cast
him a fleeting glance, then turned away weeping.

"Hush!" murmured he scornfully. "Do not waste salt water
on me. I am inflexible. Come, you have not finished yet."

"I have looked at you," sobbed she. "What more can you
ask?"

At this entreaty he recovered himself, let go of her arm
suddenly and ground his teeth as though checking further traits of
temper. Elizabeth, who was not really so frightened or hurt, gazed
at him again and perceived the almost sullen glance from his
sinister face.

"I was preparing to say that I sincerely hope you will be
happy here," ventured Elizabeth nervously. "But I fear that will
enrage you again."

"Why so?" asked he. "You have a right to speak. Happiness!
Huh, it is not so much happiness I seek as unhappiness. What

right have I, or any other fool, to what you term as happiness? Would you term an existence as happy?"

"I do not entirely comprehend you but, yes, life must be happy. I cannot live without happiness."

"But what right have you to demand it?"

"I have no right," mused she. "And I do not believe happiness can be achieved by demands. No, a great deal of my happiness comes from helping others; from helping Martha, Father and even you if you will let me."

"Damn you! I want none of your help." cried he furiously. "Your happiness is a wasted, transient thing; it has a bitter taste like poison on my tongue. Come away, I am tired of your philosophy. Show me my room and keep the lamp steady!"

She did as she was bid and led him up a long flight of carpeted stairs, hung richly with trails of gold arras and woven tapestry that gently pulsed in the internal breeze. Outside the wind roared fiercely and flung the raindrops out over the wide moor, as though indulging in a ceaseless pleasure.

At the head of the stairs Elizabeth paused momentarily, strode quickly to a partially open door and flung it open wider.

"Your bundle has been placed upon the bed," whispered she. "The sheets are warmed and there is a candle on the dressing table. Father rises at seven. You will probably be expected to be up afore. Down below are ten or twelve horses and we have clients coming every day to pick and choose. Now goodnight!"

She moved away eagerly and he, saying nothing, observed her open a small door to the far right of his, where she drew in her light, shut it quickly, and turned a key before her delicate steps faded away into the darkness.

CHAPTER 2

The transient furies of the storm had blown themselves out by the time the morning was ushered in and the consistent thunder of rain had given place to a watery autumnal sun. Long delicate threads of gossamer formed generously on sheltered surfaces; elsewhere the open ground was miry and churned with the pouring water and the whipping gale that now showed itself as a mere whispering breeze. The solitary gnarled elm that grew loftily beside the mansion's gate creaked only occasionally and reflected the name 'Westerdale' on to a bleak and barren world. Underneath colourless, limpid skies the moorland lowered sinisterly; dark, unfriendly; a world where great sorrows assumed the nature of great joys and where peat bogs strove to catch the unwary traveller. Across the dark heather, its purple soused and diluted by the weather, a few cheerless birds flew, uttering no song but the occasional raucous shriek. They were in general ugly predators like the butcher bird, but here and there a few warblers bred on, food to the hunters around them.

Directly the first vague signs of daylight showed in the eastern corner of the purpling sky Heaton Grimshaw rose and dressed. He had spent a long, sleepless night – weird visions of what he had latterly been through and queer dreams of eternal damnation haunted his waking hours. The softness of the bed beneath him, the warm sheets, coupled with strange thoughts about the woman who lay behind the locked door, all combined to send him into a writhing torment that saw no cessation when he finally slept. He would have felt warmer and more comfortable out where the wind roared savagely and cut the rain-filled night like a knife, where vast quantities of moist drops bathed his head in wetness and swept through the weird canyons of his mind.

There he would have achieved some twisted form of pleasure – some erratic happiness in his own discomfort. Here he was too warm, too safe; he cursed habitation.

Outside the cold clear air blew his tangled locks and cleared the pent-up agony of his night. He began to work.

At seven o'clock he heard sounds of rising in the grey stone house, fleet and dragging footsteps, whispering voices; he paused critically then recommenced his labour. Then at a few minutes before eight, just as he was saddling the tallest and most spirited stallion he had yet observed in the yard, the back door opened and his philosopher of the previous night came out. Observing him discreetly, she hitched up the full splendour of her red velvet gown and ran nimbly across the yard.

"Mr Grimshaw, I would not do that – the animal is barely broken. Come in, come in, breakfast is nearly ready. Will ye not eat?"

"I am not paid to eat," scorned he, vaulting nimbly into the saddle. "Stand back or else be trampled underfoot. By Christ, if this horse is not broken afore I ride him he shall be after!"

Elizabeth stood back immediately and watched him kick his willing mount into a rough gallop. She ran her hand over her left arm and winced in pain. The wound had not, as yet, healed.

When he did eventually come in for breakfast he was marked by drying splashes of mud and brown leaves concealed beneath his fustian jacket. He spoke no words to Elizabeth – her Father being in his study – but ate stolidly avoiding her eye whenever she looked upon him, primarily as an evil-tempered reason to avoid conversation, and not out of any guilt for the previous evening. He felt none, but she accredited him with that much human feeling, felt a little warmer towards him and hastened to explain his taciturn silence as shyness to the newly returned Martha.

A fleet fortnight of autumn days passed away, each one drawing in the light a little sooner in the evenings. Elizabeth scarce caught but a glimpse of Heaton; he was rarely punctual to meals, yet he worked harder and harder as the winter drew on. To

Mr Drayton he was indispensable. He was a sure institution and he slaved from six in the morning until eight or nine at night. He asked no rest, no compassion and no wages save his meagre food and board. The yard unwillingly prospered.

One evening half way through October Martha was summoned to go to her mother's in Scarshead. The old woman was at last drawing her final painful breaths. Heaton was the messenger and in a fit of duty he offered to accompany the servant through the dark, still night. Elizabeth, who had been quietly sewing until he burst into the parlour, looked up and her heart warmed a little more to the grim exterior of this man. What rested beneath? A firm conviction of goodness, ridiculed under indifference – an indifference he strove to keep steady so that none would perceive his disguise? Ah ha! Then she had pierced it and all his cruelties of the first evening were forgotten. She began to conceive a slow yet consistent kind of love for him. Were they not nearly as sister and brother? How would he feel if she caressed him as he had touched her at their first meeting?

She watched him depart with Martha but his eyes never sought hers and a little crestfallen she turned back to her chair.

"Well," murmured her father. "Our orphan of the storm has turned into quite a man do you not think?"

"Yes, Father," faltered she with a little sign.

"It's strange that he has never alluded to any part of his past though. I have not pressed him because he is an excellent worker of few words. Has he spoken to you about it?"

"Me?" cried she. "Why would he say anything to me? After all what am I to him?" And a slow tear fell.

"There, there," coaxed he. "Do you not perceive I know? Do you not know Martha has noticed a great deal amiss with you of late? Angel, are you not in love with Heaton?"

She blushed a little at this but acknowledged that she was.

"Do you not wish he was higher – socially than he is? He is so handsome, Father, yet so silent and so far beneath me I should not think of him."

"No, no, angel," comforted Drayton earnestly. "The time is coming when I shall be forced to leave you. Bodily I shall be nothing. Would it not please my spirit to look down and see you happily married? I can no longer look after you and someone must care for you. The place may as well be Heaton's as my brother's. Joseph is far from sick. He is much younger and he is rich. Heaton has not a penny in the world save what I give him. Angel, all this you see before you is yours – yours and Heaton's. If you possess happiness you will want no more."

She smiled a little at this and when he departed to bed an hour later she kissed him most tenderly and murmured gratefully, "O Father, I pray I may marry well and that you may see my husband before you are lost to God!"

"Whatever your choice shall be mine, Elizabeth!" replied he. "How I wish your mother was here but I know she is happier where she is and I, worn soul, shall soon be with her. Well my dear, are you going to bed yet?"

"Not quite so soon, Father," replied she. "I am not sleepy and I crave to finish the work that I have so neglected of late."

"Very well," acknowledged he. "Lock the doors directly. Neither Heaton or Martha, poor soul, will be back tonight, of that I am sure. Goodnight, angel."

His slow, solemn footsteps climbed the stairs, then the bang of a door and at last silence.

Left alone by the dying fire Elizabeth lay back and watched one by one the faded coals become ash and cinders.

As Martha and Heaton walked slowly over the forbidding moorlands, the latter, who went first and carried the lantern, contracted his pensive brow and putting a hypocritical light into his sullen eyes asked," Tell me, how much longer do you expect Mr Drayton to last?"

"O don't ask me, sir." cried Martha, at once. "I am no doctor. Of course I have been servant there for many years. I knew Mrs Drayton well and nursed her for three months."

"Of what did she die?"

"Of some recurring cancer and it seems to me that the symptoms could be similar. If so it is likely that he only has weeks to live."

"And his money?"

"He has very little. It will go to his brother, I imagine for Elizabeth has no husband."

"Ah but if she had?"

"Well twould go to him and possibly her – along with the business."

"O the business."

"Aye, that'n all, Mr Grimshaw."

He smiled mysteriously at this; his face finding it repulsive that he should indulge in mirth as the dark contours of his visage were not formed for laughter.

"And would you say that Elizabeth had a sweetheart whom she may marry soon?"

The grey-haired servant shook her head directly.

"No, no -yet wait," cried she. "I do know one such person."

"Ah-ha! She is fond of him?"

"Yes, she sighs for him continually, puts sugar in the salt pot when she tries to aid me; yet it is no good. He does not even look at her."

"Who is he then?" asked Heaton curiously. "Am I acquainted with him?"

"Why yes, sir – it's yourself of course!"

A long silence followed this in which Heaton attempted to conceal a strong emotion that pulled the muscles in his face and neck.

"Me!" roared he in furious distaste."Yet, wait- wait a minute. Yes, of course," he whispered calmly. He paused for several minutes as still and silent as the grave, then, turning towards Martha he grabbed her roughly by the arm and thrust the lantern into her fingers, crushing them all together.

Without a word he ran swiftly back along the path until the contours of the land had swallowed him up and there was nothing left except vacant darkness. Bemused, Martha continued on her way and eventually struck the lonely village.

Heaton slowed his pace as he returned to Westerdale and reached there just before the hour of eleven, where he observed a feeble light still to be shining in the parlour and the lonely drift of a figure back and forth in the path of a candle flame. For a moment he waited, his great heaving chest pressed up against the sightless glass, his heart pounding painfully, long wreathes of white breath issuing from his lungs; then slowly his dark, sinister form moved to the door. It was unlatched. He entered swiftly yet silently, secured it with sober hands and trod noiselessly along the passageway from where he burst into the lighted room.

Elizabeth jerked her head back from her reflections in the fireplace and turned round in panic, but when she saw who it was she remained silent and stood gazing at the dark, emotionless face of her observer. He, too, was silent for a moment, sinking back into the well matching shadows of the doorway a wry bitter grimace on his lips. Then, abruptly, he came forward.

"Well, well," sneered he unkindly, walking round her and scanning every line of her body with his cold eyes. "Have you been waiting up for the purpose of welcoming me back?"

"No, no – Where did you get that idea? I am not tired- why should I go to bed?"

"Ah-ha!" snarled Heaton directly. "I am almost moved – not waiting up for me – why you have shattered my every dream and hope!"

"I would have waited up for you many a time," cried she, misunderstanding his sneers as true emotion. "But you were always engrossed in your work – you never looked at me; you never gave me any reason to encourage a love – to cherish an emotion that was never anything but a sisterly affection. Now I cannot see you any other way."

"You feel for me as a sister then and I, in turn, should be the strong protective brother you never had!"

"Do not mock me!" cried she angrily, tears springing instantly to her eyes.

"Madam, you mock yourself!"

She flung herself into a chair and turned away from him. Heaton meanwhile gazed maliciously down upon her.

"Well," cried he at last. "I have come to prove your so-called love true. Come, you may kiss me!"

"I do not wish to," replied she coolly scanning the meaningless pages of her father's daily journal.

"I think you had better," snapped he, pulling a tress of her long hair which split beneath his unfeeling fingers. She started up at this and made a dash for the door, but, he, getting there before her, barred her way.

"Now," snarled he, grabbing her wrist. "You will kiss me!"

"Never!" vowed she. "I will scream for father if you touch me again."

"Pah! Do not suppose I value the life of a cancer-ridden wreck who has precious few days to live anyhow. Call if you like and be damned. If he hears you I will have the pleasure of snapping off his life with my fingers."

"No- I will not call...." placated she in a softer tone. "Heaton...we are nearly brother and sister...let me go."

"Kiss me first," growled he. "Or I will make you!"

Seeing she refused his advances he grew livid with anger and grinding his teeth furiously he dashed her against the opposite wall where he succeeded in imprisoning her and sinking his lips down upon hers. She struggled fiercely for a moment, felt him tearing eagerly at her clothes, and filled with horror at his hitherto latent passions she fell forward in a dead faint into his arms. He raised her swiftly, took his fierce, burning lips from hers and after extinguishing the parlour light he carried her upstairs to his room where he laid her on the bed and locked the door. Then, with a set, bedevilled grimace upon his face he began to undress himself and then the unconscious form.

A sudden, thrilling pain passed through Elizabeth's body, she sat up, opened her eyes and gave a little sob. Beside her two wide leering orbs glared out of the infernal darkness. She gave another gasp of pain and turned away but her mind suggested terrible happenings and feeling the naked blight of her prostrate form she cried out hysterically,

"Oh God, what have you done? Heaton – what have you done?"

"Away with your sobs and wails!" scolded he heartlessly. "What is a woman shaped for if not for- that? Why snivel? I have done with you now. Here, take your clothes and get out of my room."

Sobbing feverishly she rose and dressed herself, he, still naked, climbing into the other side of the bed.

"You do not realise what you have done," wept she. "Heaton...I am finished...finished! This is what I have come to – at a mere twenty years! Maid no more...no more!"

"Cease your infernal row," cried he furiously. "If you do not realise what I have done am I to be blamed for your naivety? You said you loved me....cherished an affection for me like a brother. Ho, ho, Elizabeth, you have been a good sister, but I am tired of you now. Get out, get out!" He gave her a hefty kick with his foot which sent her reeling across the room, whereupon she picked herself up silently and left his chamber.

Another few sunless days passed and the blooming heather waned cheerlessly to a universal brown haze that encompassed the scenery and reminded the moorland farmer that winter was not very far away. Hard, black frosts gripped the land morning after morning, thawing out in windswept places yet retaining their hold in the pits and crannies, the desolate nooks of the moor, until well past midday.

For Heaton life at Westerdale continued in its incessant deluge of work and sleep, the latter frequently haunting him with strange premonitions of a radical change that would raise him out of the spiritual poverty he had fallen into. Towards that he turned constantly; it almost cheered him during the long, dark mornings when ice lay thickly across every watering place and the horses were troublesome. It also cheered him to observe the grave and permanent change in his employer; the increasing pallor of his skin, the faded limbs and nerves, the inability to profit from warmth, food or work. Soon he would also be beyond the faithful love of his daughter, Elizabeth turning white-faced and tremulous to the only person she had learnt to love. Heaton shocked and frightened her. She cherished no more vague ideas of love for him – even as a brother – she fled silently from his path, kept her own council as to his actions and suffered only to remain in his company if another more pleasurable form was there.

She did not doubt that he still lusted after her. There was something almost unearthly in the dark depths of his brooding eyes which could flash glances more revolting than Lucifer himself. Yet her father was excessively tied to Heaton with his illness and every day as Drayton released his hold on some portion of his power Heaton clutched at it menacingly and revelled, commandingly, in his victory.

But soon a time came when Elizabeth could doubt her condition no longer. She strove to keep it hidden from the dying eyes of her father, yet Martha's glances became sharper and more frequent. Elizabeth, against every desire and preservation of her own life, knew she must be united to that which not only abhorred and frightened her but would, within a few years, utterly destroy her.

One November morning she soothed her father into a restless kind of sleep, sent Martha into Scarshead on purpose of purchasing some ribbon for a new gown and then slipped stealthily from the house into the regions of the stables where she knew Heaton was working at this time of day. The long, dim rows of boxes were quiet, the tiny office was cold and deserted so, throwing caution to the wind, she called out to him and in her search plunged into the tack room where she came upon him dusting a saddle.

He looked up at her approach and his black eyes narrowed with either suspicion or abhorrence; she instantly suspected the latter. Eventually he cast down his eyes and began to rub the leather work again.

"Did you not hear me calling you, Heaton?" observed she, angrily, drawing near to him.

"Aye," growled he morosely, not choosing to look up.

"Well?" cried she furiously. "Did you not think to answer me? I wanted you!"

"Damn you! I'm not your slave – you can go to hell before I come to your beck and call!" sneered he nastily.

"Ah, but you are my father's slave," observed she, cleverly, throwing back her head a little haughtily.

Heaton flung down his cloth and pinching her pretty face between cruel, strong fingers he snarled, "Ah, but your father is dying, Elizabeth, and once he is gone I shall be master of everything – even you. There is a proud gleam in your infernal eyes that I do not like but keep it there and when the old bastard has gone I shall take great delight in beating it out of you!"

He removed his fingers, drew off and flung the saddle he had been cleaning upon the highest peg; removing a bitless bridle to which he transferred his cloth.

Elizabeth stood watching him anxiously for a moment then she murmured," Heaton, I have only come to talk to you – and not solely for my sake – but for the comfort of a dying father and for what grows innocently inside me."

He continued morosely with his work.

"Heaton, Heaton- are you listening?" cried she desperately, coming nearer and attempting to touch his hand.

"Keep off!" yelled he. "And lower your voice or we shall have Martha in upon us."

"She has gone to Scarshead," replied Elizabeth in a softer tone. "And Father sleeps like a baby upstairs."

"Aye," sneered her companion nastily. "And he will die like a demon."

"You do not mean that!" gasped she. "Father has always been good to you."

"Good?" echoed he furiously, staring at her with latent eyes. "Good? How can you know the meaning of the word good? You have never suffered in your life!"

"I am suffering now." wept she. "And in many ways I am blameless."

"Blameless – huh! You are as guilty as the next man. You talk of suffering but could you see inside this black head you would know what suffering is all about."

He recommended rubbing the reins of the bridle and she, weeping freely, cried in a begging tone,

"Then do you not care that you have caused a great deal of pain to someone very near to you? I am going to have a baby. Think of that! Think of my poor father, 'twill break his heart!"

"Then Godspeed his end. If it will really kill him you must tell him instantly and have him promptly despatched instead of lingering, wretchedly, as he does."

"Oh, do you not have one ounce of feeling towards your unborn babe, Heaton?" pleaded she."I am not concerned for myself – I do not beg for mercy – I expect none. But the child, the poor child."

"Damn you, get off your knees," snarled Heaton, pulling her up forcibly and re-establishing her on her feet. "What would you have me do then? You know what sort of man I am – what, would you have me marry you?"

Elizabeth gave a sad little sigh at this and murmured, "I would almost rather you beat me to death now with those leathers you are cleaning- yes I would – there! Will that not give you infinite pleasure?"

He did not reply to this but lowered his fiendish eyes to his work. She, meanwhile, laying hold of a length of leather pulled it tightly round her neck.

"Lay off!" cried he, raising his hand and snatching the rein. "Do not suppose such bravery invokes any pity in me."

"I know it does not," replied she. "Yet there must be some way of moving your heart. Oh, Heaton will you really marry me?"

"Good God! What a sentence!" cried he, sneeringly. "Yet I can think of reasons likely to influence me. You will be truly mine when your father is gone and then you shall see what a husband I am."

"Men always love their wives," murmured she, hopefully.

"Love?" snarled he. "Yes, I will show you how powerful my love is, Elizabeth. Have you any idea of the husband I could be? You must expect no affection."

"I have long ceased looking for affection in you," sighed she.

"Good! And you must obey me without question."

"Yes."

"Capital! And you must not mind if I beat you occasionally for 'tis surely the way I show my 'love'. Now, madam, you marry me on these terms, or not at all."

Elizabeth closed her eyes and leant back against the wall, her pallid skin becoming whiter and whiter.

"Oh God," whispered she. "I am torn between the allures of two hells. Yes – yes I must marry you, Heaton."

He gave a sinister smile at this which deepened into a demonic laugh and as she made her way out he clenched the duster between his two hands and tore it to pieces with his teeth.

"Damn you that I must tie myself to THAT for a fortune," soliloquised he. "But she shall bend...she shall break....I will see to that."

His chest heaved sorely, his morose lips trembled and he surveyed the room in which he stood, no longer as a tenant, but as lord and master.

CHAPTER 3

When approached concerning the wedding, Drayton, who perceived at last he was dying, gave his permission cheerfully, thankful to commit his only child into another's hands. He believed Heaton's churlish behaviour arose from a form of shyness, and for his morose, stolid attitude to work the old man admired him. Now, at last, he could die easy; Elizabeth would be supported by an honest worker and loved by one whom Drayton foolishly approved of. He did not realise that with Heaton Elizabeth would be lonelier, needier and more impoverished than if alone in an alien world. His dying eyes saw only that she was provided for and not the abject fear and abhorrence in her face. That much she emitted but deeper, feverish torments she silenced and hid beneath a resolute front. She was as one resigned to her fate, a fate that would not encircle her until her Father died.

The wedding day was settled on as the last day of November. Heaton took no interest in anything pertaining to the union, but spent longer and longer hours in the stables.

"I would rather be there among the breath of the equines than here with you," snarled he, when Elizabeth hinted at her father's complaint at his absence in the parlour. Morose and sullen he wandered the stables as though searching for something he had lost many years ago. When in the company of his future wife he took great pleasure in torturing her or brooding inwardly and turning his devilish eyes away from the outside world. Yet to Drayton he remained as much an honest worker as before.

Throughout Heldon and Scarshead the union was much talked of with fearful rumours attached that one night had the misfortune to reach the ears of the very person it concerned.

Heaton had taken lately to passing the latter part of the evening in the nearest alehouse on the outskirts of Scarshead; a place he more gladly haunted than the warming lights of the parlour where one lay dying and the other weeping softly for her blighted happiness.

Consequently he would leave off work at eight, gallop madly to the Anvil and tethering his horse outside sit morosely at the bar over a pint of ale. The company there grew used to him and hated him all the same for his churlishness, black evil grimaces and his unearthly stares. He scorned joining in their talk or games, but clung closer to the counter and peered fiendishly into his brew. The landlord was highly nervous of him, served him unquestioningly and observed gladly that he paid his money sullenly yet fully, a loud rap upon the counter being the signal that he required more ale.

Towards the end of November Heaton finished work at an earlier hour, vowed he would do no more that night and slouched towards the house, his lantern creaking eerily in the soughing of a strong wind. He hung it in the back porch, entered the house and going straight to his room, changed into a less shabby jerkin before dousing his grimy face with icy water from a large ewer; that done he dried himself roughly, put on his coat and hat and quitted his room, whereupon he spied a motionless figure at the top of the stairs. It was his fiancée.

"Heaton, Heaton," cried she softly as he approached the stairway. "Heaton – don't go out tonight."

"Get out of my way!" snarled he, pushing her roughly by the shoulders.

"No, no you shan't go – not yet!" vowed she, attempting to hold him back.

"Do you want me to knock you down the stairs?" asked he gruffly. "Now, give over. Where I go is no business of yours."

"But it is," she affirmed valiantly. "Heaton, don't go out tonight please. It will be dangerous for you."

"It will be dangerous for you in a minute!" snarled he, aiming a kick at her.

"I am only come to warn you," sobbed she. "Come, stay at home with yer wife."

"Don't use that word to me!" fumed he, starting up and grabbing her cruelly by the throat."If ye have something to say – out with it! "

He released his hold upon her and stood back, Elizabeth choking to regain her breath. Her fiancé uttered a curse of annoyance and started off down the stairs. When he was half way down Elizabeth leant over the bannisters and whispered," Go if you must then and I hope he kills you for what you have done."

"What lunacy is this?" shouted Heaton, furiously ascending and causing Elizabeth to move off swiftly.

"You had best tell me or I shall beat it out of you!" and he stepped forward menacingly.

"Very well," cried she. "Tis my uncle Joseph, who resides over at Garstang Hall, a couple of miles from here or more. He has heard – he has heard a wild story about what you have done to me. Father, thank God, is ignorant of it, but Heaton, take care, Joseph means to have your blood."

"Oh, he does, does he?" sneered the grim figure. "By Christ, I hope to meet him so to strike the first blow. Is he tall....short..fat..tell me how he is built?"

"He needs another six inches to attain your span," murmured Elizabeth, nervously. "He is strong, I own, yet not so old as you suppose, I think about fifteen years or more younger than Father."

"Ah-ha!" cried Heaton, delightedly, a malicious scowl spreading across his face, his dark eyes glistening. He clenched his fists in relishment and glanced at the cowering form of his fiancée.

"Well done, Eliza! You have given me an excellent reason to go out tonight. Nothing could stop me now until I have smashed the old dotard's head to pieces on the flagstones outside this very house."

"Ah – take care," warned she. "I do not wish to become a widow."

"Never fear that!" sneered Heaton. "I will be back for your fortune after Joseph has been taught a lesson." He gave a vindictive laugh and descending the stairs quickly he unbolted the great front door and passed through.

Elizabeth heard the sharp sound of slithering hooves on stone, a bewildered whinny and then the dying sound of galloping which was replaced by the mournful whining of the wind in the storm-blasted branches of the solitary tree. Heaton had gone.

He drew up at the alehouse, wrenched the horse's head over to the left and flung himself off, vociferating curses at the lively steed who danced high-spirited in the gale. Eventually Heaton succeeded in tying him, strapping his head down so tightly that he was obliged to stretch his nose down to the ground in order to ease his cramped neck muscles. Then the morose figure wandered sullenly into the simple building and cast his brooding eyes over the company assembled who proved to be largely the very drinkers he had maliciously regarded on similar evenings. Heaton took his place at the bar, tapped upon the counter by way of a signal for a drink and laid down a coin. The barman was swiftly attentive, the mug was grasped and the stilted murmur of conversation broke out again.

Suddenly the morose drinker broke his customary silence and half turning towards the nearest bench of conversationalists he enquired gruffly,

"Do you know of a person by the name of Joseph Drayton hereabouts?"

"Drayton?" returned the eldest of the aforementioned group, screwing up his eyes pensively and blinking at the questioner. "Aye – well – Joseph, he inhabits Garstang Hall, a big, lonely dwelling several lengths from here, aye – a gloomy swart old place – high as one o' them cathedral things and crawlin' with ghosts!"

"The place means nothing to me," growled the lone drinker."Speak no more of it – what about the man?"

"Joseph?" mused the elder. "Aye, Joseph is all right – a bit hasty – a dubious fault in a body I knows but honest and hard working – a mite headstrong – aye but – Joseph is all right."

So saying he took a long drink of ale and spoke no more, the gloomy questioner doing likewise, requesting silently his mug be refilled.

A tense atmosphere seemed to stagnate in the walls of the alehouse, its termination being in the sound of horse's hooves, the sharp clatter dying away at the doors of the house. The outer door was dragged back and a man appeared through it unfastening a long dark riding cloak. He stepped eagerly up to the bar and casting a dubious glance at the back of the lone drinker he ordered a mug of ale.

"Good evening to 'ee Joseph, sir!" cried out the reproving elder who had voiced his opinions on the man who now stood before him.

"Good evening," returned the newcomer a shade grudgingly, marking that the fierce black orbs of his companion were fastened upon him.

"So," sneered the scornful Heaton," You are Joseph Drayton – blood brother of him that lies quaking into death at Westerdale. Stand to the light, man, so I can see what sort of constitution I face."

Joseph never moved his lower body at all but buried his face in the foaming mug and drank deeply, Heaton leaning back to scorn his adversary further.

Joseph was a heavily built man with large, powerful limbs but he was neither so tall nor so devious, as the fierce gaze he smouldered under. In age he was a good fifteen years younger than the brother he meant to succeed; in short he was only middle-aged. His smooth brown hair was as yet full and he bore a neat dark moustache. His hazy eyes were a dark grey blue; they inclined now to the latter as they sparkled up with ire at being scrutinized. On completion of his examination, Heaton slumped forward, observed his adversary had clenched his fist and gave a scornful laugh.

"Now, sir," said Joseph furiously. "You shall talk to me and bide what I have to say. You are Heaton Grimshaw?"

"Aye."

"By Christ, I am moved already to thrash you within an inch of your life – the inch I leave solely to save her you have blighted. So, she fell for black eyes and lips and a demon's caresses. Is it her fault that you have the power to charm an angel away from the upward paths?"

Heaton's dark eyes sparkled lividly; he moved forward then thinking better of it he returned swiftly to his place. An evil grimace came upon his curled lips.

"The woman was to blame," accused he. "She is paying for it now – deservedly! Yet I, too, have to suffer. I am persuaded into marrying her and being tied to her for the rest of my life!"

"It is less than you deserve," cried Joseph. "Sir, I have a score to settle with you for the sake of my niece."

"Ah-ha," sneered Heaton cleverly. "But it is not seemly to do so here where all eyes are upon us and the very walls have ears. Come then let us go outside – after you sir – there are words I can say to you better under an empty sky."

Joseph rose and cast a coin at the landlord who snatched it up eagerly, then he walked out briskly followed by his scheming opponent who bore a malicious grin that played about his dark lips luxuriously. Heaton waited patiently until they were surrounded by the stagnant darkness of the passage, then, hearing his adversary descending the steps into the yard he thrust out his foot powerfully and sent Joseph sprawling. Heaton then dragged him outside and began to beat him mercilessly.

"Have words with me, Drayton, would you? Mark how well I listen to them eh? No one tells me the steps I take. I marry Elizabeth for her money and not for the sake of any bastard child she bears. Come on Joseph! Are you listening? Speak out man! Have words with me!"

At this the injured man set up a hideous wailing which reached the ears of all inside the ale house and soon brought them out into the road. Two bore strong lanterns, another a thick cudgel with which he threatened the massive Heaton.

No sooner had he raised the weapon than a blow from the maniac's fist felled him swiftly. The others drew back with fear.

"Aye," growled Heaton. "'Tis well you note it – keep back. Keep back!" And grinding and gnashing his teeth menacingly he drew off into the darkness with his insensible charge.

The barman ran to aid the flattened figure who still grasped his cudgel incomprehensibly.

"My God – what a man!" exclaimed one.

"'Tis more like a devil," pronounced the other.

"Aye," cried a third. "For I saw him tear Mr Drayton with his teeth and revel in the blood."

"Peace, neighbours," murmured the barman. "John Long has almost come to and nowt but a broken crown is the worst of it. This night's business is best kept silent – are ye with me neighbours?"

They nodded their heads thoughtfully and shutting the outer door bore the recovering man inside.

Further out in the darkness Heaton flung his unconscious victim across the back of his tied horse whose rein he loosened. Catching the tethering rope of Drayton's mount he vaulted up behind his charge and whipped his horse into a gallop, the other poor beast being forced to follow. Ere long Heaton found himself able to guide his mount by leg only, one hand grasping the jolted body, the other pulling at Joseph's beast. The wild moor wind cut across the open plain and rocked them; the long unkempt manes of the sweating horses streaming freely in the tempest. An unhealthy white lather rose up on the neck of Heaton's horse; the beast shuddered for breath and slackened his speed, whereupon his rider dug his spurs savagely in his sides and uttered a furious curse. Gradually the boggy heather and peat churned beneath the horses' pacing hooves, gave way to a slippery surface of gravel and sharp stones. In another instant the dimmed lights of a lonely dwelling shone out and to these lights Heaton now directed his steed, knowing them to be the half spent candles of Joseph's house. This dwelling he had cause to pass whilst delivering or collecting horses from Scarshead. Soon the hooves struck a beaten path, Heaton recommenced his strangle hold upon the reins and yanked his horse to a walk, keeping him there by a merciless check of rein that pulled the very corners of his mouth. Slowly the strange group drew up at the house front whereupon Heaton, without dismounting, picked up the whip from his saddlebag and tapped loudly at the door. Both horses shied away from the sudden sound but their cruel master forced them back again. After a moment or two the door opened and a startled manservant bearing a lantern stood upon the step.

"Here," snarled the black tyrant, throwing down the unconscious body of his adversary. "Take that for what it is worth. It is yours I take it?"

"But, sir," protested the servant. "How did he come to be in a state like this?"

"A drunken brawl," sneered the offender relentlessly. "He took a punch outside the alehouse as I've never seen a man survive before. Here, pick up his corpse and grab his horse – I am away."

He flung the trailing rein of Joseph's mount to the manservant and without waiting for further questioning he pulled his horse round and galloped off.

The windows of Westerdale were still illuminated by a feeble light when Heaton arrived back and a nervous hand twitched the curtains at the echoing sound of horse's hooves. The tyrant smiled maliciously, flung himself off and led his sweating horse round to the back of the yard where he entered the stable and commenced unsaddling his beast. In another minute or two he heard the sound of running feet and his fiancée burst in upon him, a thick plaid shawl thrown round her shoulders, one trembling hand clutching a lantern.

"Heaton!" she cried desperately. "Heaton – what have you done?"

There was no answer from the black figure who carried on his work undaunted. Elizabeth drew closer and shining the lantern against his eyes she repeated,

"Heaton – what have you done to Joseph?"

"Damn you!" snarled he, snatching at the light and missing its elusive shape. "Give me that infernal brightness Eliza or you'll be sorry."

"You shall not have it!" cried she stoutly, moving swiftly out of his reach. "Neither shall you pass through this door till you tell me what you have done to my uncle."

"So," snarled Heaton, through clenched teeth. "I have not broken the creature's spirit have I? Your uncle, madam, how can he mean that much to you?"

"Because he will be all I have left when Father is dead and gone," sobbed she.

"You are mistaken," retorted he. "You will be mine then. You shall have me to contend with and I will teach you things no uncle shall ever influence. Now give me that damn lantern and get gone from my sight. Your uncle breathes yet. I carried him home from the alehouse reeking of liquor and out of his senses with delusions of my worth."

This time he succeeded in grabbing the lantern and stepping past his fiancée easily he lifted the light and sneered horribly,

"Ah ha Eliza, get down on your knees and pray to your last breath that he you set so much by does not die too soon, for then, madam, you are mine and you are a doomed woman. Goodnight."

His form receded from the stable, the light waned and Elizabeth was left alone in the darkness.

CHAPTER 4

As the cold, dark days of winter drew in, each one waning Elizabeth's temporary freedom, her father began to sink rapidly. No longer was he able to rise for breakfast or take a steady turn about his estate. The weakened man could not comprehend that Heaton was running his business to seed and his fearful heart did not perceive the growing restlessness of his daughter. Her form still brought pleasure to his feverish eyes, but even her shape seemed changed and the dresses she wore were unsuited to her.

"Why do you put on those saggy gowns?" queried he, many a time. "Why do you not wear that orange dress I bought you a few months back? 'Twill show off your trim figure a treat."

At this Elizabeth grew pale and silent, occasionally bidding him rest and trouble himself no longer with her welfare. Her heart knew only too well that she had lost her trim figure, that the orange gown hung cold and unworn in her closet whilst the child within her womb swelled visibly.

Nothing was heard from Joseph and when Heaton encountered him one day driving a flock of sheep over to Long Beck he cast a look of hatred at his victor and whistling to his two mastiffs strode manfully past with a vengeful gleam in his sullen eyes. He was not invited to the wedding. No one outside Westerdale was to attend, Heaton having authority over the final arrangements when it became painfully obvious that Drayton had sought his bed for the final time. He would never again rise from his pillow.

The night before the wedding was a bitter, frosty night with the keen moorland wind cutting into every available crevice and mourning piteously against every window pane. Elizabeth sat the long night with her father, consenting only to lie down at four

41

o'clock in the morning, when she was assured he was asleep and would not wake and miss her. Martha, who had known for many weeks Elizabeth had a baby coming, took care of her as tenderly as a mother and though Eliza never spoke of her condition it was obvious it pained her greatly.

Heaton chose to spend his last night before matrimony at the lonely alehouse where he succeeded all limits and rode home at one o'clock drunken and vicious. The door, he discovered, had been locked and bolted from inside and he could find his key no where. More over it was freezing outside and every window was shut so Heaton promptly smashed his knuckles through two panes of glass and commenced climbing in.

No sooner had he done so than steps sounded on the stairs and his bride of the coming day stood before him with a candle in her fingers.

"Oh, Heaton!" she exclaimed. "Why have you broken the window? Could you not call me? Where have you been?"

"Keep off me you bitch!" yelled he, seeing she attempted to help him up.

"But you have blood upon your face," cried she.

"Damn you, as if you care. You shall have it on yours, you useless article, unless you leave me alone. Damn you, Elizabeth, I don't want your sympathy. Get out of here sharply! I have had an infernal night and it is all your fault; if I had murdered you on your own doorstep and drunk your blood, then revelled in the gore, I could not have been more cruelly accused."

"But, Heaton," she said, almost tenderly. "When you hurt me – oh so many days ago – I forgave you. I forgive you now; if anyone has been rebuking you 'tis not on my account."

"Give over with your whining," snapped he, recoiling with horror from her outstretched arms.

"If I made you suffer am I not paying for it? In Christ's name – I'm going to marry you. What more can you ask?"

"I don't ask anything," wept she."Oh Heaton, why can't you love me? I don't mean...well, why can you never be gentle and tender?"

"Get away, you fool!" snarled he, hardening instantly. "Gentleness and tenderness – am I not a man? You do not know what you ask, Eliza."

"I only ask for the things every wife expects from her husband," sobbed she. "Oh Heaton, I wish I could understand you."

"To attempt to do so madam is fatal – fatal," sneered he, reaching out and crushing her face between his fingers. "Now, get off – you have a wistful look about you that I don't like."

"Ah," whispered she. "I almost touch your heart – I almost move you."

"Move me?" roared Heaton, furiously. "Aye – you move me as much as a snake that spends all its life crawling on its belly. As much as a flying insect that is one minute in the air and the next crushed in my hand. Pity? I have no such emotion in me. You must earn it – hard – and slog for any feeling you evoke in me. There, I have said enough, almost too much it seems. I have given you the key to destroy myself." He slowly and shakily began to walk across the room, stopping momentarily at the door, then he ascended the stairs and she, who had been cruelly hurt, crawled up weakly behind him.

The morning was wet and windy with a universal grey sky of low cloud that reflected an eerie darkness onto the swart moorland. No glimpse or trace of sun remained to light Elizabeth's wedding day. She rose early with a sad and heavy heart and dressed herself in her best white satin gown.

"Alas," murmured she wistfully. "I should not be veiled in white. I am no longer fit to wear it. My dress should be a sombre grey and yet surely for once God will be lenient with me; He knows my blighted innocence."

She shed a few tears at this but wiping them swiftly away she rose up and went to visit her father. Of Heaton there was no sign. She supposed him to be dressing and went quietly to her Father's room.

"My child," murmured he weakly. "You are beautiful. I bless you. Oh Eliza, if only I could see your wedding. If only I could be there in that moment of moments. But 'tis not to be. I shall be there in spirit, my angel."

"Yes, Father," she replied, meekly, kissing him.

"And where is your husband? I would bestow a blessing on him also. He knows I love him yet he seems to immerse himself ever more in the business. Eliza – you are marrying a good man."

"Yes, Father," whispered she, her silent heart sinking within her.

"And when I'm gone, angel, which will be very soon and could even be today, you will say "My father is dead. On earth I loved him and yet now I must give my love to my husband." Then you will forget me."

She vowed she would never do so but he smiled and continued, "Oh yes, you will and that will gladden me. I shall look down on you and see you happy with your Heaton and your bairns and my wife and I shall smile. Come, angel, do not cry, not on your wedding day. Do not weep for me. I have had a good life and I am content to die. With Heaton here to take over my business and to love you – what more could I want?"

His philosophy so saddened her that she could stay no longer and on excuse of helping Martha dress she kissed him and left misty-eyed.

In the kitchen she found Martha scrubbing the floor and Heaton carving grotesque images on a piece of wood. He looked up as she approached and marking the traces of tears on her pallid face he said to Martha, "Well, well, is not every woman beautiful on their wedding day and yet my little treasure has been upsetting herself and weeping."

"Dear, dear," murmured the old woman, rising stiffly. "What can ail ye, Miss Elizabeth? Look at yer lovely husband here. Did you ever see such glorious black eyes and hair? He's a real beauty."

"Do not smile at me like that, Heaton," cried Elizabeth. "Why do you sit there playing with that old piece of apple wood like a child? You should be away changing. Am I to marry a ragamuffin?"

At this he grimaced fiercely and curling his sarcastic lip began to cut deeper notches furiously into the wood.

Soon Martha drifted away to change and the two were left alone.

"Don't look at me like that Heaton," cried she again after bearing the malicious stare from his fierce black orbs.

"Don't ever speak to me like that Eliza!" snarled he, leaping up and grabbing her by the throat upon which he placed his whittling knife. "I do not care for people to speak to me like that in front of others. Come – stiffen up your courage and say it to me now we are alone."

Elizabeth shrank back against the wall and Heaton, hearing the heavy tread of feet on the stairs, flung her off and resumed his occupation with a sulky face.

Elizabeth hurried out and, meeting Martha, accompanied her upstairs where she aided the old lady to finish dressing. Her heart throbbed painfully. She longed to break down and tell all but a sense of pride stifled her misery, and moreover, a desire to protect him who lay dying in the next room.

At last all was ready and the hour fast approaching ten caused Elizabeth to don her cloak and set up her parasol for the lengthy journey into Scarshead by carriage. Downstairs there was no sign of Heaton, but a dull, muffled jangling audible in the kitchen, mixed with a variety of curses and blows told Elizabeth he was harnessing the horses in preparation for the journey. Accordingly she sat down on a stool and waited. After another few minutes he appeared still dressed in his working clothes and with his hair blown and wild. He went straight to the sink and washed without even noticing Elizabeth.

"Heaton," pleaded she nervously. "Aren't you going to change?"

"No," replied he with curt brevity, towelling furiously.

"But I have changed for you and done my best," said she. "Can you not do the same for me?"

"Damn you – if you wish to get married in rags I don't care," spat he.

"Then let me at least comb your long locks or else get Martha to cut them."

"Leave my hair alone," snarled he, as she attempted to touch it. "Now are ye ready?"

"Yes," murmured she.

At this he disappeared and drove the carriage round to the front door where Elizabeth and Martha climbed in. Morosely he whipped up the horses, loosened the reins a fraction and directed them onto the path that led to Scarshead.

It was raining heavily when they left Westerdale and due to Heaton's wild and furious driving a great quantity of mud and rain sprayed in upon them, Martha having had presence of mind to bring a rug to wrap around herself. Elizabeth, careless of her condition, had left her cloak open and presently her dress was saturated and clung to the tell-tale curves of her body.

She lifted her head and sobbed but the wild rocking of the carriage drowned any sound except the tremulous roar of the gale. Her sobs were dry, tearless gasps, leaving no trace of their passage.

They reached the tiny grey stone church and clambered out, Heaton inattentive to the ladies and more preoccupied in tying the horses short so they could not reach the moorland grass.

Slowly they crept inside, joined only by the precious few who felt moved to attend such an occasion and so within the next half an hour they became man and wife. There were no smiles or cheers at their union, no congratulations and no flowers, just sad and pitiful glances at the poor shaking woman who stood by the side of the man all Scarshead knew as a tyrant. A woman who had a child growing inside her, a defenceless soul forced into a union she could only fear and abhor. She walked silently from the altar, her tragic face pallid, drawn and tired whilst her husband leered triumphantly and fixed his sullen, vindictive eyes upon people around him. He seemed to drag her from the church, pushed her up callously into the carriage and leaving Martha to scramble up behind he untethered the horses, turned them so sharply they almost fell and set them upon the moorland track.

At home he put down his two charges by the front door then whipped the horses round to the yard where he unfastened them. He then went moodily about his work, the only traits of emotion in his face being a slight but regular twitching of his facial muscles.

Evening came swiftly. A cold, swirling darkness came down, bright with forming frost, insensible to wandering travellers or vagrants.

All day Heaton had remained in the yard, not even venturing inside for food and drink. Flickering lights in the sick room told him his father-in-law was sinking fast, truly dying at last so that all that lay around him would be his and his alone.

At seven o'clock Martha came out to find him loading feed stuff into the forage room with stalwart arms and a sullen visage.

"Mr Grimshaw," called she. "Are ye not coming in for supper? Your wife took hers an hour and more ago."

"Aye," murmured he stiffly, throwing the last of the sacks inside and slamming the door.

"Tell me, Martha, what do those flickering lights mean in yer master's room? Is he dying?"

"Aye," whispered she, reverently bowing her head. "He is going, Mr Grimshaw, going to a better world where there is no sorrow or pain. He'll not last the night out, I think. Do come in now – if only to comfort yer poor distracted wife."

Heaton flung his spade down, bolted the door at the top and bottom and gazing heavenwards at the dimming light he murmured," At last, at last! Down to the Devil wi' ye at last ye old bastard! And all that you have – including her – mine, mine!"

A glint of evil lighted his dark eye and lifted his sallow cheek. Then he gave a short laugh and shaking his tousled head he went inside.

The hours passed swiftly till it was almost midnight and the fire in the parlour was pale and sickly, the candle flames burned low and flickered. Heaton remained there alone. Martha had taken herself off to bed at the first strokes of ten, as was her custom and Elizabeth comforted the dying above. Heaton sat upright and stolid in his chair, one hand cupping his stalwart chin, his black eyes fixed upon the dying embers. Then, at a sudden but persistent noise upstairs he rose, walked briskly to the door and stepped out into the chilly passageway. The sound was much louder now as he ascended the stairs and it grew fiercely to define itself as the mournful wail of a woman.

Heaton entered the sick room abruptly, saw the passage of time had turned it into the chamber of death and turning away from the lifeless corpse he sneered, "Well, Eliza, how are you?"

His wife lifted her beautiful face, swollen red with sobs and shook her head inexplicably.

"In God's arms he is at rest," breathed she.

"In the Devil's hell he writhes in torment, you mean," shouted her husband furiously. "What right has he to get to heaven? What portion of his wealth did he assign to God? God? He hardly knew the meaning of the word. Why does he grin so recklessly now? Eh-I pray he burns as merrily!"

"How dare you desecrate his name!" fumed she, standing up instantly with ire as well as tears flashing in her dark eyes. "Hold your tongue! You shall not speak evil of him who aided you to rise from the cesspit of poverty!"

In answer to this Heaton ground his teeth furiously and stepping up to his wife dealt her a tremendous blow across the face.

Turning again to the lifeless corpse he dilated his features and whispered,

"It is no matter at all – the man is dead."

Then to Elizabeth, "Come, madam, have you forgotten my threat? See, he is no more. Your protector is gone and you, you are mine!"

He reached out for her and grasped her firmly in his arms whereupon she struggled furiously to escape him.

"I shall scream for Martha," vowed she, succeeding in extricating herself from his arms.

"Martha will not stand by and see me hurt."

"You may scream if you please," growled he, observing a shadowy figure in the doorway.

"Martha is no longer needed here. Her services are past; is that not so, Martha?"

The form at once withdrew and returned noisily to her room, whereupon Heaton stretched out his arm to his wife again.

"Come, madam, you are mine now to corrupt or treat as I please."

Sullenly, carelessly she flung out her hand and let him drag her unyielding yet obedient to their room, whereupon he slammed the door directly and locked it.

And all night long the mournful howling of the wind gave way to a sound far more eerie, far more desperate; the low, unceasing sobbing of pain.

CHAPTER 5

The long dreary days of winter drew onwards in their never-ending succession of black frosts and grim, cheerless rain. With December came the first bitter showers of snow and the moorland became transformed into a frozen waste of white underneath which the icy heather withered and died. The few recognisable landmarks became obliterated. No longer was it possible to drive the bleating flocks across the virginal wastes.

Elizabeth grew thin and listless, yet he who tortured her grew stronger and more indomitable. Her marriage was one based not on true love but rather on aversion, cruelty and frequently hate. Heaton refused to neglect her; carelessness would have been a welcome joy, but instead he abused her, dictated the paths her footsteps should follow and after suffering her to perform a hard day's physical labour he would force his brutal attentions on her half the night. He knew this haunted her till sunrise while he, thoroughly exhausted and through with his sport, slept peacefully. That he was master of all he surveyed was a strengthening joy to him. The will, when it was read, proclaimed Heaton as heir to everything Drayton possessed apart from a tidy sum which was settled on Elizabeth but this her husband secretly forced her to yield to him. Accordingly Heaton reset his principles of business. He did not deal honestly but by sly trickery with which he fooled the inexperienced client. The experienced he treated cautiously but with brutal frankness. Upon inner counsel he resolved to employ no servant so Martha was sent packing and, of course, he had a wife who could be forced into doing any job he himself did not care to perform. He cut her off without a penny, gave her nothing more than her food and his brutish attentions.

One day in early December, when the north wind blew as keenly as a knife across the moors and froze the remaining patches of snow in the hidden hollows Elizabeth, who had suffered yet again from Heaton's cruelty that very hour, noted that he was forced to go out suddenly. Unusually he did not lock her into her room. She waited breathlessly until the furious churning of hooves had died down and then, quitting her room, she descended the stairs and throwing on a cloak let herself out of the front door. A bitter gust blew her back into the shelter of the porch but she was insistent on leaving and after regaining her breath she plunged out again and began to traverse the narrow moorland paths that she had frequented since a child. She walked slowly yet determinedly, the baby within her already a heavy burden for her tiny frame. Her wary eyes skimmed the familiar landscape and the queer yellow half-light of the sky (it was then two o'clock), but she saw nothing to alarm her; nothing at all save the stark outline of a naked, wind worn tree upon the horizon.. Accordingly her steps seemed to acquire a purpose; soon she breasted a tiny hillock, came across an almost hidden valley and spied ahead a roving figure. At first she cringed nervously and stopped in her tracks but then, observing the form to be an elderly woman holding onto a small child, she gave a joyful smile and descended the hillock in a rush.

The old woman looked up at her approach and narrowed her time worn eyes, then she, too, gave a smile of greeting.

"Martha – I – am – so – glad to see you!" panted Elizabeth as she reached the figure and took hold of her free arm.

"There! There!" cried her former servant soothingly. "Ye shouldna' run. Not at all in your condition. Where is yer husband that he allows ye to go across the moors in this weather – and wi' a baby coming?"

At the mention of her husband Elizabeth turned pale and shook with uncontrollable fear.

"Heaton is out," murmured she, at length. "I do not know where."

"Ye do not look well, angel, not at all," sympathised the old woman."Yer eyes are darker than they were when I saw them last – all rheumy with tears and ye are so thin I'd not have recognised ye! O! Elizabeth, is Heaton really good to you?"

"Good?" cried she, in horror. "He has no knowledge of the word at all beyond it being an ideal he wishes to desecrate and ruin. He will not rest until he has drawn every conceivable fragment of good out of the world. O, Martha – I could tell you such tales of his cruelties but it is to no avail and I see you have uncle's first-born with you. Are you nurse there now?"

"Aye," replied Martha proudly. "Come forward Master Gerald and say good afternoon ter yer cousin."

But the child was very shy of the pretty yet worn looking lady and he hid his fair curls and huge brown eyes beneath his nurse's pinafore until she, out of patience with him, let go of his hand.

"Can ye not come back with us fer a little while?" pressed Martha. "I am sure yer uncle would be glad to see ye! He is kept indoors today by a trifling cold and yer aunt is as sickly as ever I'm afraid."

"Alas," murmured she. "I dare not. Yet I crave to see them. Perhaps I will come. My husband may not be back until dusk. Here, Martha, give me your free arm and help me along. It is a long time since I felt the warmth of living, caring flesh."

They wandered back over an undulating moorland path which frequently broke into wide, muddy puddles and bogs which they were forced to skirt. As they walked it began to rain in large, heavy spots that blew furiously in the reviving wind. Rounding a brake of heather they descended a dip and glimpsed the warm inviting red sandstone of Garstang Hall – a far larger and gentler mansion than Westerdale which revelled in its starkness. Garstang was strangely beautiful and haunting; Garstang could be a welcome refuge, Westerdale a cold prison.

Martha led the way into the kitchen where a huge fire roared powerfully up the chimney and cast an orange glow over the culinary utensils. She removed the child's wet outer clothing and bid him run through and tell his Father to prepare for a surprise.

"Now," murmured she gently. "Sit down by the hearth and I'll rub your hair, Eliza. Is it not like old days when you were a little girl in ringlets and I was sent to scold you after some misdemeanour ?"

"Yes," replied Elizabeth wistfully and a poignant tear fell. "'Tis like any day, Martha, any moment, before HE walked into my life and ruined me!"

"Hush, now," coaxed Martha, pulling a comb through the shining auburn locks. "Dry your eyes and put on a brave face for your uncle. He'll not like to see you cry."

"He is not aware of what I suffer," whispered Elizabeth, rising awkwardly and brushing her dress. "There, Martha, I am ready. How do I seem?"

"Very pale." answered the nurse gravely. "Your eyes are still misty. But they will be overjoyed to see you. Go in now, Eliza!"

The girl did as she was bid, knocking quickly at the parlour door before entering, a slight sense of fear entrapping her quaking heart.

By another immense fire composed of peat, wood and coal a middle-aged man sat stroking the hair of his young blond heir who turned over the pages of a picture book. A little way off, reclining upon a rug-covered settle an attractive woman in her early thirties drank a cup of steaming liquid with easy gentility. Elizabeth came further into the room, shut the door and approaching the former figure murmured softly,

"Hello, uncle."

She held out her hand towards him but, overjoyed to see her, he leapt up and embraced her warmly crying, "Eliza! How good to see you again. I feared your marriage would excommunicate you from our company but, no! See, Emily, our niece is back at Garstang again!"

Emily swung herself off the settle and kissed her relation fondly.

"Well," murmured she. "I was, of course, bitterly disappointed at not being invited to your wedding but this makes up for it. Are you happy Eliza?"

"I am content," replied Elizabeth awkwardly, casting down her eyes.

"Your father's death shocked us all," continued Emily. "He was not so very old after all and his pains must have been great. Of your husband I will not speak – I have thoughts in that direction that would make you very angry if they were spoken!"

"I think not, aunt." cried Elizabeth. "For many days I have thought similar things. I have prayed aloud to be neglected. Alas, he has not done so. I have yearned for his death but he continues hale and hearty. This very afternoon he galloped off onto the moors and forgot to secure my prison so I gained release and came here."

They bid her sit by the fire and warm herself, Emily presently taking Gerald upstairs for his rest.

Directly they were gone Joseph broke his long silence and asked,

"Eliza, have you yet discovered what sort of man you have married?"

"O yes," whispered she. "I knew it before....but the rash step was taken to give the child I carry a name."

"Then you no longer cherish any love for him?"

"Love?" cried she, in horror. "I could as much love a snake or embrace a viper as HE! O no – it is not love I feel for him. What is it? A peculiar, twisted emotion of fear and hate with a sharp touch of revenge thrown in. Yes, THAT asserts itself every time he defiles me!"

"My angel," replied Joseph, anxiously. "You've not married a man but some soulless ghoul – a Devil! I knew so from the moment he played that trick on me. But my suffering is over – yours, I fear, is yet to come."

She lowered her eyes at this painful truth and shook her head.

"O uncle! Talk no more of....him. Let it be. Maybe I am culpable. I am glad my poor father knew nothing of the man Heaton really is. 'Twould have broken his heart."

"Perhaps it would have moved his hand to write such a monster out of his will! So, Eliza, he takes it all?"

"Yes."

"Well – do not forget us in your troubles. We are always here. Now will ye take some tea before you go?" enquired he, ringing the bell.

There was, however, no answer to his summons. Outside it began to grow dark and a fresh downpour rattled against the window.

Suddenly there was the sharp clatter of hooves on gravel and a loud prolonged banging followed by the slam of a door and angry shouts. Elizabeth rose from her chair but her uncle bid her remain where she was whilst he sorted things out. Halfway across the room he perceived the door to be flung open and a black apparition strode through, shaking off the serving woman on his arm.

Heaton was back. He gave a final, malicious push to Martha which sent her sprawling on the floor. Shocked, Elizabeth ran forward but flashing his evil eyes upon her Heaton froze her progress.

"Stay where you are, Eliza!" bellowed he, flinging out his fist and ignoring Joseph. "Now, madam, I am come to demand an explanation of your conduct. Come-quickly! I am waiting and sorely out of patience!"

"Sir," cried Joseph, stepping forward. "I, too, am waiting for an explanation as to your uninvited presence here in my house! I neither heard plea nor request. What the devil do you mean by barging in here like this?"

Heaton transferred his gaze to Joseph and scornfully curled his lip.

"Well! Well!" sneered he. "'Tis the hero of the alehouse! By Christ you take a good punch, Mr Drayton! It makes a man sorely tempted to repeat his triumph but never fear – I have only come after what is rightfully mine, worthless tho' it is! Now, stand back. Elizabeth, come here!"

Trembling with fear she did as she was told, whereupon Heaton grabbed her and viciously twisted her arm. She gave a short cry of pain which drew Joseph forward. Heaton, believing him to be ready to fight, duly thrust out his fist and sent Drayton reeling across the floor. Elizabeth struggled to reach her prostrate uncle but Heaton, rejoicing in his power, clamped her more firmly in his arms and laughed out loud.

Slowly Drayton regained his breath only to watch Heaton drag his prize from the room. Martha ran to aid Joseph recover his feet.

"Ah, yes, Martha, thanks – no – let them go. I cannot save her!"

Together, man and servant, hurried into the yard in time to see Heaton vault onto his black stallion with his almost insensible wife in his arms. Her head drooped down and her limbs flailed against the saddle.

Seeing both figures helpless and hopeless Heaton's lips curved and twitched with amusement, then he whipped up the horse and without a backward glance galloped off, the rich dusk enfolding him.

It was pitch dark by the time they arrived back at Westerdale and the cold wind restored Elizabeth's senses. She was flung down carelessly in the yard while Heaton dismounted; then he grasped one wrist and jerked her up, pulling her along as he led his horse to the stable. Silently he untacked the beast, flung the tack into the forage room and dragged his wife back to the house.

"Now," growled he. "Get inside."

Shaking with fear and cold Elizabeth did as she was told, directing her steps to the parlour where she found a huge fire had been lit. Wearily she sank into a chair, rubbed her wet shoulders and closed her eyes.

In another few minutes Heaton entered the house and burst, noisily, into the room, startling her from her light doze.

"So," snarled he ferociously. "You have led me a pretty dance today, Eliza! Yes, I was slack and left the door unlocked but I have had my punishment. Do you think it was any joy for me to enter the house of THAT man?"

"THAT man is my uncle," pronounced she. "It was natural that I should visit him. My own Father is dead."

"Yes, God rot his soul!" snarled her torturer. "I presume you went to complain of my infernal behaviour. Well, that was my punishment. Yours has only just begun."

"I did not complain of you," cried she, tearfully. "They asked me if I was happy and being truthful I told them no!"

"You deserve your unhappiness," spat he, grasping a handful of her plentiful hair cruelly. "You bring it all on yourself. If you had not infuriated me these past hours I would not be torturing you now."

"I have done nothing wrong," wept she.

"Nothing wrong?" he yelled, yanking out a handful of her twisted locks. "By, Christ, Eliza, at times I feel moved to murder you – not directly, no, but slowly, insidiously, with a lingering pain that lasts for years. You have disobeyed me. From now on you will remain locked in your room all day and every day until your grotesque body produces my offspring! Now – you have said enough. Get up there and be thankful you have your life."

"Of what value is that? "cried she as she ran from the room, receiving on her journey a sound slap in the face that set her nose bleeding.

From then onwards Heaton doubled his vigil over her. If he had been cruel before he was a hundred times worse now. Frequently he forgot to bring her fresh food or water and she had no fire in the great, lofty bedroom. Her wistful eyes were ever searching and wandering over the bleak moorland so that at times she imagined her spirit was soaring there, free, unfettered, light. At night she felt she was skimming over miles of frozen moorland, leaving behind the shackles of her human body and the heavy child she carried.

Christmas came and went, unnoticed by Elizabeth. The water in the great ewer was often frozen now so that it was afternoon before she could drink. Heaton's atrocious conduct continued so she was permanently bruised both inside and out, her skin acquiring a purplish hue where his rough fingers plucked her.

January and February passed, then March arrived and a little light crept into the evening skies. Towards the end of the month Elizabeth began to experience strange pains in her womb that caused her to cry out. She could not believe that the child was coming as she was not near her time but the day arrived when she could doubt it no longer. Her tiny frame shuddered with pain she could no longer conceal and her breath was laboured and spasmodic. Heaton, who cared nothing for her suffering, had a sudden fear she would die and his unborn child with her. He contemplated the situation, gazed at her twitching and sweating body, then walked over to the door.

"So," stammered she, clenching her teeth. "You are going to leave me now, Heaton, are you?"

"By no means," replied he. "You shall have some help."

"What!" cried his wife, struggling up. "You are concerned for me?"

"I don't give a damn for your fate, Eliza, but I want this child delivered safely. He must be my heir!"

"And if – she is a – girl?" moaned Elizabeth, falling back on the pillows.

"Then you had best not die yet, woman, for you'll be required to give me a boy! A girl, bah, what use will that be?"

He quit the room, descended the stairs and went out to saddle up his stallion. In a few minutes he set off in the direction of Scarshead.

Within an hour he returned accompanied by a tall, stately gentleman upon a chestnut horse who served as the local apothecary and doctor. The pair dismounted, entered the house and ascended the stairs to the bedroom where Elizabeth lay. It was almost noon and every conceivable movement of air had ceased. Outside there was an unearthly hush, backed by a gentle violet sky and a weak, watery sun that cried tears of light onto the gathering clouds.

Heaton wandered out into the yard and commenced the midday feeding; his tall, gaunt form stamping loudly over damp gravel as he fed his beasts. Soon his ears focused on a peculiar succession of sounds – the sharp cry of a woman, the prolonged wailing of a child and then, instinctively, the echoing sobbing of sorrow. He flung down his bucket, entered the house and encountered the smiling doctor who called his name joyfully and held out his hand.

"Well?" snarled Heaton, impatiently.

"Mr Grimshaw, your wife has just made you the father of a beautiful baby girl! I would like to congratulate you-"

"Damn your congratulations!" yelled the Father, furiously. "In Christ's name what do you offer them for? She has produced a GIRL! A girl! What use is that to me? Wipe that smile off your face and get out of my house. You have done what you came here to do. O Christ – a puny, feeble girl! All this while for a- - girl!"

He leaned heavily against the bannisters and closed his eyes, his fists clenched, his teeth grinding rhythmically together. The doctor, bemused, and half-afraid of this swarthy-skinned gypsy, took this opportunity to get out and fled, shutting the door behind him.

Heaton remained motionless, leaning on the rail for a very long time. Eventually he stood up, opened his eyes and continued his climb to the top of the stairs.

In her chamber Elizabeth lay propped up by several pillows, the tiny seven month child in her arms, her eyes misty and wet with tears. She looked up directly her husband entered the room and then her eyes fell sadly upon the sleeping baby.

"Well," snarled Heaton, furiously. "THIS is what you present me with after all my care. A puny little bastard – a girl – a useless creation to me. What will I do with her? In Christ's name I feel moved to drown her in the horse trough like an unwanted kitten."

"How can you say that?" cried Elizabeth, hugging the child closer. "Doesn't she move you to any emotion, Heaton? She is ours- ours! God sent her to us!"

"God?" sneered he, nastily. "As for me she might have come straight from the Devil. God damn her I say – for being female and God damn YOU for bringing her into this world! Keep her away from me, Eliza. She is YOURS – never refer to her as mine. I disown my part in her. But be ready soon for since you have survived you shall fulfil a useful purpose and give me a son! O yes! The next one shall be a boy or else she'll go out the window! Damn you Eliza – damn you I say!"

He slammed out of the room and ran down the stairs to the yard where he saddled up the wildest horse in the stable and took his fury out on the tawny coloured stallion. He whipped him into a frenzy then galloped and galloped over the dark, satanic moorlands that, alone in this world, he felt any emotion for.

CHAPTER 6

During the next few months Elizabeth conceived again and almost a year from the birth of her first child she produced a second. This time she bore a strong, healthy boy which alleviated some of the cruelty Heaton bestowed on her innocent head after the birth of a girl. He still delighted in abusing her and kept her under constant vigil, swearing that as soon as the boy was old enough he would take over mastery of him. The girl Heaton did not bother to mention. Elizabeth was allowed complete freedom in raising her which afforded some pleasure in a dark and cruel world. Accordingly she chose a name – Errin – the name of a sister lost in infancy and although Heaton refused to get his daughter christened he did not dispute the name choice.

With the boy he was not so careless. Elizabeth must feed and clothe him before the girl and if Heaton heard him cry the mother would suffer. She grew used to the constant physical and mental abuse; true she shrank from it but it had for so long been part of her world that she had learnt to be stoical about it.

The swift years passed by and the children grew into personalities and temperaments. As soon as the boy was five years old Heaton claimed him completely and throwing aside Elizabeth's pleas that he be named Edward he called him Hardy and set about modelling the child into a copy of himself. Elizabeth was locked into the house with Errin, whilst Heaton taught Hardy to ride, shoot and generally rape the moorland around him. Thus the mother tried to bring up the little girl to be as good and gentle as the other child was wild and cruel. Errin was a very pretty child with wide violet eyes, pale skin and black hair. The gentler, pallid looks of her mother had faded and toned down the harsh, rugged contours of her Father's features. It was true she had, on occasion something of her father's spirit and temper but she had also inherited her mother's kindness. If ever she hurt her mother by some misdemeanour she would quickly repent and end up far more hurt than Elizabeth.

She soon learnt to love her mother and fear her father. Hate had not, as yet, entered her tiny world but she shrank from her rough, unwashed brother who, although a year younger than herself, was far taller and stronger.

Rarely did any news arrive from Elizabeth's uncle. Eliza heard that he was prospering in his farm work and that his wife had born him a second child some two years after the birth of Errin. How Elizabeth craved to see them! She pleaded with her husband who delighted in thwarting her and sent her to her room for daring to ask.

Hardy grew taller every day and wilder too so that by the age of fourteen he adopted the duties of manhood and half-ran the business. The language he used was equal, if not worse, than Heaton's for it was backed up by youth and high spirits. By sixteen he was well over six foot, had inherited his father's swarthy skin, coal black hair and black, scornful eyes that flashed with temper. He was taught no means of control and if he swore at table no one rebuked him; in fact Heaton positively encouraged him. Elizabeth soon learnt to ignore his filthy manners for any sharp word to him would not be heeded but met by a blow from his father and jeers from the lad himself. Poor Errin was bemused by such behaviour and strong feelings of abhorrence began to root themselves in her heart, mostly for her black-hearted father who caused such suffering to the mother she loved.

On Errin's eighteenth birthday her mother, who had planned a special surprise for her daughter, felt unable to rise from her bed after her cruel treatment of the night before. Heaton had caught her rebuking Hardy for his inhumane treatment of Errin and for this the tyrant had whipped his wife soundly upon retiring. The day before she had received a soaking from Heaton's cruelty in locking her out of the house for some trivial offence and, suddenly, all the torture of her eighteen years of marriage fell upon her. She became very ill. Elizabeth had all her life nourished a tendency to sickliness and now, approaching middle age, she developed consumption, the seeds of which had been sowed by her husband's cruelty. She took to her bed, forcing Errin to take on the domestic work which the girl did gladly. Her favourite task was waiting on and trying to cheer up her mother. The sickroom was never without its bowl of flowers, tenderly removed at night and Errin spent long hours cooking tasty dishes to tempt her mother's appetite. At times fear weighed heavy on Errin's heart – the gnawing pictures of life after her mother was gone.

"O Mother do not leave me here alone!" cried she, lamenting her selfishness but lamenting more the loss of a beautiful friend. "How can I face Hardy and my father when you are gone! The world will be an empty void with no one I care anything for in it!"

At this Elizabeth would smile gently in between her fits of coughing and say, "You will find someone worthy of your love, Errin, but be wise and never hasty! Learn to ignore your father, since it is impossible to love him, and think of me often for, in that way I shall always be with you!"

Heaton at last realised the seriousness of his wife's condition and requiring confirmation he summoned the doctor to her. It was the very medic who had helped her give birth over eighteen years before.

Doctor Jacobs came warily and found the same Heaton Grimshaw, a little more lined and with the corners of his once jet black hair fading into grey for he was now thirty-eight years of age. But there was the same evil glint in his eyes, the same massive heavy form and the same hands – hands that could knock a man insensible with a single blow. The doctor examined Elizabeth thoroughly and imparted tragic news; her aunt had passed away just over a year ago and left two children – a girl of sixteen and a boy of twenty-two.

"Her end was full of peace and love," soothed the doctor. "She lingered for several months, luxuriated with every care her loving husband could bestow upon her but in the end God called her home. Joseph mourned her deeply, as did the children, but in the end he set up a fine tombstone for her and fresh flowers appear on the grave at least twice a week. Ah! He is consoled now though at first he was distracted by grief!"

Elizabeth was comforted by this knowledge but she wished passionately she had been free to attend the funeral and pay her last respects to the aunt who had been a stranger to her for eighteen years.

Closing the door the doctor was approached by Heaton, who barred his way and snarled,

"Well? Where are you sloping off to? If I pay I expect answers. Tell me if she will live! Spit it out man!"

"Mr Grimshaw! I cannot say after one examination but sadly both lungs are badly affected. Now she needs- -"

"God damn you!" cried Heaton, furiously. "Don't blind me with the morbid details of her health or her requirements!" His eyes flashed dangerously. "I don't give a fig for her needs. Come, stand up like a man! Don't cower before me! I asked you if she'd live?"

The doctor was very alarmed by his tone and retreated to the top of the stairs. Heaton clenched his fists and his lips curled sardonically.

"Well?" he bellowed.

Jacobs excused himself, bowed and ventured that she would not live long. He extended his sympathy to the black tyrant

"Damn you – I want none of your pity," snarled Heaton, turning away. "You came here to do a job and cast a verdict. You have done it. Now get out! You'll be paid, never fear."

"But am I not to repeat my visit to allay her sufferings and treat her with blisters and…"

"If she is to die, then let her do it," replied Heaton through clenched teeth. "I have no more to say on it. Good day!" and he brushed past the doctor and descended the stairs to the parlour.

That evening Elizabeth was visibly worse, a rising fever bruising her thoughtful brow and sparkling her misty eyes. Errin sat by her side in solitude. A beautiful bouquet of spring flowers graced the dresser and lent their perfume to the air.

"Today has been so mild, Mother," murmured Errin. "The air was so warm and balmy upon the moorlands I seemed to drink it in like wine. It soothed my troubles for a moment and it heartened me further to come across these early blooms. Do you not think them splendid?"

"Yes," murmured Elizabeth, vaguely."They are a bright patch of colour in the darkness. My dear Errin- I am dying- I can feel the change coming over me. These limbs seem barely mine. Come, let me kiss you!"

The girl bent and gently embraced her frail mother, feeling, instinctively, the cold despair of death in the white flesh.

Elizabeth lay back on the pillow and drew a long breath.

"And yet I cannot die without speaking to him who has wronged me. During these past sombre days I have had a dream, waking and sleeping, that heartens, yet frightens me!"

Errin begged she would tell but Elizabeth closed her tired eyes and bid the girl run for her father.

"Tell him, Errin, I am dying, at last. Say I have something to impart to him that will alter the colour of his existence and remould his future when it comes to pass. Then get to bed for Heaton will be in no mood for socialising when I am done. Now- ask no more questions, angel, just go and find him!"

Errin rose willingly to do her mother's bidding and descending to the lower regions of the house encountered Heaton and Hardy gambling and drinking in the parlour.

"Well," cried her father sarcastically as she entered. "I heard no knock? Did you Hardy? What are you doing here? It's time women were off to bed. The men are at play and we do not require the pleasure of your company!"

"I have not come for pleasure," replied she, spiritedly. "I've long ceased looking for that in this depressing region that scarcely bears a warm heart within its walls. Father, my mother is sinking fast. She wishes to speak to you urgently."

"O really?" sneered he. "Well, well, you have done her bidding. Now – begone! I'll away to her after my game."

"She wishes very much that you come NOW!" persisted Errin, standing her ground.

"And I wish very much to be left alone to continue my game, madam. Now get out while you have the chance," fumed he, rising and pushing back his chair.

Errin withdrew hastily and ascended to her chamber where she lit a candle and undressing carefully she prepared for bed. A glance in the mirror revealed a tense, white face marked with tears of sorrow and anger. Pushing back her long, black hair she knelt down and, putting her hands together, murmured,

"O God in your mercy take the innocent soul of my mother and avenge yourself upon my worthless father at whose hands she has suffered abominably. O Lord, show me the way, give me new life and strengthen me in all I do. And support me in the sorrow that will follow. Amen."

She climbed into bed and lay down, her heart pounding painfully, then gradually, her features softened and she slept.

A little before midnight Heaton finished his game, drank the last of the whisky and sent his defeated son to bed, whereupon he fastened the locks in the house and extinguished the parlour candles.

Ascending the stairs he could hear every gasping, rattling breath from his wife and upon entering the bedroom he saw she had struggled up and managed to light a taper by the side of the bed.

"So," murmured she, after her feeble eyes had recognised him. "You are come at last, are you Heaton? How many hours after you received my message?"

"Damn you!" snarled he. "I am not your servant, to come to your beck and call." He removed his shirt and prepared for bed.

"No," whispered she. "But you do need to be wary of me, Heaton for in death the oppressed will become the oppressor and the defeated victorious. Listen to me – for these may be the last words I ever utter on earth."

"Well then," sneered he. "If they move you so powerfully say them then I can sleep in peace!"

"Peace?" laughed she. "Peace? A year from now you will not know the meaning of the word. When I am a year in my grave, Heaton, I will haunt you unceasingly, incessantly and with an intensity you have never experienced in your life before! THIS, this is my prize! Yes, I dreamt it but it is my reward for all these years of oppression and suffering. And yet I was nothing but a good wife to you."

"What nonsense is this?" cried he, rising sharply and approaching her.

"Yes-hear it again, Heaton, if you doubt it. In a year from my death I will return and haunt you infernally. You shall not sleep, eat or work without me there. Even when you breathe I will be in that breath. AH! You may laugh and shrug but you cannot deny it. Such is your fate."

A furious rage kindled within Heaton and grinding his teeth uncontrollably he brought down his hands upon his wife's face, crushing the very life from her. As she struggled in vain to breathe he lividly pressed harder, tearing at her face furiously until she trembled, sunk back and was still. She breathed no more.

Heaton removed his hands and felt her pulse. It flickered, wavered, went out. Elizabeth was dead.

He withdrew from the body, commenced dressing and lighting a fresh taper went into his daughter's room where he shook her roughly till she woke.

"Come!" cried he. "Get up quickly! It's your mother.....she's dead."

At this news Errin began crying and breaking away from her father's vice like hold, rushed ahead of him and knelt down beside her mother's bed. Heaton followed sullenly, his lower lip curled sardonically, his dark eyes vaguely misted and his fists clenched.

Poor Errin leant against her mother's cold form and wept, her long black hair becoming saturated with tears. Heaton's lips tightened and after a moment or two he darted forward and dragged her away crying,

"There! There! That is enough. She was never that good to you. Hush yer howling."

But Errin, overwhelmed by her loss, would not be silenced and ere long her father lost patience and slapped her. After a while she got up, pushed away her damp hair and rubbed her face, stinging from the force of his hands. She turned her swollen eyes upon him and put into her stare as much hate as she could muster.

"I will stop only because you can make me!" cried she. "But inwardly I will never stop mourning her death nor blaming you for it. To think that one who is my flesh and blood could mete out such cruelty! Father- from now on you are no more than dust to me. You will never again experience love – from me or anyone! The love for my mother is locked up in my heart beyond your reach!"

"Ha! Do not suppose I crave any affection from YOU!" sneered he, triumphantly. "I thrive on abhorrence and fear. Errin – you are mine now! Never forget it! From this moment onwards you will do my bidding, go where I wish you to go and even think what I desire you to! Do not beg for mercy or try to play upon my sympathy – I have none! You may cry and wail till Domesday – I don't care! It doesn't move me. I could crush you with one hand and get great pleasure from it!"

"I neither seek anything good from you nor expect it," cried she. "Since she I loved is no more the world is an empty place and all men in it but shadows. Even you, Father, will not move me with your cruelty. I know what my mother suffered all those months. All those slow years of pain with you! Where does it fall now? Yes, it falls on me! Did she not prepare me for it? Such evil becomes my lot. Yes – I am ready for it. Do your worst, Father, I may yet foil you by dying and then where will your cruelty go?"

"There now you have said enough!" cried he angrily. "Be thankful I assume it is grief that makes you speak so powerfully. Why, if I thought they were your true sentiments I'd rip your heart out this very second! Get out, you insufferable witch and go to your room! Your mother wants nothing further from you and I am content to let you sleep undisturbed for tonight. NOW – GO!"

Errin scrambled to her feet and went out, sobbing to herself and, slamming her chamber door, she fell, insensible, on her bed.

Heaton, left alone with the stiffening corpse, raised his candle for the last time on the woman he had used, abused and utterly ruined in his lifetime.

"Haunt me, Elizabeth, would you?" snarled he between clenched teeth. "For your unholy threats you shall lie in unhallowed ground so that Old Nick may fetch you easier in his own time!"

So saying he covered the peaceful face, blew out the candle and returned to his bed.

CHAPTER 7

The next day Elizabeth's death was confirmed to the world and the cause of it stated as consumption of about three month's duration. The doctor was somewhat perplexed at the suddenness of death, having prognosticated its slow approach a few days earlier. However, his understandable fear of Mr Grimshaw made his visit short and he was offered no time alone with the body. He did notice a number of strange blue marks on the arms and upper torso but under Heaton's evil gaze he put them down as bruises, covered the alabaster face and left thankfully.

Later the following day Heaton hitched up two of his best driving horses to the wagon and locking Errin into her room, called up his son and set off at a fair speed for Scarshead. There he journeyed to the carpenter's and after a lengthy conversation tied up the wagon and crossed the road to the alehouse.

As he did so he was overtaken in his walk by three individuals – the oldest of whom, a grey-haired man, tapped him smartly on the shoulder. Heaton turned immediately and curled his fists but kept his temper by scanning the group with a scornful eye.

They consisted of two men and a young girl, who could not have been more than sixteen years of age. She had a strange and perplexing resemblance to Elizabeth, especially around the eyes and mouth and the autumn beauty of her hair. She wore a simplistic plaid gown covered by a thick shawl and her hair was partly braided at the front. Her deep hazel eyes seemed to pierce his soul and made Heaton wince. The sensation was more painful than any kick or blow. The other two were colourless by comparison to the girl. The younger man was possibly twenty and bore a thick profusion of blonde hair with a short beard and moustache. He was very tall, well-formed and good-looking in an angelic sort of way. The other man who had touched him Heaton recognised as Joseph Drayton, now grown old and stout.

The latter man spoke first.

"Mr Grimshaw," said he, in familiar tones. "I am come to express my sorrow at your wife's death. As you know I lost my own partner a little while afore. I send you my sympathy, sir, and would be honoured to attend the funeral if you could give me the time and date?"

"Well, well." sneered the black villain contemptuously. "Mr Drayton as I live and breathe! I am shocked to see the change in you. The passage of years has not been kind and I would not have recognised you but for the voice. I am pleased to see you remember me!"

"Remember you?" gasped Joseph. "O God that I could forget you, Heaton! Yet I am bound to do my duty to one who, in life, was my own flesh and blood. The funeral, sir?"

"There will not be one. At least not as you would recognise. But this I will say. There is nothing to do with Elizabeth that concerns you now! Good day. Come, Hardy!"

The two men moved off and entered the alehouse opposite, leaving the group of three staring after them.

"A strange man, Papa," whispered the girl as the father and son departed."Who is he? Why is he so black and grim? Why, he might be the Devil himself! His words were very powerfully spoken!"

"Think nothing of him, Rachel," replied her father immediately."He is not worthy to be friends with. Let us go back to the carriage."

But Rachel was young and inexperienced and her heart had been raised in a loving, secure environment where hatred and cruelty never raised their ugly heads. Her memories of the black, demoniac figure became compelling and attractive; not a middle-aged man with grey in his coal-black hair but a shadowy gypsy figure encompassing all the desires and feelings growing in Rachel's maturing mind. The picture of him haunted her for the rest of the day and, like a child possessed of a new toy, she turned the encounter over and over in her brain. Who was he?

In the evening, when her father was asleep and her brother Gerald absorbing himself in the delights of a calf-bound book, Rachel grew tired of gazing into the shifting fire and ventured a cautious question to Gerald.

"Do you know who that man was we met today?"

"Yes," replied he briefly, still absorbed in his book.

"And do you know why Papa has such an aversion to his company?"

"Yes."

No further communication was forthcoming so Rachel sighed deeply and resumed her silent occupation. Then, after a while, she could bear it no longer.

"You must tell me, Gerald!" cried she as loud as she dared. "Was that boy at his side his son?"

"Yes, he has a daughter too, a year or two older than you."

"Oh, then how come we did not see his wife?"

"He does not have one – now. She is dead."

"Ah-ha!" said Rachel delightedly. "Now I perceive it! His wife was Cousin Elizabeth that Papa mentioned and therefore, by marriage, he is our cousin too!"

"He is a bad man, Rachel, so do not be happy about the relationship," warned her brother.

But secretly Rachel was excited by kinship to a man like Heaton and she vowed if she saw him again she would speak to him. That her Father disapproved so strongly of Heaton did not trouble her. Many times she had challenged her father's judgement and surely the disagreement must be over business or inheritance? Accordingly she said no more to her brother but stored up the gleaned information in her heart and reflected inwardly upon it.

The next day was a mild spring day with huge fleecy clouds gracing the heavens and shifting lazily across a blue firmament sparkling with sunshine. The moors opened up bountifully in the warmth and revelled in their luxurious air of freedom.

After breakfast Joseph Drayton set off for the nearby town of Scarton, accompanied by his son Gerald on horseback. Gerald proposed to help his father with some business transactions and then return home at lunch time, leaving Joseph to follow in the evening.

Rachel was left in charge of her governess who came from Scarshead to teach her the accomplishments of painting, music and needlework five mornings a week. Other than that the sole inhabitants of Garstang Hall were two servants and a housekeeper, each involved with their considerable workload. The governess, a mild, gentle woman was easily influenced and when Rachel complained of a sick headache she was allowed to go to her room with no questions asked. A few minutes later Rachel heard the governess pack up and leave, then a blissful silence followed.

Rachel went to her wardrobe and changed into her best riding habit then she slunk stealthily down the stairs and out of the side door where she could reach the stables unobserved.

A gentle breeze wafted across from the sleeping moorlands, sweet with the perfume of opening spring flowers and reviving heather. The brown fronds were greening; they had been held tightly in the grip of frost or frozen beneath layers of fallen snow. All that was now gone. Summer was ahead. Warmth, new life, until autumn would once again transform the moors into a sea of purple lustre.

In a few moments Rachel had saddled and bridled her small brown pony Zephyr and mounting easily from the gate she set his head in the direction of Westerdale. By casual questioning she had gathered information on this establishment from the Hall's servants, one of whom used to work there.

In her heart Rachel saw herself restoring peace between the two families. Was this man not her cousin? Ignorant of the deep, unfathomable rift between her father and Heaton and unaware of the infernal true nature of the latter's indisposition she imagined the two families reunited. Although she had heard a lot about Westerdale itself and cousin Elizabeth very little was said about

Heaton. What a strange dark enigma he presented! She knew her Papa grew angry at even the mention of Heaton's name but he had never disclosed why which puzzled her and made the attraction stronger. Forbidden fruit...

She put her pony into a faster pace and cantering on over the fragrant ling she imagined her clamorous reception at her destination.

At Westerdale a furious argument had broken out and been ended, as usual, by the single blow of a tyrant. Heaton refused all rites of funeral regarding his late wife, turned away the undertaker with threats and now cursed his own daughter for daring to disobey him.

"Let her lie where she is!" snarled he, yielding a spade and urging his sullen son to do likewise.

"You may attend us this once Errin – snivel if you think it proper and go and change your gown for a black one. Bah! It will not help her. There – I am out of patience with you. Do as you will." And making for the door he gave her a hearty kick. Hardy followed, gazing carelessly at her with dark sullen eyes and made a point of treading on her as she lay prostrate.

Errin picked herself up and went into the scullery where she washed her swollen face. Heaton had lived up to his threats and had beaten her regularly for even the smallest offence. She was forced to adopt the role of servant, serving their food in the parlour but taking her own meagre meals in the cold kitchen. Here she spent the evenings sewing and washing till her once pretty hands grew red and blistered. Heaton allowed her no luxury of a fire, and it was only lit for cooking. Her eyes were rheumy with constant tears and her once fine gowns became impoverished with dust and damp. Heaton had stripped her room bare of comforts. He possessed the key and instructed his cruel son to accompany Errin on any errand that involved leaving the property. Hardy performed the role ghoulishly, watching over her every movement and even inventing disobediences in order to pinch and kick her. Life without her mother was hard but life without love was unbearable.

She brushed her thick, dark hair and fetching her prayer book, the sole possession Heaton had not stripped her of, she put on her cloak and passed through the open door, traversed the yard and walked out onto the moorland.

Her black jailer was assaulting the damp, peaty ground with a spade, every shovelful of earth being dispatched with a curse between clenched teeth. Hardy dug stolidly, a sly, satisfied grin upon his usually unsmiling lips.

After a while Heaton stopped, wiped his face and glanced up at the innocent apparition who stood above him.

"Damn you!" he cried, digging in his spade and leering at her. "Damn you, Errin, for looking at me in that way! Why have you inherited the very eyes I seek to bury? Why do you look at me as she did? And there is another, not so very far from here, possessed of her infernal orbs! Get back I say and keep those damn pools of light from my face!" He climbed out of the trough he had created and Errin, experienced in his heavy blows, drew off and turned away.

"Ah-ha!" cried Heaton, gloating. "The miserable wretch has learnt to fear me has she? That is good! Fear is desirable. It is my life- blood – it sets me on fire! Fear and hate! Excellent! Take the strain, Hardy, and continue digging. I'll return to your side in a moment."

He marched off in the direction of the house from whence he emerged a few minutes later pulling a long, flat cart upon which rested a simple wooden coffin. His black eyes met his daughter's and he turned sneeringly to the spring flowers some tender hands had heaped around the box.

"Well?" he cried in fury. "You have really done it this time Errin! Who gave you leave to gather flowers for her! Come, speak up! I permitted no floral tributes nor this haphazard arrangement!"

"They are wild flowers," replied Errin. "I gathered them from the moorland hollows when I was out with Hardy. There is no harm in them!"

"Hah!" sneered he, gathering up the blossoms and crushing them between his fingers. "No harm indeed! There is no good in them either! Well, Hardy you have exhibited a weakness! How could you allow your sister to idle away her time in picking flowers for a rotting corpse?"

"Do not speak so!" cried Errin, bursting into tears. "They are not for you. Do not deface them! They are mother's! I'd not so much as put a daisy on YOUR grave. Anything alive on your grave would die instantly but these would have stayed fresh for days upon the damp turf!"

"Damn you! Shut yer foul mouth or I'll shut it for you!" spat Heaton grabbing the remainder of the blooms and scattering them over the grass. "Come Hardy, what have you to say?"

"I saw no harm in it," murmured the accused, ceasing work. "She wished very much to have the flowers and was very persuasive in her tone. Besides I am sick of her constant moaning and crying and at least that stopped when she saw the blooms."

"Indeed! You have weakened considerably. If she looks beseechingly at you again with limpid eyes you must tear out the offending organs and be done with it! And if she pleads with a silver tongue you must wrench that out too! In short you should have cuffed her and brought her to me. You'll not move me so easily, will you madam?"

"You have no heart, no feeling!" cried Errin. "Hardy you have ruined and debased but there is a spark of decency in there somewhere that might spring to life if you would let it!"

"Hark how she heaps praises on you, Hardy! Well....I must take great pains to crush this spark of decency before it ignites and ruins the boy. Keep at your work, Hardy, and you Errin, for your insolence shall join him. There, take my spade and dig! Dig your mother's grave. Can you not see the worms that will consume her? I tell you if I were to remove this lid you'd smell such a stench as'd sicken you for days! Get on wi' it. Get in the hole now!" And he pushed her roughly into the trough, throwing her his heavy spade that she could hardly wield.

Looking at his two offspring working beneath him Heaton felt a deep sense of satisfaction. Raising his eyes he took a quick look across the greening moorland where he espied a figure on a small brown horse heading towards Westerdale. His gaze fell again upon his children. Errin, already fatigued, paused nervously and glanced up at her antagonist.

"Keep at it," snarled he, skirting the deepening grave and heading out onto the moorland track towards the visitor.

Ere long the pony reached him and he stretched out his powerful hand and enclosed strong fingers upon the reins, his eyes staring, hard and cold, at the rider.

Rachel stared back at him with no trace of fear or anxiety in her face. Heaton winced.

"So," declared he. "You are trespassing, madam. Your beast is stamping his hooves on MY land. Do you perceive that?"

"Yes, cousin," replied she, simply."I have taken the liberty to call on you unannounced. I trust the surprise is agreeable to you?"

"What?" cried he in amazement, stumbling backwards and thus freeing the pony's head. "You know me? Yet...wait...I have seen eyes like that before and your face.....yes, in some reoccurring nightmare!"

"True, we have met before. Do you not recall it?" asked she, continuing to gaze into his face. "My father and brother were with me at the time. Come, sir, I am no stranger although you have obviously forgotten me. Shake hands with your cousin, Mr Heaton, I am Rachel Drayton."

"Rachel?" cried he, apprehensively. He felt as though a bullet had passed through his soul. "Aye, now I remember it. Old Drayton, yes! Well, well I am honoured by your visit." He essayed a small bow. "However your pleasantries are wasted on a rough fellow such as I, grown black and twisted with age. But please venture forth and I can introduce you to a far more amiable cousin!"

A sly smile spread across his grim features and Rachel mistook it for the seeds of friendship and accordingly, urged her pony onwards to Westerdale.

77

"Hardy!" snapped the black master, clicking his fingers and nodding his head at the half-hidden form of his son. "Come out of there, now! You've done enough. Drop yer spade I say and come and take Miss Rachel's pony so you may escort her into the house. Be a good guide and leave out yer cussing for that is stable talk and not for the ears of young ladies! Look lively, lad! Go in. I will follow shortly. Errin, stay at your post."

Heaton crushed the pony's reins into his son's dubious hands and watched the pair move off with narrowed eyes. Heaton as a schemer was pervading and dangerous.

They drew off, Rachel dismounting and venturing forth a stream of questions to her companion who replied in halting monosyllables. Slowly they progressed to the stables.

"There!" sneered he, delightedly picking up the vacant spade and commencing work. "I have put into action that which will be the means of killing him who despised my union with this coffin. By Christ! The daring of my plot kindles me! You are safe from cruelty today, Errin – do you hear? I am nearly happy!"

"Then you must be very miserable indeed for your sole pleasure lies in creating and enjoying other's misfortunes!" cried she, emotionally. "Now you've destroyed mother and debased ME your cruel eyes glint on that poor girl! Who is she? And what has she ever done to hurt you?"

"Be silent!" snapped he, turning and giving her a savage slap. "How much longer can I put up with your eternal misery and reproach? I will NOT be criticized – I will NOT be rebuked! Remain at your work. That girl is the blood of my greatest enemy. How can she be so ignorant? Ha – if I can only break HIM by bending HER. Do you think I care if she suffers? Damn you all! The world might fall to pieces tomorrow and I will feel no pity for it. Satan might tear you limb from limb in front of me – do you think that will move me? Do you think I revere compassion? It is weakness, weakness and man must suffer for it!"

"Did you never feel a twinge of love in your lifetime?"asked she, tearfully, shocked at his inhumanity.

"Don't speak to me of love!" spat he, attacking the earth again. "Whatever connections I had to that vice – that wasted, useless emotion – I bury now with this box. And may no one ever resurrect them."

In the quiet, dark interior of the stable Rachel got a closer look at her taciturn guide. He was a fully-formed youth, athletic yet stolidly built, handsome yet reserved. He untacked her beast wordlessly, tried hard to avoid her questioning eye and mumbled that she might care to come into the house.

"Yes," replied Rachel. "I should love to see the interior of Westerdale. How many servants do you keep?"

"Servants?" exclaimed Hardy, in surprise. "Why – none. Why would we need to keep any servants when we have Errin? She does the house and Father and I do the stock."

"Errin is your sister?"

"Aye."

"The pretty dark girl outside?"

"Aye."

"You're very talkative, Hardy!" replied she, disappointedly after a minute or two's silence. "Don't you want to know anything about me? We are cousins after all."

A grunt was the answer to this and then Hardy led the way through the yard to the back door.

"This is the scullery," murmured he, morosely, deeming it necessary to inform her of the fact.

"Indeed!" she replied, a little haughtily, lifting up her skirts and flaring her nostrils. "At home ours is the haunt of servants. I have never been in ours!"

Hardy could think of nothing to say to this and bidding her be wary of the dogs he led the way into the kitchen.

A broad, light alcove opened up from the passageway which comprised the primitive "kitchen" here. In one corner stood a wooden mangle; upon a ledge dark, identical canisters lined up in single file and below this a dying fire spat. Over this hung an empty black cooking pot, burnt by the constant contact with the flames. A low, three-legged stool stood by the grate and another higher seat by the pump handle. Elsewhere the orange lustreless tiles were stained by generations of muddy boots. A small, open larder led off from this recess in which an old table stood, housing portions of meat, prepared chitterlings and bottled fruits. Bunches of dried herbs, twists of spices and tied vegetables hung from the ceiling prolifically.

Upon one wall various crude figures and numbers had been drawn in smoked charcoal and Rachel, observing them, moved over for a closer look. They were things she might have done in infancy when five or six years of age.

"Who did these?" asked she, turning to her guide who blushed red.

"'Tis no matter," replied she.

"Who did them?" repeated Rachel, undeterred.

"Very well – I did them!" affirmed he. "What do ye make o' em?"

"They have lasted well!" she commented, scanning the surface. "They were doubtlessly formed in your infancy!"

The door opened at that moment and Heaton entered, throwing down his spade with a clatter. A wry smile played about his lips from the latter remark which he had overheard.

"He formed them last week!" sneered the father, gazing tauntingly at his blushing son. "You see, Rachel, a dunce before you. Why – he cannot write to save his soul. Now, if you took it into your head to teach him he'd be far more use to me than he is at present. Well, Hardy, I am very disappointed in 'ee. Fancy keeping our guest in the servant's quarter! There – you have tried for long enough. Go help yer sister and do not return until everything is done. Now, Rachel, come through to the parlour. My son is out of practice at receiving guests but he will learn if you come often enough!" And he smiled dark eyes and lips on her and she....she was captivated.

CHAPTER 8

Gerald arrived home from Scarton a little before one o'clock, having left his father discussing business over a mutton pie in some respectful alehouse. A warm shower of rain dampened him in his journey but the gentle moorland breeze soon dried his wet clothes and the silky coat of his steed.

Arriving at Garstang Hall he rode round to the stables and having untacked his beast noticed, on passing the box, that Rachel's pony Zephyr was missing. He walked a little way onto the moorland track, climbed a grassy hillock and surveyed the distant heath lands carefully. There was no trace of movement in any quarter save for a flock of dun brown birds feeding on a group of stunted bushes. Elsewhere all was strangely dark and lifeless. An immense mass of black cloud had rolled over the sun and the cornflower blue became a light, unattractive grey. The landscape felt grim and stark; even the growing flowers at his feet emitted only a pallid beauty, their glories over shadowed by the louring firmament.

Gerald was bemused. He turned and entered the house front where he spied the plump, elderly housekeeper.

"Ah! Good afternoon!" exclaimed Gerald, trying to keep his voice steady and control his panic."Can you tell me where my sister is, Mrs Gudrun? I have some news for her from my father that is urgent!"

"Miss Drayton is confined to her room," answered Mrs Gudrun at once. "She has a trifling headache or some such pain. The governess accompanied her there then left I believe."

"And Rachel is still in her chamber?"

"I think so, sir."

"No one has ascended to see to her?"

"Well, Ruth did run up a few minutes ago but her knock received no reply so deeming it likely Miss Drayton was asleep we left her. Will you wake her up for luncheon, sir?"

"Yes," replied Gerald, although his heart sank. "I will see to her. You may serve now, please."

He climbed the oak staircase, traversed the landing and burst into Rachel's room without knocking. It was, indeed, empty, as he had feared.

A tartan plaid dress draped carelessly from a chair – the very dress he had observed she wore that morning – and a pair of shoes lay idly at the foot of the bed. Gerald moved to the open wardrobe, observed her riding outfit had been removed and having satisfied himself his grounds for anger were righteous he left the room and ran down the stairs.

"You must hold luncheon back!" cried he to the surprised housekeeper. "Miss Drayton is NOT in her room! She has changed into her riding kit and Zephyr is gone! I will re-saddle my horse and go after her. Attend to the meal. Perhaps – and I hope this fervently – I will not be long." He threw on his coat again, neglected his hat and running out of the side door re-entered the stable and tacked up his horse. Vaulting on nimbly he legged his mount into an easy canter and turned his head towards where he knew the grim walls of Westerdale lay.

Hardy and Errin had been forced by the ominous approach of storm clouds to hasten their labours and immerse the coffin in a shallower grave than their black master would have allowed, had he been present. This they accomplished and were in the act of shovelling in the peaty soil when the earth trembled with the approaching roar of thunder. They shovelled faster and the sky turned a vivid purple in which sulphur flashes of lightening rose and fell like heaving waves. A sultry breeze whipped up forewarning them of rain but Errin, who had abandoned any notion of comfort in the grim world she inhabited, continued to flatten the earth whilst the downpour broke. Hardy left and ran for cover.

In the parlour Rachel sat by the glowing fire, her eyes turning periodically to her grim cousin who sat opposite and produced an alluring smile on his black lips.

"Well?" asked Heaton when Hardy appeared removing his outdoor clothing.

"'Tis done!" replied his son simply. "Errin still moans over it but I have left her. It is raining and she will come in when she's soaked."

"Aye, aye," returned Heaton."Let her be a little longer and then go fetch her. Well, now, Rachel, you have your cousin back to entertain you! Do you not think him handsome in a devilish, ghoulish way? He is almost seventeen, are you not, Hardy?"

"Aye, seventeen, and past!" lied he, proudly.

"And he cannot even write his own name!" laughed Rachel scornfully, fixing her eyes upon him. At this he grew furious and curled his fists, throwing his form into a far-off chair.

"I can outshoot you, outride you, hunt, fish and keep the stock in order. THAT is far above book-larnin' and all that trash!" he exclaimed, angrily.

"Ar," replied she, evidently a little sorry for her scornful words. "But wouldn't you like to learn, Hardy?"

"No," snapped he, in a bad temper. "I've no time for books!"

"If I taught you we could write to each other sometimes," pleaded she. "Wouldn't you like that?"

"Why can't you come over here instead of doin' all that writing?" asked he, in a milder tone.

"Well 'tis a long way and besides Papa may not like it," ventured she.

"You are correct there, Rachel," affirmed Heaton, his black eyes darting maliciously from one to the other. "He still believes I was not good enough for his niece and blames me entirely for her death. Yet what more could I ha' done? The doctor was called at the first twinge and remained till the last breath! Alas! He could not save my poor Elizabeth. Yet your father still finds me culpable. Rachel, I am much misunderstood. Would such a man as I am named – devil, demon, entertain the daughter of a man who unjustly hates me? He would do me harm if he could, believe me! Think of that next time he maligns me."

"O, he does not complain of you at all to me," she cried. "But my brother, Gerald, paints vivid pictures of your wickedness. Cousin, you have been cordial and kind to me – I will deny knowledge of your evil for I have seen none."

Heaton smiled slyly at this declaration and bid Hardy fetch some of Errin's cakes for their guest and a bottle of wine from the cellar.

Outside it grew even darker. Errin had no desire to seek the company of the loathsome black duo so remained at her mother's grave, her eyes low and sad and her heart heavy. Occasionally she brushed the damp earth with her trembling hand as if to caress the lost soul she had loved.

"O Mother," she breathed. "If you could see from your seat at Abraham's bosom, the abject cruelty and torture I suffer you would surely send angels to snatch me away from HIS clutches! Yet your suffering was greater. O mother- I wish both you and I were safe in heaven away from this hellish world!" A few slow tears fell but they gave no comfort. She rose up and began gathering the crushed flower heads her father had scattered over the grass.

Whilst she was doing this her ears, ever alert, picked up the approaching clop of horse's hooves and turning she beheld a large, brown charger being driven onwards by a tall figure whose coat had fallen open and flapped loudly in the rising gale. As he neared her she could see the fine cut of his beard and blonde hair. She gazed at him in surprise for a few seconds, remembered her muddied and tear-stained face and turned abruptly away as if to run off.

"Wait a minute!" cried he of the blonde hair. "I desire a word with you. Please wait!"

She did so uneasily and he drew level with her and dismounted, allowing his horse to catch a mouthful of moorland grass.

"Good afternoon," murmured he gently, observing the girl kept her face averted from his gaze and that she was dressed in mourning.

"Good afternoon," faltered she. "If you are looking for my brother or Father they are both within."

"Who is your father?" he asked quietly.

"Why, Mr Grimshaw – Heaton Grimshaw. Surely you have heard of him? My mother was Elizabeth Drayton. She lies buried under this damp earth," replied she, at last receiving courage to turn and face him.

"Ah ha," he murmured, gazing at her dirty, tear-stained face. "Now I perceive it. You must be Errin Grimshaw – my cousin. No, you do not know me. I am Gerald Drayton from Garstang Hall."

"I have never heard of you before," she replied, feeling bemused. "But why would I? I never go out of the house unescorted. Well, until today. The day of my mother's funeral. He has left me to mourn for a few minutes in solitude," she finished, bitterly. A few tears fell onto the sod and Gerald perceived them. His tender heart bled for her.

"Please don't upset yourself," he begged. "Is your father unkind to you?"

"Unkind?" spat she, her spirit rising within her. "He is an inhuman monster – a fiend – a devil! Do you know he possesses not ONE atom of compassion or kindness? He is black and twisted – so evil he must have come straight from Lucifer himself!"

She spoke powerfully and her swollen eyes sparkled with pain and ire.

"Heaton is only happy miserable, only joyful when tormenting me or bringing cruelty into some one's life. My mother suffered terribly. Pray God she is at peace now! He has stripped me of every human comfort. Were he to starve me I would gladly die but he is too clever for that! He gives me just enough to exist and survive so I can bake his bread and wash his clothes." She became conscious of the power and emotion of her words and blushed.

"I should not speak so to one who is a stranger!"she said. "But I crave death so to be in union with her who lies buried here!"

"I have heard atrocious reports of Heaton's conduct before," confessed Gerald. "My father speaks of severe injuries received at his hands many years ago. It has resulted in a morbid fear of that black villain who surely killed your mother with his cruelty. Yet I am not come to see Heaton or discuss his behaviour. I seek my sister, Rachel, who seems to have developed a fascination for Westerdale and Heaton's history ever since we met him in Scarshead. Can you recall seeing her?"

"Aye," replied she, shaking back her wet, dark locks. "There is a young girl within who arrived on a small brown pony that now resides in our stable."

"Then I must find her," avowed he. "And escort her home before my father returns. He will be appalled if he finds out she has been in Heaton's company! Will you show me the way in? Can I tie my horse up in your yard?"

She picked up her spade, bade him follow her and led the way round to the stables, after which they entered the house by the side door.

In the passage way before the parlour door Errin paused.

"Take great care," whispered she urgently. "My father is a man of great cunning and hypocrisy. With one hand he may be caressing your soul but with the other he will be ripping out your heart and drinking your blood. Wait here. I will announce you."

She knocked quickly and went in. The three of them were partaking of refreshments, Rachel sitting by the fire eating cake and caressing a little black cat. Heaton turned at her entrance and put down his goblet of wine.

"Well, Errin?" demanded he. "What do you want? We are entertaining a guest! I presume you have tired of sobbing over a corpse and have come to me for sustenance. Well, take a cake and get out. Servants eat in the kitchen. Hardy, escort her there!"

"No, no," cried Errin as her brother laid rough hands on her."Someone has come to see you, Father."

"Well, well," sneered Heaton. "What a day we are having! Leave her, Hardy. Show the person in, girl, then return to the kitchen. Lock the outer doors, Hardy and bring the keys to me."

Errin withdrew gladly and opening the door summoned Gerald to enter.

"Tread carefully," whispered she as he passed her. "Father is possessed of a devilish plan. Beware-he will assume any mood to obtain it."

Hardy rose promptly and stared indolently into the visitor's face. Then he grabbed his sister's arm, twisted it behind her back and marched her out to the kitchen. He locked the outer doors, leered at Errin and returned to the parlour.

"Good afternoon, Mr Grimshaw," said the young man, trying to keep his voice pleasant. "I believe introductions are unnecessary; certainly I am acquainted with you!"

"I haven't the slightest notion who you are, sir!" replied Heaton, angrily. "You are a trespasser on my land and an uninvited intrusion. You had best state your name and business, sir, or I'll be obliged to set the dogs on you!"

"If you wish to know my identity, Mr Grimshaw, then ask my sister who sits blushing at your hearth and turning her face away! Well, Rachel, this is a delightful situation to come home to! I supposed you to be sick in bed but no! A long ride is my duty and to a stranger's fireside. The servants told me you were indisposed."

"Servants always lie," sneered Heaton. "You would be best rid of them. You'll find none here!"

"Sir," replied Gerald, his temper and impatience rising at the sullen expression on his sister's face. "I have no quarrel with you such as my father entertains. I only desire to take my sister home before our father returns and finds us both missing."

"And suppose she does not wish to leave?" snarled Heaton. "She came of her own free will and must leave in the same way. Now-ask her in a civilised way, if you please!"

"I shall ask her how I please!" snapped Gerald. "This is my business and no concern of yours! Rachel – get up at once!"

"On the contrary, sir, you forget yourself," replied Heaton with dangerous calm. Only his black eyes sparkled with ire. "You are in my house and as such must abide by my rules! Hardy, guard the doorway! I shall keep you here till you remember your manners!"

"Mr Grimshaw," reasoned Gerald, struggling to keep his temper. "I have only met you once before- briefly- yet I have heard numerous tales of your cruelty and insolence. The picture that is painted is incredible! Can such a man truly exist? I will reserve judgement until further acquaintance. In short I have no quarrel with you! You have never lifted a finger against me and as such I cannot hate or fear you. I form my own opinions; I don't listen to tales or stories. Now seeing there is no feud between us take your guard off the doorway and let me go!"

"Stay where you are, Hardy!" called Heaton, fixing his dark eyes on the quaking form of his guest. "Now then, Rachel, do you wish to go back with this brother of yours or shall I send him on his way?"

"It is raining!" cried she, gazing at the blurred windowpanes behind her. "I have no desire to get wet so you must wait a few minutes longer, Gerald!"

"Very well," resolved her brother, impatiently. "Since you persist in remaining I'll leave you to come home alone or, if you prefer it, Papa shall fetch you himself! I hardly think he'll be in a good mood when he hears of your present location."

"There is no need for you to tell him!" she cried angrily. "I only wish to remain till this shower passes!"

"Stay here eternally if you wish!" snapped Gerald. "And let Papa cut you off completely – I don't care! Mr Grimshaw, I am anxious to be on my way, I leave you my sister. She may do as she pleases!"

He turned from the fireside and cast a suspicious glare at Hardy who had not moved from his post.

"Stand aside!" cried Gerald but the guard continued to stare at his captive insolently so Gerald, tired of this constant provocation, promptly sent out his fist and floored his captor with a mighty blow.

Freeing the door he stepped outside and made for the side entrance which led round to the yard. Luckily it was unlocked. Entering the stable he tightened the girths of his mount and was swinging himself into the saddle when a plaintive voice called,

"Wait for me!"

"Quickly, then!" he called, unbolting the door to the next stable. "Hardy will be after me for that blow and Papa may be home early in this weather!"

Rachel vaulted onto her pony without the provision of saddle or bridle and clinging to Zephyr's luxurious mane followed her brother's horse out onto the moorland. In another few minutes the outline of Westerdale was lost in the gathering mist.

Hardy picked himself up and wiped the blood from his face.

"There," sneered his father, laughing. "He has felled ye! And serve ye right!" His eyes darkened and his smile faded. "By Christ if any one had done that to me when I was your age I'd never have rested till I'd broken every bone in their body!"

"'Twas an act of surprise," muttered Hardy. "He's a hand higher than me and several years older--"

"Aye and he would have fallen harder if you had given him back such a blow as he gave you! You will learn. I have plans for you Hardy but you must learn to protect yourself! No, if life proves kind and fate sails in you may yet wed a fortune!"

Gerald and Rachel arrived back at Garstang in time to escape a second soaking, the first heavy shower having died down soon after they left for home. The largest stable, reserved for Joseph's seventeen hand hunter Megalin, stood empty, its door creaking in the rising wind. Both rider's dismounted by the stone trough and allowed their mounts to drink; Rachel was wet-eyed and upset, Gerald angry yet restless.

"Well," murmured Gerald at length when it became apparent that Rachel had no power for words. "What Papa will make of your deceitful conduct I can hardly tell! It will grieve him deeply to know you crave acquaintance with such a fiend and exhibit pride in naming him cousin. I hope you are cured of such a friendship, Rachel, by Heaton's violent words and conduct!"

"On the contrary," replied she, choosing not to meet his eye. "I never saw him raise a hand against me – or indeed a word – only YOU Gerald struck a blow! Heaton's conduct was altogether amenable."

"Amenable? How can you be so blind, sister? Did you not observe the way the black duo torture and abuse poor Errin?"

"Heaton has no refinements, that I will allow," she acknowledged. "His manner is rough and blunt but I would hesitate to call him uncivil and I saw no cruelty!"

"Think as you like, Rachel, but that was an experience I never want to repeat. Obviously my words can't shift your regard for that man, but as a distant regard it must remain! There are to be no more visits to Westerdale. Papa will forbid it when he hears all and will take steps to curtail your freedom."

"There is no need to inform him!" she cried, directly. "'Twould only grieve him knowing what I did and much as I think he wrongs Mr Grimshaw by his judgement I love Papa too much to offend him!"

"Then you must make me a promise," vowed Gerald, trying to remain calm. "Swear to me you will make no further visits to Westerdale and I will leave Papa in ignorance of today."

"I cannot do that!" cried she, starting up in alarm."I gave my word before I left that I would come again and teach Hardy his letters. I cannot break my promise."

"Do as you will then," stormed Gerald, losing patience and leading his tired mount to the stable."And I will turn the whole thing over to Papa as soon as he arrives home!"

Rachel pondered deeply for a minute, then she swallowed hard and nodded her head sadly,

"Very well. So be it. I swear never again to visit Westerdale."
And a slow, despairing tear fell with the first few spots of evening
rain.

CHAPTER 9

Having extracted a promise from his sister, Gerald found himself the one most likely to break it, for, after seeing the tragic face of Errin, he could not forget her. Night after night he lay awake, harbouring vengeful thoughts against the man who abused her and in his sleep she appeared to him shackled with heavy chains, always out of reach though he sweated blood to reach her. By day he worried about her welfare. Was she warm? Cold? Had she eaten today? Had she shelter? Watching the advent of many a dawn he wondered if she slept or wandered, pensive, as he did.

His father thought him ill or pining for some secret cause and thus set him to work harder. Joseph became exasperated when easy tasks were missed and more difficult ones performed incorrectly. The cattle were often left unbedded in the byre, the sheep could be wandering on the moorland when they needed to be at market and the horses frequently went hungry.

It was early summer now and the long, level hours of daylight produced a fervent restlessness in all living things. The moor, preparing for its annual transformation grew green and strong. Wild flowers ejected their varying colours among the verdant carpet. The nights were moonlit and occasionally warm, sweet rain fell; heat shimmered in the valleys.

Since her meeting with Heaton Rachel had been unduly quiet, almost reserved. She declined going out, affirmed she was not ill and chose to remain in her room at every opportunity. She rose earlier and earlier, getting downstairs before the servants stirred and conversed with no one save the stable lad who came every day from Scarshead. A couple of times a week she went to the stable block to see him and was once seen by the servant to be giving him books and jewellery. As this same servant saw him kiss her on the cheek downstairs talk was that Miss Drayton had a sweetheart to whom she lent her pony to and lavished playthings on.

Had anyone been able to observe her meetings they would have seen her giving him letters and occasionally being given missives back in return for rings and books. These letters she kept secret and took up to her room to read so that no one saw her. The servants talked of the meetings among themselves but mentioned nothing to the master as they respected Miss Drayton's privacy. She looked so pale and unhappy who were they to add to it by uncovering her secret?

It took no genius to deduce these letters were from the inhabitant of Westerdale – one Heaton Grimshaw to be precise. These missives had started innocently enough. Rachel, upset that she could not keep her promise to her cousin, had written a note to say her absence was due to her Father and Gerald's bullying and not her desires. To get it to Heaton was her next problem but overhearing the servants saying that the new stable lad was friends with Hardy Grimshaw she hatched her plan. Waylaying the lad with the letter and the promise of kisses and books she got him to take Zephyr and deliver the letter. To her surprise her missive produced a reply and so it went on.

"I cannot forget," wrote she "that you gave me a most cordial reception and that my brother was unbelievably rude! I hope Hardy bears no grudge against me for Gerald's conduct as it was not of my making. Please tell him so, dear cousin, I wish he could write to me or that I could see you again and learn more about you. Everyone speaks ill of you here. I know they do it deliberately to poison me against you. Have no fear-I will not be swayed. How bitterly I regret that rash promise to Gerald – alas I may never again enter Westerdale and Papa affirms you will never be welcome at Garstang."

At first Heaton was perplexed to receive such a letter which indicated there was little hope Rachel could visit and thus kindle the romance with his son that he so desired. Yet, as much as he hated the name Drayton, he was determined that a union would come about that would bring riches to Westerdale. To do that meant acquiescing to the girl's odious desire to send and receive letters and Heaton had to perform this task as Hardy's writing was no better than a child's. But every sentence Heaton penned brought Rachel nearer and nearer to his son's clutches so soon, very soon, she would be within Hardy's reach.

My dear Rachel, wrote he, shuddering at the sentiment, *I, too, was overjoyed to make your acquaintance though it seems to me many years too late. If only we had met years ago how glad Hardy and I would have been. He and you could have grown up together and the eternal rift, which has deepened over the years with your father's hatred, would have been healed and our families united. I have many times extended the hand of friendship to Mr Drayton but it has always been promptly and proudly repelled. That he and your brother seek to poison your mind I am not surprised. Therefore show these letters to no one and be discreet with your delivery. Hadan is a close friend of Hardy's and can be trusted to keep silent. Hardy wishes he knew his letters well enough to write to you. He was quite overcome with your beauty and wisdom and mopes about the place asking when you will come again. Alas! I can give him no good news on that front. But he is practising his writing and learning swiftly so he can take on this communication. He thinks of you by day and dreams of you by night. Please reply quickly so I can read him your answer.*
Your loving cousin,
Heaton.

At the termination of such a letter Heaton would read it out aloud with much mirth and sneering. Hardy would join in and paint a revolting picture of what he would do to Rachel if she were his wife. If Errin were present this would be played upon time and time again to draw forth the girl's disgust and if she ventured a syllable Heaton would banish her from the room.

94

The summer wore on in its pleasant way and the end of August was reached. A period of hot, baking days ensued with dry, airless nights that banished sleep. Windows were thrown open at all hours, sashes rolled up and the great harvest moon floated in the heavens for all the world as if it were on fire.

Gerald had managed to put behind him the image of Errin and had convinced himself it was sheer folly to believe he could help her. She was quite out of reach and her close kinship to that infernal man Heaton distanced her further. He remained cool and aloof and rarely spoke to his father or sister. The former was annoyed with his preoccupied manner and the latter seemed even more distracted than Gerald himself. He knew Rachel still blamed him for destroying the seeds of friendship with Heaton and he suspected, too, that she still harboured feelings for that black villain and his son.

At night by the silent fireplace Joseph would sit and doze, Rachel retired early to her room in silence and at times the loneliness of the old house rose up and choked Gerald. He became envious of the servants and their excited chatter and laughter in the back regions. Errin was then a half-forgotten dream, many miles away and removed further by the evil spirit that surrounded her and threatened to engulf Gerald if he moved to aid her.

Sometimes he would take a walk over the star-spangled moorlands when the moonlight glinted as bright as day and a cool, refreshing breeze wafted deliciously from the ling. It smelt of strange distant lands, far removed from the pungent smell of bog water and peat.

On the last day of August when the first purple hues of heather vied with the amber sun for supremacy Rachel received a different letter in a foreign hand that held in its contents the means to change her whole life.

Dearest Cousin – it read -

I am at last able to write to you as I wished I could have done months ago when I was first granted a peek at your beautiful face!

Rachel gasped. It was from Hardy himself and although the spelling was poor and the grammar weak she believed the sentiments it contained to be true.

Many nights have passed by – he continued – since I saw you and you have tinged my waking hours and haunted my sleep. I miss you and desire to know you better and see you again.

Return an answer tomorrow saying you will meet me the day after on the moorlands near my home. I know of your forced promise but there is no need to enter Westerdale and so break your word. Can we not take a turn about the moorlands in this clement weather and talk? My father will be absent on business and my sister will be at home so please, dearest Rachel, come and end this yearning!

Sadly I know my rough and uncivilised manner can have no attractions for a lady like you but can we not be friends? Do not let my unworthiness stop you. Say you will come at two o'clock the day after tomorrow.

Your loving cousin,

Hardy.

Bemused by the letter but desirous of meeting her cousin again Rachel could, at first, see no means of gaining enough freedom to do so. True her father had no suspicions of her conduct but Gerald was very curious of her behaviour lately. If she succeeded in saddling Zephyr Gerald would almost certainly notice and follow her with the same calamitous circumstances as before. How was she going to achieve this? She wandered up and down her room and at length she formed an idea.

Fetching her writing desk she switched her pen to her left hand and choosing some plain paper she wrote,

Dear Sir,

I have recently moved into this neighbourhood and desire a good supply of mutton and beef for the business I propose to start. Reliable people of this area have suggested you may be interested in striking a deal with me over this.

Could you possibly meet me the day after tomorrow at the Scarshead-Scarton signpost at two o'clock? I am in lodgings at present so cannot give you a reliable address to reply to but I will wait at that post for half an hour in the hope you will come. If you do not attend I will look elsewhere for my meat supply.

Your faithful servant

D L Evans.

Her writing was easily disguised by her left-hand and she was pleased with her effort. She sealed it up and went down to put it in the parlour by the door so that her father would find it and assume the servant had brought it in. Then she returned to her room, took out some fresh paper, dipped her pen and wrote--

Dear Hardy,

I am happy to inform you that due to my Father and brother's absence from home on that particular afternoon I can meet you. Please do not ask me to remain long – for myself I would be content to linger all afternoon but my parental duo will return and seek me within a couple of hours. Although I can never enter Westerdale again the thought of seeing you again heartens me. Life here can be cold at times as Papa is busy and Gerald preoccupied.

I am sorry Heaton will be away but maybe it is for the best as Papa continues to heap evil on his head and Gerald agrees. Nothing is said about you.

The weather has been too hot lately. The rooms here are stifling and airless. I long to be up on the moors in a stiff

*northerly wind with the ice in the hollows and the valleys singing
with snow! Gerald mopes about on the moors by night and never
rises till ten in the mornings and Papa is displeased with him.
There is a sharp, tense atmosphere here so I must look for
comfort elsewhere.*

*Godspeed the day after tomorrow. I love September – a
month of early morning mist, fresh dew and the purple blaze of
heather.*

I will come as promised, Hardy,

    Your loving,

        Rachel.

The letter was dispatched with a kiss for the stable boy and a
volume of stories. Then she ascended to her room and waited for
breakfast to be called.

At the meal she noticed her letter had been put by her
father's plate. Gerald was late down as usual so that her Father
had read and digested the missive before his son appeared.

"Ar! Here you are at last!" cried Joseph as Gerald came in,
looking tired and tousle-headed.

"What do you make of this?" and he handed his son the
letter.

Gerald read it.

"Is it possible for us to comply?" he asked, pouring himself
some coffee. "It seems a very good opportunity. Shall we attend
Father?"

"Aye. It's only a five mile trip and could be worth it. Draw
up some figures, Gerald. We'll entrust Rachel to the servants'
care for one afternoon."

Gerald's eyes flickered to his sister's, his heart remembering
the last fateful time she had been left alone. Rachel's eyes
remained on her plate but she felt the stare and her cheeks
rouged.

That evening, by the first fire of autumn, the letter Rachel
had written so lovingly was being read aloud by its recipient in a
prim and mocking tone. The grim audience of one remained

unmoved by its simplistic sentiments. And when Errin was allowed in it seemed to her the letter was full of impending tragedy. She sewed on quietly in the corner, her hands trembling slightly and every now and then a tear fell on the coat she was patching.

"Well, Father?" said Hardy when the reciting was at an end. "How am I to greet this cousin when she arrives? I am prepared for your plan if it will bring us greater wealth. Indeed I am quite resigned to it as these letters tire me considerably and I don't wish to write any more even if you do dictate them! They appal me! ME love a Drayton? The sentiment we create is false and sickens my stomach. The Draytons are our enemies. Must I really.....well...I cannot say with Errin in the room."

"Ah-ha!" sneered Heaton, gazing deep into the fire. "The spirit is indeed willing but the flesh is weak! You must stiffen your sinews Hardy! The day is come when you must prove yourself a man as I did over eighteen years ago. There – that evoked a reaction in you, Errin! Yes, you may listen if you will but nothing you can do or say will thwart our plan. You'll be under lock and key. Rachel Drayton is doomed to a life such as yours. Well, well, Hardy, we'll soon have two servants."

"She was doomed from the moment she set eyes upon you!" cried Errin, angrily. "Everyone that sees you is immersed in tragedy. You are a human Black Shuck! A black angel of death, Heaton! When you are like this I cannot call you Father."

"Then keep your mouth SHUT!" yelled he. "Don't you think I rue the day I created such a waste of space as you are! Errin – you are as worthless as spent wood heaped upon the fire! You are as odious to me as the smallest creeping thing that crawls upon the earth! I cringe from contact with you and those eyes remind me damnably of HER! Keep your eyes and your comments to yourself else Hardy shall show you to the kitchen and I'll show you the power of my fists!"

"You will threaten me once too often!" she cried."One day someone will rise to protect me and cast you into the pit of hell where you belong!"

"And one day, lady, you will provoke me so unreasonably that I will put you to sleep for good! Hardy, take her out before I.....Get her out and confine her to the scullery for her insolence. I am tired of her reproaches. Woman.....you are not even worth your bread. Get out!"

Hardy grabbed her roughly by the shoulders, pinching her flesh with strong fingers and led her out.

When he returned Heaton was standing by the window staring out at the growing twilight and flickering shadows.

"'Tis strange," murmured he, turning away from the darkness. "But every day she grows more painfully akin to her I buried in that peaty earth! I thought she lay out there in peace. Lay! I wish she would lay down and rest. I fancied the other night she was beside me, bending over me, her warm breath encircling my cheek, her mouth forming words that made no sense to me. I half thought she called my name but her eyes were on another form that I could not see. She kept sighing and wringing her hands but whether for me or her I could not say. Ah! Well it is no matter. She may lie in her grave for another fifty years before I chose to join her!"

He became conscious of his son in the room.

"Well, Hardy, are ye prepared for the tribulations of married life as they lie before you? Expect no joy or happiness and you'll not be disappointed. Extract from your wife her duty and do yours but do not be so foolish as to love her! O, no. Keep her humble and begging for every crumb and as the master you'll cope tolerably. What say you?"

"Nothing," mumbled Hardy, bemused at his father's long soliloquy as he had entered the room. "It's impossible for me to love Rachel anyway as she bears the name Drayton and too close a relationship with that dolt who felled me! But if I can strike even with him by paining HER I'll do it!"

"Be patient," urged Heaton. "Revenge, sweet revenge, may not ensue for several weeks but come it will!" He clenched his fist.

"We'll break him and bring him to his knees. And then when Gerald is gone and the only other thing he possesses is under our control he is a rabbit in a snare waiting to be taken. Do you not feel a rich man, Hardy? It's taken long enough. For eighteen years Joseph has hated and despised me but always, always he's been out of reach. Now, at last, he is but a breath away! Wine, Hardy, wine and the best goblets for tonight, son, we celebrate!"

CHAPTER 10

The day after the morrow dawned fair with a pink streaked sky and persistent breeze laden with sun-kissed heather scents. The air was fresh and seemed strong enough to renew the dying and fill the living with joy and hope.

At Westerdale Heaton rose at his customary hour of six and lighting a half spent taper in the uncertain gloom he woke his son. From there he barged into his daughter's simplistic room and shook her roughly, bidding her get up quick or she would be sorry. Errin was accustomed to such threats and did as she was told, washing quickly in cold water. Her work worn hands were rough and sore with the hard physical labour they were forced to perform. Deep callouses showed between the fingers and a row of half healed burns reflected a moment's carelessness.

At seven Hardy went out to see to the horses and at eight the family breakfasted, Errin left in the kitchen with her crusts after serving the menfolk. After this she worked unceasingly until lunch time.

On this particular morning the milk was late so that Hardy and Heaton had already started work in the stables when the boy arrived with the churns. Usually he would carry them to the back door, await inspection and then carry on with his Father to his next delivery at Garstang Hall. Since she rose a vague idea had taken root in Errin's mind and it soon germinated into a bold plan. She must, she MUST communicate the danger Rachel was in to Gerald. Usually she was never left alone but Hardy and Heaton were struggling to break in a difficult horse and had lost all track of time. Better still the kitchen door had been left unlocked and they had forgotten the milk delivery.

At the boy's gentle knock Errin opened the door and cautiously bid him come in.

"Have you a pencil?" she asked anxiously.

"Aye," replied he.

"And paper?"

"Well I've some milk labels, miss."

Errin grabbed one of them and wrote, desperately,

Gerald- Do not trust Heaton. He has deceived Rachel into meeting Hardy this afternoon at two o'clock. Do not permit it. Your absence from home will bring disaster on her!
Errin.

"Here!" cried she, folding the note in four and slipping it into his hand. "You must deliver this for me urgently to Gerald Drayton at Garstang Hall where you call next. It is a matter of life and death!"

"And what do I get for doing it, miss? My dad may kick up if I tell him it's all for nothin'."

"I have nothing to give you, poor wretch that I am!" cried she, wringing her hands. "HE has entirely impoverished me. I don't have a penny!"

"Well, I will go for a kiss even though your lips are thin and pale," replied the boy. "Aye – two kisses on the lips!"

"Take them then," she said, carelessly. "But make it quick!"

He stepped up and kissed her once, twice, trying to make the kisses last but her lips were like ice.

Putting the milk label in his pocket he turned and went out of the kitchen, shutting the door.

"I have no pride, I have no dignity!" she moaned to herself. "Yet what could I do?"

Suddenly she heard a loud struggle and yelling from the courtyard, followed by a string of obscenities in her father's crude tone. Then the sound of running feet reached her ears. She hurried to the door when it opened under her nose and the grim form of her father entered carrying in his hand the note she had just written.

"So!" cried he furiously, his eyes mocking her defeat. "No sooner is my back turned and my mind occupied in labour than you are selling yourself for a favour, Errin! Well! This is a trial to be sure. Did you really think you would succeed in fooling me?"

"I would do anything to thwart you!" replied she, savagely. "I would sacrifice my life if I thought it would cause you to fail!"

"Brave words!" sneered he. "But put to the test they'll crumble to dust. Come- what have you gained by this latest disobedience?"

"The satisfaction that I tried, that I attempted to forewarn the girl you mean to wrong. I can do no more but I could not rest unless I tried!"

"You have achieved nothing!" cried he, vehemently, ripping up the message and scattering it over her head. "Instead it will bring you a fresh crop of sorrow – a new level of pain! Every day my hand is raised higher and comes down heavier upon you – and still you disobey me! Why do you stand your ground now? Why are you not cowering in fear away from me? Why don't you tremble? You have a look in your eye that I don't like. I try and try and try but I can't beat that look out of you!"

"I have long since learnt to take whatever pain you throw at me," cried she. "Yes, it physically weakens me, it shakes my mind and breaks it but it cannot harm my soul. Every night I pray I will be safe with Mother!"

"Damn you!" replied he, shaking visibly and running a quivering hand through his hair. "Why do you mention her name to me? By day she constantly reveals herself and at night I feel the clogging aura of her presence. Why do you call upon her? She cursed you when she knew you were growing inside her. She cursed you as loudly and vehemently as I did – as I still do!"

Errin observed he had broken out into a cold sweat at her words and he shook as a leaf does when stirred by a sudden breeze. His eyes lost their wild, dilated look of anger and shrank back into his head. His uneven breathing came in a series of gasps. He stared, not at his daughter, but rather at something beyond her, beyond even the narrow confines of this world. His dark, dry lips moved but no sounds came. Then, slowly, like a man awakening from a dream, he seemed to recollect himself and an evil smile twitched the corners of his mouth.

"There!" sneered he. "For your disobedience today you shall take my place in the stables. Hardy is a severe taskmaster and he will punish you amply. ME? Ar, I spurn touching you! I shy away from your creeping flesh. Yes, you revolt me. Get out-get out now before I recover the ability to enjoy torturing you!"

She did as she was bid for her father had a strange twisted look on his face that she had never seen there before and when she passed him he uttered a low groan and gnashed his teeth together.

After she had departed Heaton flung himself into a chair and fixed his bloodshot eyes on the gentle red glow of the fire.

"Why do you persist in this?" murmured he, turning his head away as if from some invisible force. "Your year is not up. Why do you haunt me? Yes, I murdered you. What, would you have me leave you to your sufferings? I ended them! God didn't! Aren't I more powerful? Didn't it feel good to be released from such pain? For God's sake – I am suffering now – have mercy upon me!" His eyes were suddenly wet, his great chest heaved with emotion, then slowly he stretched out one hand and enclosed it upon thin air with a groan of despair.

"Yes," snarled he. "Get you gone! Your time is not come yet! Your hour has not dawned. O God! I shudder to behold it. Torture me by hairbreadths if you will. Much may it amuse you but I can twist YOU by my remorseless cruelty to the only thing on this earth that bears your form."

He rose swiftly and hurried out as if to accomplish this mission.

The day drew on in rapid pace and the blue sky at noon was soon replaced by ominous rain clouds in a darkening sky. A little before two o'clock Hardy left his work and led his long suffering sister indoors. Many times had she felt the full weight of his hand upon her, mainly due to the weakness of her frame and her own inabilities.

"Here," cried Hardy, thrusting his sister's arm at his father. "You had best immure her or she'll be the means of blasting our plans to hell! I'm off to change and put on the part of me that will destroy the Drayton witch and ensure our future wealth."

Heaton took his daughter's arm as though she were some creeping insect or odious snake ready to bite him. His flesh recoiled from contact with her flesh and he shook volubly. He dragged her up three flights of narrow stairs to the top of the house where he paused before a dark oak door and searched his pocket for a bunch of keys.

"Do you know this room?" asked he.

"No," replied she simply, gazing at him in fear but yet maintaining a degree of outward strength.

Heaton at last secured the right key, unlocked the door and thrusting her into the musty darkness cried,

"There! Do your worst now, elfin witch and see if I care. You may scream till kingdom come from your lofty tower and SHE will not hear you. I, however, am a different matter and if I hear your voice you'll wish thirty times over you were never born. Thirty times over! God – I wish a million times over you had expired in your cradle."

"Don't you think I've wished that – and often!" cried she as he fastened the lock."I'll do it one day, Father, very soon and then you must face both of us!"

"Heaven help me," whispered he as he descended the stairs. "How could I find the strength to overcome two such ogres. One bending over me, the other towering above. It is bad enough that SHE gives me sleepless nights but that one would lull me to sleep in order to cast the most ghastly nightmares over me. Ah, you are listening are you? A dark shadow falls on the stairs. Never suppose I will give in to ye. No, I will go stiff and silent to my grave. Ah, you drift off again. O, that you would enter the gateway of hell and trouble me no more."

He uttered a low, despairing moan and went to his room where he commenced pacing up and down, his eyes wild and excited and his dark cheeks flushed. At length he heard the door bang, then the click of footsteps and then, finally, silence.

Hardy stood facing the restive moorlands, his face compressed into silent mental horror at the prospect of what he faced. His keen eyes searched the moving scenery, here dark and grim, where an overhead rain cloud cast shadows on the heather. Further away the higher ground was bathed in an orange glow that gradually faded into grey.

On the horizon appeared a small russet brown pony galloping towards him and bearing upon its back a laughing figure, her long hair streaming like a banner in the wind. She reached him, jumped off and leaving her mount to graze, stepped up to the tall, grim figure and planted a kiss on his cheek.

"Well, cousin Hardy!" cried she. "I am exceedingly glad to see you! I have thought of you constantly since we met. Have you thought of me?"

"Aye, Rachel, all the while," lied he, rubbing his cheek frantically, as if to remove the fateful kiss.

"I fear it will rain soon," said she, turning a wise eye to the darkening skies. "I shall be obliged to go. I trust your father is well?"

"Aye," replied Hardy. "He's away....on business. He'll be sorely vexed to have missed ye, I'm sure."

"It can't be helped," returned she. "I've not told Papa about our growing friendship as he persists in thinking ill of Heaton. I attempted some praise of you but he passed no comment. He may yet be reconciled to our contact."

"I don't doubt it," said Hardy, trying to smile. "He should be overjoyed that the two families no longer oppose each other. Time and time again my father has sought to heal the breach by offering the olive branch. You know what results this has brought! Father did not demean my mother by marrying her. She accepted gladly."

"Indeed. How can one demean the state of love?" pondered Rachel. "Papa is wrong to rebuke Heaton. I feel ashamed of my own flesh and blood but I take no part in it."

They strolled on a little at this point and Hardy, secretly observing his companion's face, saw she was preoccupied and pensive. Unwittingly she let herself be guided a little further from the moorland path and a little nearer Westerdale.

A gentle patter of rain among the stunted bushes around the homestead announced the eruption of the storm that had threatened since midday. Hardy grasped his cousin's hand firmly and taking the pony's reins in the other hand urged her to run inside for shelter.

"I cannot!" cried she, pulling back. "I have made my promise and must keep to it."

"Mere words will not protect you from a soaking and chill. Come, Rachel, please! The house is so lonely as Father is often away and Errin is no company. They mean nothing to me since I beheld you!"

"But I have given my word!" insisted she, remaining motionless whilst the rain drops soaked her dress."You must understand the importance of such a vow!"

"It is only important in your eyes," replied he, becoming desperate. "The truth is your vow means more than I do and that cuts me like a knife. Who will know? Father is away and your Papa distant. You're dampened now but in another few minutes you'll be soaked!"

She weakened visibly at his accusations and the hurt in his voice. At last she acquiesced, pledging she would shelter till the storm abated, her pony remaining tacked up for her departure once the rain ceased.

"Come, angel," cried Hardy in triumph, squeezing her fingers and jerking cruelly at the reins.

They ran together into the rising wind round the back of Westerdale where the gale threw them into each other's path and tangled Rachel's riding outfit around her taller cousin's breeches.

Hardy reached the first empty stable, unbolted the door and sent Zephyr in with a smack on the rump. Grabbing Rachel's hand again they ran to the kitchen door as a flash of lightening illuminated their path in silver.

"There!" cried he breathlessly, shutting the door as they tumbled in. He latched and bolted the barrier, then turned the great key and put it into his pocket.

"We are safe now, Rachel. No need to fear the tempest outside."

"Why have you done that?" cried she, her anxiety rising. "There's no need to lock the door, surely."

"The hinges are very weak," soothed he."The door flies open in a draught! Come nearer to the fire and get dried."

He threw more kindling on the blaze and stirred it up and all the time there was a sly smile on his face that Rachel could not see.

She edged round to the fire and attempted to smooth down her dishevelled outfit which was twisted and torn in places. Small pieces of twig and green moss clung to it and she picked these off and burnt them silently.

Hardy looked down at his spurs and observed several strands of her dress were entwined on the wheels.

"There!" he cried triumphantly. "Fate has thrown us together and mingled our clothes!"

She did not reply and he regarded her flushed, sullen face ponderously.

"You are stark and silent," observed he. "Yet that cannot but enhance beauty like yours! Of what are ye thinking?"

"Of broken promises," replied she, in a whisper, lifting her eyes to his face. "And of lies and hate."

"Unhappy thoughts!" murmured Hardy. "Do not dwell on your promise. Your papa has no quarrel with me."

"No ," mused she, gazing in to the centre of the fire. "Yet I do him wrong by even being in this place. I must return. The rain is drying on the windowpane and the gale is dying but my heart is sorely troubled."

She rose and moved swiftly to the door but Hardy leapt in front of her, barring her way.

"You shall not go yet," affirmed he. "Why you have only just arrived and I cannot bear the prospect of losing you. Don't leave, Rachel, with all this sadness in your heart."

"Give me the key, Hardy," replied she firmly, holding out her hand. "You cannot keep me here a moment longer than I desire. And I desire to go home NOW!"

"You shall NOT have it!" sneered he, turning on her and grabbing her arm.

Rachel was furious.

"Let me go!" she screamed, attempting in vain to push him off. But he put his arms about her and caressed her wildly.

"Not so soon, cousin," whispered he into her ear as he kissed her. "You must wait a little longer for your freedom."

"I will NOT!" cried she tearfully, using her nails to loosen Hardy's hold at great expense to his flesh. "Let me go!"

Hearing the sound of footsteps Hardy released her and observed as she reached the door leading to the passageway it opened and the grim, unsmiling form of Heaton stepped through.

"Well," sneered the black villain, extending his hand. "What a surprise and joy it is to see you, Miss Drayton. I trust your health is good?"

"I am much vexed at present," replied she candidly, refusing the proffered hand. "The conduct of your son is atrocious. He has locked and bolted the door and I desire to go home!"

"Dear, dear, a sorry tale, Hardy! Have you been treating your cousin infernally? Tut! What did I tell you!"

"She would have galloped home in the storm," replied Hardy, assuming a mild manner and tone. "I deemed it better she come inside till the rain ceases."

"I see. Well, Miss Drayton, you'll take some tea with us shortly."

"I won't!" replied she with spirit, shaking her head and stamping her foot. "I just want to go home. Mr Grimshaw, order your surly jailer to hand you the key so you may open up the door and release me!"

"Yes, Hardy," murmured Heaton. "I had better have that key."

Rachel's countenance lifted slightly at this and she moved forward but Heaton, upon receiving the article, transferred it to his own waistcoat pocket and turned his black eyes upon her. Rachel, furious beyond words, rushed at him and beat her fists upon his chest.

"I will have that key!" screamed she. "Give it to me! You are a wicked man, Heaton! Papa spoke the truth about you. I should have listened to him. O, you have tricked me!"

"That's right," snarled Heaton, rebuffing her with a sound slap and throwing her off. "Shout and scream for all you are worth. There is not a soul here to come to your assistance. Between Hardy and me you are undeniably trapped. Ah! Rachel will you ever see your darling papa again?"

At this she broke into a long, loud fit of crying as she realised the trap she had walked into.

"Were you stupid enough to think all those letters I sent to you meant a damn? Do you really think I could ever love a Drayton?" cried Hardy, standing over her as she sobbed.

"It is all trickery, trickery," shouted she. "Let me go, Mr Grimshaw! Have I ever done you any harm?"

"Hardy," said the black scoundrel, lifting his cruel eyes from the weeping girl. "Your cousin grows hysterical. She can hardly be sent home in such a state. O dear! How much grief would it give her dear papa to see her like this? Take her up to your room to rest and give her a little wine. Child – get on your feet now and obey. Think deeply on your home and if you want to behold it again then behave!"

Hardy moved to her side and attempted to lift her up but she sprang to life and caught him across the face with her nails. At this he ground his teeth furiously and commenced slapping her until she was almost insensible and he could gather her up easily in his arms.

They passed out of the kitchen, turned to ascend the stairs and paused upon the landing. Hardy held Rachel in one arm and took a large, heavy key from his jacket pocket which he used to gain access to his room.

Rachel was now half conscious of her surroundings, her companion and the terrible threat they posed. She tried valiantly to cling on to the outer door handle and from there to reach the bannister but Hardy had a strangle hold on her. Her attempts were futile and his strength against her seemed to double. The door closed behind her, he flung her contemptuously on the bed and locked and bolted the door.

Going over to the window he bolted the sash and drew the blinds down, throwing huge shadows across the walls. Then he sat on the corner of the bed and slowly removed his boots, jacket and shirt.

"What are you doing?" cried she in terror, edging herself away from his close proximity and casting a longing look at the door.

"It is no good looking at it – I have shut and locked it!" replied he calmly, lapsing into his usual laconic way of speaking.

He continued undressing slowly, Rachel petrified by a wild, numbing fear that burnt inside her like a volcano. Her eyes in the half gloom rolled white and huge, like the eyes of a hunted creature vainly searching for any crevice it might crawl into. But, for her there was no escape.

He stood up suddenly and every article of clothing fell away from his body, leaving him naked. His eyes glinted cruelly upon her and he seemed to revel in her shock and in the futile way she twisted her trembling body when he seized her.

"No, no!" she screamed, the powerful muscles of her throat rippling uncontrollably. "No, Hardy, you must kill me first! Be merciful-please be merciful!"

Hardy never uttered a word at her heart wrung protests but flung himself on the bed whereupon Rachel managed to slip from under his embrace and crawl to the far corner of the room. He had torn her outfit at the shoulder and his cruel fingers had deeply marked her colourless flesh in a crescent of bruises. She panted desperately, backed further away from his oncoming form but found herself cornered.

His eyes glinted red with a strange, inhuman fire and exuded hate. His naked brawny arms were outstretched and he seemed to assume the size and proportions of Goliath as he reached her. His arms canopied above her, his body pressed against her and his open mouth dipped down on her own trembling lips. With one hand he pinned her against the wall, with the other he tore, incensed, at her clothing and then, when she had no strength for breath or struggle, he threw her carelessly onto the bed. Climbing hastily beside her he flung the crumpled covers over their naked bodies.

CHAPTER 11

When Rachel woke, several hours later, she found with relief, she lay alone in the cold bed and, as far as she could discern in the growing gloom, nothing living moved in the shadowy corners of the room. Her mental anguish was understandably great and her blighted body was filled with pain. She had never before experienced such an ache but she knew, all too clearly, that she had been raped.

Rising slowly from the bed she searched for the remains of her clothes and put on her outfit as best she was able. It was torn considerably at one shoulder and the material hung loosely down her back whilst the skirt was almost rent in two and had to be tied. Her shoes lay under the bed and she put them on before approaching the door and trying the handle. It was, of course, locked.

Crossing to the window she let up the blind but a sudden sound behind her caused her to start and turning swiftly she beheld Heaton entering the room. His eyes registered both revulsion and amusement and he pocketed the key as soon as he was in.

"Well, now, Miss Drayton!" observed he, trying to sound pleasant. "I have heard a sorry tale of my son's conduct to you. He begs leave to excuse himself. It seems your beauty went to his head like wine and quite intoxicated him!"

"How can you face me after this, you rogue!" cried she, wildly. "Don't think I am stupid enough to believe this act was solely of that boor's making. I have been tricked into falling for a fantasy romance. O Papa, Papa, you were right! Mr Grimshaw, you are in league with the Devil and your black powers have imprisoned me. How long have I been lying here?"

"A few hours," replied he, smiling grimly.

"Hours!" echoed she, aghast. "Poor Papa will be frantic! And Gerald – oh! Mr Grimshaw, let me go home. You have had your infernal sport with me – let me go home!"

He did not reply to this but looked away from her and at length bade her keep her revolting eyes from his face.

"O God! They remind me of how HERS used to flash," murmured he. "Keep them down child, or I'll gouge them out and be done wi' it!"

"Let me go home!" sobbed she, throwing herself on her knees. "Papa will be so upset. He will not know what has become of me and I hate to make him miserable. Please, Mr Grimshaw! Your son has done to me what no other woman would take silently, but I will! I will! If you let me go home Papa will never know of your son's cruelty, and your own!" She stretched out her tattered arms and clung to his leg; the limb trembled furiously and, kicking her off Heaton yelled,

"Don't touch me! Don't touch me! I can't bear your flesh against mine! How Hardy could......?? I shall never know! How can you appeal to me? I spurn you – you revolt me! Go home? No, Rachel, you shall never go home. I have other plans for you. These plans do not include the presence of your infernal papa!" His eyes blazed in anger, he regarded her with a certain satisfaction now she cowered away from him.

"Yes, yes!" he gasped. "That is better. Fear – it nourishes and sustains me. I – feel – almost – recovered!"

Rachel wiped her bleeding face where his boot had caught her and she perceived he was smiling again in an odious fashion.

"As much as I detest and abhor you," he continued, recovering breath and venom. "I am determined that you and my son shall become man and wife. Daughter-in-law! Ye Gods, what a hideous prospect! What a punishment! Now, what do you say? Come, speak! I'll not strike you again providing you keep your distance."

"Never!" vowed she. "I could never marry the beast that defiled me – I'd rather die first!"

"Brave words!" sneered he. "But you will change them when you realise that unwed you'll never behold your father or brother again." He spoke the last words with a blend of sarcasm and triumph.

"So think on of your rash vow," growled he. "As prisoner here you will surely change your mind. Ah, it invigorates and heartens me that by incarcerating you here elsewhere – in that great gloomy hall – I am causing great pain to my enemies. THAT will cheer me when I am forced to behold your elfin face! Now I know Hardy is very anxious to come up again and continue with his lovemaking. I am quite powerless to control him! Come – you should be proud of yourself. You've awakened passions in him I never knew he had! Well – good day – Miss Drayton!"

"No!" screamed she, starting up in panic. "No , don't leave me to his devilish embraces! I can't stand it! Mr Grimshaw – if I marry Hardy may I see Papa again?"

Heaton turned from the door and smiled grimly.

"Do you swear on your papa's life to wed him?" he asked, boring his black eyes into her quaking soul.

"Yes," she replied. "I swear it. But let it be soon so that I may go to Papa or he may come to see me!"

Heaton made no further comment on this but let himself out and relocked the door.

Rachel, left alone in the gathering darkness, wondered what she had promised and to what evil force she had pledged her life. The safe and familiar picture of her father floated up to her and was a spark of warmth in the cold, hard world she found herself in. Bitter tears beaded her lashes, she flung herself on the bed and ruefully extinguished her beliefs as to Hardy's excellent character. True she now hated him but part of her still cried, "FIGHT! FIGHT!" and she seemed to hear the word echoing around her. After a while the salt water ceased, she stood up and taking a position by the window she watched the evening slipping into night.

Downstairs Heaton stood before a blazing fire, his dark eyes gazing at the burning embers, then upon Hardy dragging in a basket of logs.

"There!" cried the latter triumphantly. "'Tis done Father! Do ye hear me? 'Tis done!"

"Aye," murmured he, distractedly. "What did the vicar say? When can he be here?"

"Tomorrow morning at ten. Is that suitable?"

"Aye," whispered he again, contracting his brow as though an intense pain had hit him. "Now send up some food and drink to yer bride! Leave yer sister – God damn her. Let her starve for another night. She won't die. She'll be around to plague me till there's not a grey hair left on my head. O God – they revolt me. They repulse me! Begone, Hardy! I desire to be left on my own!"

Once the door was shut Heaton resumed his solitary position by the fire, his eyes now focused on some object invisible to other eyes. It stood between him and the blaze and produced a cold atmosphere. Slowly his lips began to move but no words came; then a great sigh escaped and he began to speak.

"Alone?" cried he. "Would that I could be on my own for one second, one minute, one hour! But no – you must come picking over me in your delightful torture! Yes – I'll stiffen my sinews against you till every nerve is taut but O God, you pluck them unmercifully! When will you leave this house? Can you not see the suffering I am inflicting on your blood? Is it not enough to make you run straight through the gates of Hell? Can you really bear to see your own flesh so abused? But, no, you feed on it and in torturing others I make you stronger!"

A gentle tapping at the door awoke him from his soliloquy and he found his eyes were wet.

"Come in!" he growled, wiping his face.

"Mr Drayton is here," cried his son, entering. "He'll not go away till he's seen ye though I told him we'd not seen his lass since our last meeting in town."

"Bring him in then," snarled his father. "I am in no mood for entertaining people. My talk this evening is blunt and coarse without refinement for a gentleman's ears but he may have it straight as it is!"

The door fell open and Joseph Drayton appeared.

He essayed a small bow and came, hesitantly, into the room.

"Mr Grimshaw!" he murmured nervously. "Believe me this is no social call or duty of pleasure since nothing on earth but the loss of my daughter would persuade me to enter these walls while you are master here!"

"Then since I am master, Drayton, you had best employ a civil tongue in your enquiries or I'll have my son and the dogs show you out!"

"I have but one question," replied Joseph, staying near the door. "Have you seen my daughter?"

"Your daughter?" sneered Heaton. "What the devil would make me entertain HER? If that is your quest it is a useless one and I pray you'll go and trouble me no more!"

"Mr Grimshaw," pleaded Joseph. "Unfortunately it seems I, alone in the district, am thoroughly acquainted with the evil of your black heart. You sold your soul to the Devil many years ago when you married my poor cousin whose body lies not far from here."

"Ah ha! I see it now!" cried Heaton. "You are come to complain of my burial arrangements are you? Your cousin was no saint or goddess so if her God wants her let him come down and dig her up for himself. I've longed to do that many times! Why did she have to die? I had not finished with her! She had a purpose in my life and I sorely miss her! Damn her for dying when she did!"

"You are mistaken, sir!" said Joseph, becoming angry. "She was glad to die and in quitting this world for a better one she has escaped from your devoted torture. Ah, she is safe now in eternity where even you cannot reach her!"

"No, no," muttered Heaton, a look of pain crossing his face. "No – I can't reach her to inflict my torture but she, ever watchful, bends to me to administer hers."

Joseph regarded him coolly.

He was, by now, a man of almost forty years, yet his black hair was thick and only slightly greying and his swarthy skin was relatively unblemished by the passage of time. His figure was tall, erect and strong – scarcely a pound heavier, and his muscles were steel with an indomitable will. Yet, here and there, Joseph detected a knot of facial muscles and a compulsive tic as though his mind was diseased while his body continued in rude health. His breathing seemed fast and shallow, causing his massive chest to heave and in his eye Joseph saw, at times, a confusion and anguish he had never noticed before. Joseph deemed this to be due to a life time of quick temper and black moods. He felt slightly less afraid of his adversary.

Heaton dropped into the chair by the fire and covered his face. His breathing was audible and rasping. Ere long he raised wet eyes and fixed them on his enemy.

"Mr Drayton!" snarled he. "I am past common civilities at present. I have answered your question so please go! My son will show you out. Be off with you for I feel something of the beast stealing over me when my humour knows no boundaries. It takes great delight in torturing the innocent. God damn your presence – it has put me in a sour mood when I meant to be happy. I shall simmer away for hours now! Goodnight."

The latter word was said between clenched teeth and with curled fists and Joseph, who had felt the weight of those hands before, withdrew from the room and entered the corridor. Hardy lurked there with a tray of gruel and some rough bread. He put this down at once and accompanied Drayton to the door. Opening it he pushed the elderly man through with a muffled curse and recommenced locking and bolting everything.

Hardy waited till he heard the regular beat of hooves drawing off into the distance then he collected his tray and mounted the stairs.

Without knocking he unlocked the door of his room and stepped inside, instantly locking up as though he expected an ambush. It was quite dark and, as he put the tray on a nearby stool he brushed against living flesh. The owner of that flesh reacted as though she had been stabbed and leapt to the far side of the bed.

"I'll bring a candle," muttered he, sullenly. "You cannot see to eat yer supper and, damn it, I can't see where you are!"

"Kindle no light in here," said a melancholy voice. "I don't want to behold your evil face. Don't look at me! We will be one soon enough though I shudder at such a husband! If you want to know where I am I will tell you – as far away from you as possible!"

"Ah," replied he. "You may say that now but tomorrow things will be reversed. All that you have will be mine and you will be my wife. Then we'll see the lengths of cruelty I can go to!"

"Yes," sneered she. "I expected that from you. But you know nothing of the person I am and what sustains me. I am no Elizabeth to take to my bed and die. I am equal to your strength mentally – nay I surpass it! Yes, you and your father can do your worst."

"Your boasts are impressive, cousin," smiled he, withdrawing to the door. "And if I had the time I'd find you in this infernal gloom and punch an apology out of you! But I can wait for the morrow when I shall possess you legally and bodily. Yes, enjoy your freedom one more night!"

Nothing further came from Rachel so Hardy went out silently and fastened the door.

After his steps had faded on the stairs Rachel approached the tray. She was faint with hunger and thirst. True the gruel was salty and the bread stale but she was glad to have something other than water in the ewer by the window. A little colour crept into her cheeks as she ate and a little spirit entered her heart. She would not give up hope! She must remain calm and resolute. Her inner strength would not fail her. She wandered up and down the room till midnight, fearing Hardy's return but when the silence remained unbroken she lay down on the bed and slept.

No other soul within the grim walls of Westerdale spent such a peaceful night. To Errin, imprisoned and starved, in the lofty garret, life had never seemed so hopeless and the black night was endless. Strange noises seemed to fill the air; deep, unearthly sighs, tragic groans and persistent scuffling that she soon attributed to mice. Her throat ached from sobbing, her wet eyes could squeeze no more tears and, at length, she watched the dawn sweep in through the tiny window.

Hardy remained on guard downstairs upon the parlour sofa in case Drayton took it upon himself to return with men to storm the place. His eyes watched the fire's embers dim and die and his ears were assaulted by the howl of wind. He pulled a horse blanket about him as the night got colder and mused.

About midnight heavy footsteps traversing the landing woke him from his reverie, and then sighs and groans seemed to float down to his ears. Hardy sat up, threw off the blanket and lit a taper with the last embers.

Slow, faltering footsteps descended the stairs, loud whispers rent the air intermingled with more groans and sighs. As the sounds approached the parlour Hardy ran across the room, flung the door open and thrust the taper out into the hallway.

"For Christ's sake what infernal conduct is this?" snarled a familiar voice with a yelp of pain. "Do you mean to burn my whiskers off or turn my hair to flames? Lower that light! Don't stare at me like you don't know me! Aren't I the same flesh and blood that begot you, damn ye!"

The refulgence ceased to illuminate the wide, tortured eyes of Heaton Grimshaw and darkness hid his features. The shadows slipped into the tight, knotted muscles of his face and neck.

"Well?" he cried when no answer was forthcoming.

"I did not know it was you, Father," replied his son, shielding the light. "Why do you stare and look deranged? God – I hardly recognised you! What do you see?"

"Yes," replied Heaton. "You do right to talk about madness. And whom I see – why it's HER. She's torturing me, lad! Torturing me till I become a nocturnal wreck!"

"Who?" asked Hardy, in a puzzled tone.

"Yes, who?" snarled he. "I wish I could live in such blissful ignorance. Ah, nothing troubles you does it Hardy? You sleep easily, untroubled by spectres of your past. Why have I paved such a road? 'Tis no matter, it will not beat me! Come, get away. You may have my room for tonight. It seems I am not permitted to sleep in it."

"Where will you sleep then?" asked Hardy. "There's a blanket on the sofa but it's hardly comfortable."

"Damn comfort!" cried Heaton, trembling visibly. "Hardy, do you not see a dreadful change come over me? By day I am comparatively myself but at night – well – I shall not sleep tonight! I am not even at liberty to lie down in any room and close my eyes but SHE is picking over me! Last night I even tried to sleep on the moors but she was there. Ah, said I, I will spread eagle myself over her grave and slumber and in so doing I will keep her restless spirit at bay and trap it beneath the ground. Fool that I was! It seemed that I did not lay on the warm earth but on her ice cold, clutching body! All the soil between us was suddenly dissolved away and I was two foot under in the revolting caresses of her embrace! I screamed aloud with shock – a grown man! And ever since then she has sent sleep to the Devil for me! Now – I need to be alone. Get up to bed and lock the door. I shall wander a little longer before the sun rises."

Hardy was deeply perplexed but the unearthly shine in his father's face discouraged further questioning and he felt uneasy in Heaton's presence. He mounted the stairs at a rapid pace and locked himself into the room.

The restless murmuring continued throughout the early hours of the morning and slow, solemn footsteps echoed incessantly over the sleeping household until the advent of dawn's gentle light when a peaceful calm filled the mansion.

Hardy rose at six o'clock and lit a candle to banish the lingering shadow of night. A rich, red sun rose hesitantly in the east, pink wisps of cloud glowed in the west and a queer yellowish mist encased the moorland.

Out of this mist came a morose and dripping figure. Hardy met his father by the gate to Westerdale, his gun dog shrinking away from the path of such a man.

"Well?" cried the black figure, wet through from the morning mist. "What the devil are ye doing here with your gun and dog? Do you mean to rape my land?"

"Father," said Hardy. "'Tis I – your son. Where have you been and why are you in such a state?"

"O!" replied the grim wreck, shaking his matted hair. "'Tis Hardy. Well, Hardy, would you leave your old father when he needs you most? Come – I desire your company to bring me back to reality. Turn about with me – come give me your arm. O, Hardy I have had an infernal night!"

"'Tis yer own fault," murmured Hardy."To choose to ramble about in this damp air instead of enjoying the delights of a warm bed. If you fall sick it is no wonder. Would you eclipse this life and let your property fall to another?"

"Die?" cried Heaton, aghast at the idea. "Why? Why should I die? Do men die of sleeplessness and nightmares?"

"No," scolded Hardy. "But they die of cold, starvation and frequent soakings!"

"Why!" exclaimed his father. "What nonsense you talk! Cold? Why you should feel me! I am burning with passion and as to soakings – well, 'tis only the mist that has wetted my hair!"

Hardy regarded him quizzically.

His hair had grown long and unkempt, like a mane falling over a wild beast's eyes. It was beaded with moisture but also matted with mud, heather and a few leaves. His eyes were sunken and the skin surrounding them was raven black but the whites were blood flecked after nights of sleeplessness. His cheeks were hollow, the mouth a little twisted as though by constant pain and his figure dirty, unkempt and bedraggled. The cloak he wore was stained and smeared here and there with ochre coloured earth and deep crimson hues that could have been dried blood.

Together, the pair entered the hall, passed into the house and ascended to the upper regions. Heaton appeared to have recovered and demanded that Hardy unlock Errin and guard her whilst she lit the fires and prepared breakfast.

"Then," cried his father. "Get away to yer room and don yer best jacket – I have men coming today to perform a union 'tween you and that Drayton lass. Yes – it all returns to me now and I tremble before its power! How I relish such a proposition! I am almost excited! She has lost her hold on me. Yes, I am nearly myself again." He locked himself into his chamber and commenced changing his clothes.

Hardy, having taken the key from his father, mounted the attic stairs and unlocked the door.

"Errin!" cried he, entering the room. "Errin – you are to come down immediately and light fires and prepare breakfast. I am yer jailer today so you'd best look lively for I have a heavy hand. Father is exhausted today. He did not sleep so if ye cross me you'll have his black mood to deal with aswell."

"I saw him last night," murmured she, from her position by the window. "He walked like a man – nay – an animal tortured by some invisible force. What haunts him? This morning he stumbled in like he was drunk! Is he taking opium?"

"It's none of yer business what Father does!" replied Hardy. "Get about yer work or you'll be sorry!"

"He had a look upon his face when he returned earlier that made me glad I was not he," continued Errin.

"You'll be sorry to be yourself in a minute," fumed he, raising his hand.

"Well done, well done! That's the spirit," came a voice from the landing. "Show her who's boss, son. No weakness now! Well, Errin," continued Heaton, coming into the room. "You'd have me in my grave would you?" He grabbed her angrily by the arm and flung her against the opposite wall.

"Look!" cried he, fair spitting in her face. "Do you see the eyes of a haunted man? Are these the limbs of a dying body? Feel my sinews. They revolt from the touch of your flesh as much as they revolt from death. I shall be breathing, Errin, when you are ten foot under. When you are dust blowing in the wind I'll be the richest man in Scarshead. Nothing shall stop me! My arms ache to beat you for your insolent words. Get yer face gone from here before I crescent it with red! Hardy – guard her with yer life!"

The two went out onto the landing.

"Do not wish me dead, Errin!" called Heaton. "Hardy is an even harder task master and my ghost will never be content to rest. No, the more you crave my death the more I'll turn away from that sting. Now – hunger possesses me. Get away and cook my breakfast! Be gone!"

When their footsteps had faded on the stairs Heaton sunk to the ground exhausted.

"By day you free me," whispered he. "Do not encircle me – my year is not up! How can I hide it from them?" He pulled himself up and went over to the window. Flinging it open, a cool blast of moorland air hit him and he reeled back. Recovering, he surveyed the stark, barren scenery with a strange, twisted pride then his eyes narrowed and his face changed. Covering his eyes he turned from the lattice, shut it with a loud bang that rattled the glass and hurried from the room.

CHAPTER 12

At ten o'clock a loud hammering came upon the front door of the house and Heaton, who was wandering sullenly round the yard whilst Hardy dressed, took the men quickly and silently round to the back door and through the kitchen.

"Well, gentlemen!" cried he. "I wish you good day. I trust my terms for this little arrangement meet with your satisfaction?"

The three affirmed so very nervously and gazed longingly at the outer door Heaton had locked. Weighed down as they were with guineas they felt it necessary to agree with the man before them but his reputation made them wary.

Heaton walked up and down the gloomy kitchen, occasionally casting a malicious glare if one of the men moved. The minutes ticked on and still the surly jailer paced the floor, his hands folded behind him, grim resentment lining his face. Ere long he bolted from the room, locked the door and mounting the stairs at a rapid pace burst into the room above. Errin was assisting Rachel into one of her dresses and both jumped.

"Well?" cried the intruder. "My guests are here – very unwelcome ones but still....Are ye not ready? Come – 'tis no time for tears!"

The two women turned to face him, one more bravely than the other. Rachel looked soft and pretty and any other heart would have melted at the sweet smile on her lips but Heaton cast his eyes down and ground his teeth.

"There – damn you!" he snarled, recovering. "What does it matter if yer dress is crumpled or yer faces dirty? What are you both? Nothing, nothing! Brace yourself, Rachel, and stop crying – don't snivel in front of me!"

"I wouldn't shed a tear for you!" cried she, bravely. "No, not one, Mr Grimshaw! You're not worth a fig. You don't possess the power to make me eternally unhappy and if Hardy is evil....well, he is your son and cannot be any worse than you!"

"Keep yer mouth shut!" cried he, clapping a rough hand over her face. "I shall very likely torture you myself and get great pleasure from it. Aye – we can share you. Hardy! Come and take this bitch's arm before I break her and send your wedded happiness into oblivion!"

Hardy came in and grasped Rachel's arm in a vice-like hold and Heaton went ahead with his daughter. He showed them all into the parlour and was about to leave when a flame fired in his cold black eyes.

"Now!" snarled he. "The first one of you to fail me today shall receive such a beating from these" here he held up clenched fists. "Not just once but daily! I can never love any of you. Everyone of you possesses a part of...HER. O God, my flesh abhors you! But you will not escape me Rachel because you bear my name! I hope Hardy will beat you into the wife he desires. Now, no more words till you are spoken to. Errin – cast your eyes down girl! They betray your feelings too keenly!"

Heaton left them briefly then returned with the three men who also looked nervous in their surroundings.

"Now!" declared the black villain, shutting the door and standing guard by it. "Let business commence. I need you to be quick, gentlemen! I want you here no longer than necessary. My home is my own and I do not welcome strangers here. Begin!"

The day wore on till noon when a fine, misty rain began to fall. A vivid purple light appeared in the sky and a storm brewed sullenly in the west. Flashes of sulphur graced the skyline, thunder rattled overhead shaking the windows and an icy hail hit the moors.

Inside a cheerless spitting fire burnt in the Westerdale parlour and around it sat four preoccupied people. A heavy, oppressive silence fell within the walls but outside the wind wailed mournfully. At length Rachel lifted up her eyes to the grim figure opposite and murmured piteously,

"Mr Grimshaw – cousin – I have done as you asked. I have married your son and in doing so have sealed for myself a fate worse than death! Please can I let Papa know I am safe? No, I will never call this house "safe" but tell him I am, at least, alive. Tell him what I have done and ask for his mercy and love. O, cousin, I yearn to go home. Since you dislike me so much let me move myself back to Garstang."

"What?" cried Heaton, lifting his eyes from the fire. "And leave your mate? What sort of a union is that? Hardy will be keen to consummate it, I fear. You are compelled to stay here by the vows you've taken and I am your Papa now. You need no other. If "Papa" comes he may visit you here but only under Hardy's guardianship. Look around you, Rachel – this is your home now."

His eyes glowed with satisfaction as he spoke these words. Rachel, however, was not to be silenced.

"But Papa will think me dead at the bottom of a bog or that I ran off as I didn't love him. I can't bear that. Please, Mr Grimshaw, send Hardy. Besides I want my things – my clothes, books and needlework to while away the dreary hours in this place."

"You'll want no playthings here," sneered Heaton. "And neither will you have time or energy for reading. You must work for your bread Rachel and beg for a crumb before I condescend to throw you one. Hardy can ride over there tomorrow for your clothes. I think it best to do that so he can glorify in the news. Do you hear this Hardy? Just a few workaday gowns and the like but the playthings you can toss into Scarshead Marsh. How wonderful that you go as Rachel's husband!"

"Then shall I ever see Papa again?" cried she, tears springing to her eyes.

"Hardy may arrange a meeting if he thinks fit. Just one mind. And that ass of a brother may come if he chooses but he looks too yellow. Anyway I have other plans for him. But you, Rachel, shall never enter Garstang Hall lest you throw both Hardy and me into hell first!"

Heaton lapsed into a brooding silence broken only by the chime of a clock.

"Now away, Hardy, and feed the stock," cried he. "And be sure to lock all the doors lest your pretty wife escapes and you'd not be left alone on your wedding night surely?"

The lad got up sullenly and commenced putting on his outdoor clothes, Heaton presently following him, carefully locking the parlour door behind him.

As soon as Heaton's odious presence left the room Rachel arose from the settle and went over to the window where a depressing sight met her. A deep, almost navy blue sky full of black clouds racing at a furious pace. Further away a line of gaunt and stunted trees were blown almost horizontal by the gale and a great sea of rain came over Westerdale, lashing at the panes with frenzied fingers. The satanic moors were almost invisible.

"I would rather be out there than in here," wailed Rachel, tracing a falling rain drop down the glass with her finger. "For though Nature is wild tonight she is not cruel. She would not blow upon me any more than upon those poor trees over there nor lash me with her water any more than the sodden heather. O how desperately I want to go home! I curse the day I ever heard the name Heaton Grimshaw." She turned back to the fireside, Errin's eyes following her wistfully.

"Yes," continued Rachel, sitting down again. "I am doomed! Sentenced to a lifetime of cruelty – oh Errin! How shall I bear it? When I first came here I thought, no, some one will come for me. My courage was strong and my resolve unbroken. I would not break down and give my torturer any strength but where is my strength now?"

"You will learn to conquer your emotions and to remain impassive in the presence of Heaton because he feeds on fear." replied Errin. "He delights in terror. He revels in receiving your hate and witnessing your horror. However, strangely of late I have seen a change in him. He seems to see or hear things I cannot perceive and they haunt him."

"Does it not appear to be the onset of madness?" asked Rachel.

"I cannot tell. It seems to be the onset of something far more sinister but maybe it's the first twinges of his conscience? Heaton is now middle-aged and youth has left him so, if it please God, maybe his strength will recede a little?"

Rachel's gentle eyes filled with tears but none fell.

"Poor Papa," sighed she, rising and wandering restlessly around the room."How he will blame me for my part in this sad affair. I shall appear as a fool – a guilty fool at that, when, in reality, I am innocent. Papa is growing old and none too strong either, Errin, and I fear the shock of this will break his heart or even kill him."

Ere she completed this gloomy speech she became aware of another presence in the room.

"Kill him, Rachel?" sneered her father-in-law in delight. "I pray it will. O joy! Revenge is so sweet."

"My father never behaved badly to you," replied Rachel angrily, drawing herself up to full height and flashing her eyes at Heaton.

"Ha! Not what you said a few days ago, madam," countered he.

"Mr Grimshaw – you are a wicked man who delights in abusing any decent soul. You are a blot on creation. You are a fiend moulded into human shape. No wonder Papa spoke of you as he did. How right were the names he gave you!"

A furious light flashed in Heaton's dark eyes and stepping up to his daughter-in-law he slapped her full in the face. She bore the blow well but her lips trembled and tears fell.

Seizing her by the arm Heaton dashed her several times against the wall, motioning Errin to keep her seat or be damned. Ere long he let Rachel fall and holding his daughter off, stood over his victim triumphantly.

"Next time you speak to me like that you shall go all the way to the Devil. And much joy may he have of you! I will NOT be talked to so. Damn you! My foot aches to kick you and my arms to beat you again. One day you will push me to such passion that I'll lose every degree of self control. Damn you!" cried he, rolling his eyes as Rachel fell against his leg. He clenched his fists and shook with rage whilst muttering unintelligibly. Then, suddenly, he recovered himself, stepped over her and went out.

In the kitchen Hardy had just come in and was locking the back door against the great gale of wind which pushed against it. The heavy rain had ceased, replaced by a fine drizzle from the thick cloud.

"Well, Father?" queried the son, stepping up to warm his hands at the comforting blaze. "Are ye not happy with this day's business? Has it not gone well?"

"Aye," murmured Heaton, sitting down on one of the high backed stools. He said nothing further but seemed to be suppressing an outburst of emotion.

"I must pay dearly for this sleeping fortune," said he, at length."To be forced to behold their stupid faces. It's the eyes I can't stand, Hardy! I want to gouge them out with my nails – O God, I do! They are HER eyes. Somehow they have survived the annihilating forces of death. O Hardy, keep that pretty wife of yours away from me! Yes, do not let her cross my path else she is in danger of losing her life!"

He rose swiftly, kicking his stool into the ashes. Then he let his eyes wander around the room.

"Tell me," continued he, in a quieter tone. "Do you see unearthly visions rising within these walls? Is Westerdale haunted? Do ghosts wander these corridors?"

"I see nor hear anything," replied Hardy. "There is nothing here, Father! Why do you jump at the slightest noise? What is the matter? If Rachel repulses you I'm sorry for it. She can stay in my room and you will never see or hear her. Or she could go back to Garstang if you wish it."

"Let her go back?" cried Heaton, furiously dashing his head against the chimney breast. "By Christ you have a weaker spirit than I thought Hardy! Do you imagine my sufferings would end then? No, the only way I can endure such suffering is because, if I keep her here, her father suffers MORE. THAT is my daily pleasure. I revel in it! It heartens me. And I will be victorious when you ride over tomorrow and inform that man that his bundle of joy is mine. MINE. God, that instils a strong, heady power in me." He rolled his eyes and ceased speaking, picking up his stool. A little blood dripped on to the stones from his head and some sizzled in the fire.

"Now, begone!" he said, turning to his son. "Take the womenfolk upstairs and secure them. I would hear no more of their voices tonight – nor yours either. Shut and lock the door on your way out and then leave me. I shall wander where I please within these confines." He flung his head to his hands and commenced a low, unearthly moaning that startled Hardy into action. He walked past his father silently, offering no comfort and let himself out of the kitchen. In a minute or two footsteps could be heard on the stairs, then silence.

The next morning, as soon as it was light, Hardy saddled his horse and threw on a rough worsted jacket, concealing within its pocket the note he had allowed Rachel to write to her father. He revelled in her growing despair at the nightly cruelty, which she knew she was destined for, and the fear and hatred she exhibited gave him power. As he tightened his girth he heard a heavy footstep behind him and the deep, painful sigh of breath.

Turning he beheld the dishevelled form of his father journeying forth for a walk, having little to do in the yard lately. Indeed many of the boxes stood empty and few customers came since the talk around Scarshead was of melancholia and madness at Westerdale. True, Heaton was an expert horseman but his reputation preceded him and clients went elsewhere.

"Well, Hardy," cried his father, grabbing the horse's bridle. "Where are ye off to so early? Surely it's not seven o'clock yet – the sun's not out of the mist."

"I'm off to Garstang, Father," replied Hardy, vaulting onto his horse and riding up to the latched gate. "Be so good as to remove the chain and I'll be on my way."

"Not so fast, not so fast," cried his father. "Tell me – are ye in fighting spirit? Could you fell that oaf Gerald with a single blow if he threatened you?"

"Aye. My fist aches to plant itself in his face. I've not forgotten the blow he gave me!" snarled Hardy, in anger, yanking at his horse's head.

"Good, good!" replied Heaton. "So, are ye ready? Godspeed!" and he unlatched the gate and watched his son gallop through and whip his horse until they were both but specks on the horizon.

At Garstang Hall life continued in the same round of work, rest and sleep although the father and son received very little of the latter. The time passed swiftly. They duly despaired and hoped and knew not what to do or where to go. Half of Scarshead thought her drowned in a peat bog and the other half thought she had a secret lover whom she had run off with. The fact that she had daily conversations with the stable boy had been explored but he said very little and the subject was dropped by the servants.

At first Joseph was frantic for his Rachel. He neglected his work, left it all to Gerald and would entertain nothing or nobody unconnected with his daughter's disappearance. Latterly, however, a quieter spirit filled him of "what will be will be" and nourished him in dark hours between dusk and dawn. He did not believe her dead.

Gerald, at first, took care to keep out of his father's presence, shunning his company at meal times and spending his evenings in his room. His heart ached to tell his Father of Rachel's secret meeting with Heaton yet how could he do so without incriminating himself? And Joseph had been to Westerdale and found no trace of her. Gerald frequently rode to the borders of Heaton's land but he gleaned nothing. He scanned every frond of heather, now rich in its autumn hues, and every blade of moorland grass as though it held a clue to Rachel's whereabouts.

When Hardy arrived at Garstang Hall on the cold September morning the family was at breakfast and the servants chatting in the large back kitchen. It had been a misty and dewy ride and Hardy was beaded from gossamer from rough bushes and stunted trees.

He clattered his horse round to the stable yard, flung himself off and tying his mount to an iron ring by the drinking trough, hammered loudly on the back door. A light step approached, drew back the bolts and ushered him in.

"I must see Mr Drayton!" cried the visitor with no preamble or niceties. He barged in, undid his jacket and sat himself down in the kitchen.

"Well?" continued he. "Don't stare so! Don't you know me? Ye certainly know my father – he's been here afore. Go tell Drayton I'm here and I'll wait." and he rested his muddy boots on the bench in front of him. The servants froze in their work and the housekeeper was sent to do his bidding.

She approached the parlour, where Joseph and Gerald were eating, knocked quickly and entered, curtsying low.

"Shall I clear away, sir?" asked she, observing little food had been eaten.

"Aye," replied Joseph, laconically motioning her out by a wave of his hand. "You may take it all – I've no appetite." He turned to the window behind him and murmured,

"I thought I saw her face at that casement – oh hundreds of times since she went. But whenever I open the window only the wind rushes in and chills me! Only the rain dampens my hair and she does not come, she does not come!" He ceased speaking and turned his wet eyes away.

A tense silence fell around him and Gerald laid down his knife and fork upon the untouched food.

"Thank you," said Gerald, softly, as the housekeeper still stood there. "Thank you. I think my father would like to be left alone now---"

The words froze upon his lips, the sentence was never finished.

Into the room strode a tall, youthful figure as black as though he came from the Devil himself. Both Gerald and Joseph were stunned into silence. The visitor enjoyed the scene he had created and threw back his head and laughed.

"Sir," said Hardy, turning to Joseph with a mock bow. "I do apologise for my intrusion but your servant has been very lapse in announcing me. I've waited in the kitchen for some minutes but time is money, Mr Drayton! You know what I've come about I've no doubt and you must know who sent me!" He picked up an untouched lump of meat and began to chew on it. "Now, Joseph, I would ask to speak to you alone so send these superfluous people about their business."

"Return to the kitchen, please," stammered Drayton to the housekeeper. "Leave the table. This gentleman must make do with cold coffee."

Hardy sneered at him and helped himself from the earthenware pot. He swilled the liquid round his mouth, then spat it out.

"By Christ, Drayton, you keep a poor house and foul coffee!" He flung down the cup.

"Now," he snarled. "Tell yer son to be off too – I'll not speak to 'ee! My message is for you alone. Besides he dealt me a blow at our last meeting that makes me anxious to return it with treble the weight and a great deal more fervour!"

"Remain where you are, Gerald." murmured the old man uneasily. "I don't feel comfortable being left alone with the offspring of – that man."

"Hardy," replied Gerald. "My father is old and infirm so you will entrust your message to ME." And he stood up to emphasis his point.

"Very well," sneered Hardy. "Hear this both of you. My father has Rachel at Westerdale and, as such, she is likely to remain there for the rest of her life!"

Upon hearing this Joseph gasped and tried to struggle up but his strength failed him and he fell back into his chair and covered his face. Gerald, however, waxed livid, and pushed his chair over, then strode over to Hardy with clenched fists.

"Mr Grimshaw!" shouted he. "By what means did you entice my innocent sister to Westerdale and what is her fate within those sinister walls? Speak up or I'll deal you such a blow as will knock your evil head off! I am not afraid of you. I scorn you and your black-hearted father. This evil will not prevail. Peace, Father, Rachel will be back at Garstang before nightfall."

Hardy took a step forward, nostrils flaring furiously and grabbed his adversary's arm, bending it powerfully behind him. Gerald gave a yelp of pain.

"Don't threaten me, Mr Drayton!" said he, between clenched teeth. "Rachel is now lawfully mine – I possess her." He reached into his breeches pocket and took out a crumpled paper.

Freeing Gerald with a laugh he threw the sheet at him.

"Aye, look at that. We are married. My God – Gerald you are a lilly livered brother-in-law but I'll not murder you yet! And you," turning to Joseph with a mock bow, "let me introduce myself properly – Hardy Grimshaw – your new son-in-law. Yes, she has wed me, legal and proper. And now I am come for her things. What's the matter, Gerald? Why are you trembling so? Ah, you gave me a blow that took me off my feet but my blow has felled you completely! Who is the victor now eh? Well, I'll tarry no longer with my in-laws. Bring her clothes. As for her playthings they can go to the Devil. She'll need no luxuries at Westerdale. We are a rough, simple lot there. Well, brother-in-law what a gloomy old house you inhabit. No wonder Rachel was so keen to run off to Westerdale."

"By what foul means did you entrap her, you rogue?" shouted Gerald, throwing the marriage certificate at Hardy, who grabbed it and put it away. "There is no way a Grimshaw could love a Drayton. She is lost to us – do you hear Father? - she is lost to us! Better that she had drowned in a peat bog than be possessed by Heaton! Heaton! How can she endure THAT?" and he dissolved into noisy sobs.

"Well, Mr Drayton," replied Hardy. "You have reared a fine man there! Are you not proud of its golden curls and I'm glad it has a beard else it could easily be mistaken for a lass! Come now – there's no reason for us to be enemies, linked as we are by marriage. My father is quite disposed to be cordial to you. He extends an invitation to Westerdale so you may come and see how happy your daughter is. And," continued he, producing another piece of folded paper from a pocket, "He has allowed Rachel to send you a note. If she speaks piteously 'tis only homesickness and I can easily beat that out of her."

He threw the piece of paper at Joseph as Gerald was still overcome with emotion. It landed on the table and with trembling fingers Joseph picked it up and read ----

Dear Papa,

I hardly know what to write to you. In fact I can hardly see the paper for tears of regret and homesickness. O Papa! I have been a fool. My heart aches so much I can hardly breathe! My sole thought now is to crave your forgiveness. Do you forgive me? Do, do! I was rash, I was weak, but I am still your daughter.

Heaton's conduct is atrocious and both he and Hardy delight in attaining new levels of cruelty. I cannot comprehend that the latter is actually my husband. I was forced and tricked into marrying him by events that I cannot go into now – they are too painful.

Dear, dear Papa! Please, please forgive me. I was fooled into meeting my black cousin who soon showed his true colours. Oh, I have been infernally treated.

Come and see me soon, Papa and bring Gerald with you for I fear I will die of a broken heart. I cannot survive for long in such a dreary house. I could stand a harsh environment but I cannot stand the loss of love, honesty and decency. My surly jailers are pure evil. O Papa you were right in your judgement of Heaton and had I listened to you I would be at Garstang now by some enormous fire with you and Gerald.

I long to see you both. My heart returns constantly to the green hollow where Garstang stands. I hate it here.

Have pity upon me Papa! I await your coming.

Do not fail me – I am desperate!

Your loving,

Rachel.

Joseph lowered his shaking head and gazed uncomprehendingly at the grim figure before him.

"Well," sneered Hardy. "She writes lovingly about me as a devoted husband, does she not, Mr Drayton? She's far too soft for her own good. I shall try to toughen my wife up. My wife! It trips off the tongue so sweetly do you not think? Now if you wish to write her a reply I'll wait and consume this left-over food while you compose it." And he began cramming the remains of the meal into his mouth, grinning at Joseph as he did so.

Joseph screwed up the letter and threw it into the fire. Struggling to compose himself he went over to his sobbing son and put a comforting hand on his shoulder.

Biting his lips he turned to his guest and said,

" No, Mr Grimshaw, there is no necessity for you to wait. Contact with my daughter is over. There will be no more letters. Nor do I wish to receive any more communications from her. It is..over. While she is your wife she is my daughter no more. Do you hear that? I sever the tie. You will not torture me by torturing her so you may do your worst. Please deliver that message to your father. There will be no visits from either myself or Gerald. You may possess her, Mr Grimshaw – I give her up to you entirely. And now you can get out of my house. I will get my servant to pack up her things and deliver them to you on the morrow. I shall cut my daughter off from my person and my purse. You have a hollow victory, Mr Grimshaw. From now on Rachel is dead to me. I go into mourning for her as though she had died in a peat bog. Now we would like to be left alone to grieve for our loss. Good day!"

Joseph moved back to the table and sat down. He attempted an air of indifference as he poured himself a cold coffee but his shaking hands and quivering lips betrayed him.

Hardy cast his sullen eyes over the room. Nothing further was said and after a few minutes he made for the door, ran through the kitchen and slammed out of the back door.

Tugging at his horse's head he bestowed a string of curses on every inhabitant of Garstang Hall.

"We are not finished yet," screamed he, at the wall in front of him. "We will possess this place – WE WILL! I am the victor here – I!" And he applied his whip and galloped out of the yard.

CHAPTER 13

It was well past midday when Hardy eventually arrived back at Westerdale and his tired horse was soaked in sweat which the wind had dried in dark streaks on his chestnut coat. His rider was dirty too.

Hardy slunk round to the stable yard, glad it was deserted and that his Father was employed elsewhere. He clattered past the row of stable doors without noticing that between the top and bottom of one box a pair of black eyes glared with the fierceness of the midday sun.

Hardy led his mount into an empty stall and commenced untacking him, taking his saddle and bridle to the tack room. As he did so Heaton followed him, pitchfork in hand.

"Well?" demanded he as Hardy put up his saddle. "Where have you been, Hardy? Four hours an' more for a trip to Drayton's? And I've never set eyes on you since seven."

"My time is my own," replied Hardy, sullenly. "I was never aware that I had to report to you hourly for dispensation of my time."

"Do not be insolent!" shouted his father, snapping his fingers angrily. "You owe me your labour for the bread you eat and the clothes you wear. Never forget that – son or not! Come, why are you so sullen? Have you spent the past hours at Garstang?"

"No," murmured he, trying to get past his father, without meeting his eye. "Father, my horse needs attending to. He is hungry and dirty."

Heaton grasped his arm as he attempted to get past

"If you've not been to Drayton's then in Christ's name where have you been? Come – I am waiting!" he snarled.

Hardy flung his father's arm away and stepped past him to a corner of the stall where he leant against a partition and struggled to suppress a violent, conflicting mix of emotions. Then, turning back to his father he said,

"I've been riding over the moorlands – just riding for mile upon mile in order to come to terms with what I learnt at Garstang. Yes, and to bring my own bad temper and violence under control. Father – I would go anywhere for you – but do not send me back there! Such a gloomy, mouldy place is calculated only to bring forth my worst mood and black tempers!"

Heaton stared at his son in surprise.

"How were you received there then?" he asked.

"Infernally!" cried Hardy, banging his fist against the partition. "Father – they all mocked me! One was weeping on the ground like a lass and the other summoned up his last bit of strength to tell me that since Rachel now bears my name and lives here he's cutting her off wi' nowt! So, all this suffering – all this taking of that bitch in marriage is useless, wasted. Yes, you do right to stare. I am tricked too – as was that girl I ravished at your request! Do you imagine I enjoy the work I perform for you? And where is my reward? Heaton – for I scorn to call you "Father" - I'll tell you where my reward is shall I? In the lap of that lad who looks more like a lass! I have married a liability who is cut off without a farthing and I must clothe and feed....THAT. By Christ, I'd rather murder it today and sell its carcass for hound food than sleep with it one more night. So – you smile, Heaton! Do you mean to laugh and sneer at my misfortunes as they did?"

"I'm not laughing I assure you!" cried his father. "On the contrary I share your anger but I do not share your black-hearted despair. That I will never share. The rat, when he is backed into a corner, only jumps higher. You go to Garstang and let yourself be upset by an ancient dotard. No wonder I smile. Of course Drayton still cares about her. Do you suppose he could cut this love out of his heart after sixteen years? He could as soon forget her as his son Gerald he sees every day. He could as soon abandon her as the food he eats, the air he breathes. Bah! Do not come here and tell me such a story, Hardy. It just smacks of your vulnerability and inexperience! Joseph has won a paltry victory. Did you not hand him all the winning cards by behaving like that? Never fear, Hardy! Summon up your courage and go tell your bride of her rejection. Ye Gods, the thought of her pain heartens me and gives me strength. You will yet be master of Garstang Hall!"

Heaton turned and departed for the house with a sly and scornful smile playing about his lips. Entering the kitchen he beheld the two women preparing vegetables for the meal. His smile widened when he witnessed Rachel's flinching and cringing as he came near her.

"Well, daughter-in-law," said he. "You are to be relieved of your culinary duties for a few precious minutes. Errin, take her upstairs and help her to prepare to meet her lord and master. No, do not quake, he has something for you. Something that will benefit us all. Come, look lively!" he yelled, raising his hand in impatience when neither of them moved.

"Yes," continued he, in delight. "Your lord has been over to Garstang. There, that made you move! Do not waste any questions on me. I am not at liberty to disclose anything but that cannot stop me laughing at your misfortunes."

He produced the key from his jacket pocket and unlocking the door pushed the two girls roughly through and escorted them upstairs till they stood before Hardy's chamber. This Heaton also unlocked and ushering them in he crossed over to the window and drew back the curtains.

"You worthless bitch!" snarled he, surveying the untidy nature of the room. "Could you not lift your idle fingers and draw up the bed? Huh, have you already tired of pleasing him? If he possesses one ounce of sense he will force you to do office as his chamber maid."

"I will do nothing save what I am forced to do. You cannot make me servant in here. This is HIS domain. How is it that you keep a key? If I were Hardy I would not allow it. This is our room!" and Rachel drew herself up to full height.

"Do not taunt me, madam," replied Heaton, grabbing her roughly by the shoulders and shaking her. "This room, as part of Westerdale, is MINE. It is not Hardy's and it can never be yours! I would rather destroy it first! By Christ, I believe you enjoy putting me in a passion!" He flung her on to the bed and let himself out of the room, grinding his teeth as he did so.

Silence took over the house apart from the slow, funeral ticking of the hall clock that pervaded all the rooms. Hours seemed to stagnate at Westerdale. From cock crow to sunset seemed like the passage of weeks rather than a few hours. Darkness seemed to dominate the house and enjoy control in the unlit corridors most of the day. Occasionally the rising sun crept over the grimy walls, fixing its sultry power in the dusty corners.

Soon another step moved on the stairs and Hardy let himself into his room and gazed with hate at the two women within. His wife, upon seeing him, rose eagerly and approaching him held out her hand in anticipation of a gift.

"I know you've been to Garstang!" cried she. "Please give me what Papa has sent. You promised I could receive letters from him."

"Aye," replied he, morosely, turning over his empty hands. "If he had written – aye – you would have had it. But he vowed not to."

"What do you mean?" Rachel was horrified and it registered in her huge, dark eyes. "Hardy, don't mock me. I appeal to you! Please give me his letter." and she flung herself at his feet and held out her arms beseechingly.

"Get up, get up," snarled he, withdrawing from her needy touch. "Don't be ridiculous Rachel! I can't bear you to grovel. Get away, get away!" and he aimed a kick at her and sent her sprawling across the room.

"Now," said he, decisively, moving to stand over her. "Understand this Rachel. Your father in his love and respect for you has chosen to cut you off. You are penniless. He no longer recognises you as his daughter and rejects his own flesh and blood. He desires neither to communicate with you again nor see you. Your wonderful papa says you have chosen your fate and must accept it. Ah, the meaning has hit home I see!"

Rachel trembled uncontrollably but dragged herself to her feet and walked over to the window to turn her back on her husband. Her bearing was straight and upright but her shoulders heaved as she struggled to subdue her weeping. Hardy gave a short laugh and after locking the door descended the stairs with calm indifference.

Rachel waited till Hardy's footsteps had died away and then she collapsed and began crying fervently.

"O Papa," wept she, biting her hand as if glad of physical pain to ease her mental anguish. "O Papa, how could you do this to me after sixteen years of love? No, Errin, don't comfort me. I require no assistance. Let me be, please, let me be! I will – I MUST come to terms with this!" She sobbed silently for a few minutes and then, rising shakily, she sat next to her sister-in-law and took her hand.

"O Errin," breathed she. "For my sake I could take it! Yes, I could! But not for Heaton's sake – no – I can't bear to think how he will laugh and gloat. How easily must he dismiss Papa's regard. What a victory he and Hardy have won and how he'll scorn me as the loser!"

Scarce had she finished speaking when the grate of a key sounded and the black villain himself was in their midst.

"Errin," snarled her father. "I would speak to your pretty sister-in-law alone. Begone to the kitchen but beware Hardy roams the corridors in such a foul mood that I appear an angel!"

He held the door open for her and smiled as she passed, for the fear was clearly etched on her face as though she suspected a blow or kick to her person. Heaton relocked the door and then turned, unwillingly, to his daughter-in-law, the smile quickly fading from his face.

"Well, madam," began he. "I see by the state of your face that you have been celebrating my son's news from Garstang Hall in your usual fashion. Tears! Bah! They are wasted on me. They reinforce the weakness of your soul and body. And they spur me on to crueller and crueller atrocities!"

"My tears are not shed for you," replied Rachel, angrily. "I would not cry for you, Mr Grimshaw. NO, not even if my life depended on it. I'd not give you the pleasure of believing you'd hurt me. I do not cry for myself either – no, I cry solely for Papa!"

"Yes," sneered Heaton, fixing his narrowed black eyes on her. "He is a wonderful papa, is he not? He's worth a sea of tears for the love he reflects for you isn't he? Such an adoration that proves he can't travel a few miles to see you? An adoration that causes him to swear he never wishes to set eyes on you again!"

"I expected your scorn," said she, spiritedly. "I awaited it, and your exulted cry of victory. So you may laugh, Heaton, and you may scorn and you may say hundreds of times, "Ah, Rachel, THAT is how you are loved!" But oh, Mr Grimshaw, you'll not get a penny through me, not a penny! You have made the biggest mistake of your life in declaring to Papa that I am here and the wife of your offspring. Now he knows where I am, under who's contaminated roof I reside, I will be written out of the will. I will not exist. Lost I would be worth a small fortune but HERE, I am as good as dead!" She spoke with a dreary kind of triumph, yet her eyes flashed powerfully and Heaton, who felt their fire on his cheek, drew off a little, half in awe of their passion.

"Madam," murmured he. "You have said enough. I will speak to ye when grief ceases to tinge your mind, when you behave and speak sanely and this nonsense is gone from your mouth. Until then you can stay alone and ponder on the madness of your thoughts." He drew off to depart but Rachel, conscious she had won a shallow victory, ran up to him and cried, triumphantly,

"Yes, Mr Grimshaw, go! Yes, leave me. Starve me, stone me, hit me, kill me even! I alone will be the victor knowing that no matter what you do to me you won't get a penny of Papa's money and more important you cannot hurt Papa! Garstang Hall will be Gerald's and his alone!"

At her words Heaton grew livid and raised his hand as if to strike her but somehow he could not do so and his hand fell uselessly by his side. He took a deep breath, withdrew rapidly, relocked the door and let the darkness of the stairway swallow him up.

CHAPTER 14

A week of drear sunless weather followed culminating in the first hard frost of the season, for the month of September was already half spent. The wind picked up, the insipid skies cleared and the sunlight became weak and fragile. As the days sped away and no word arrived from Garstang nor the clothes and books she had been promised Rachel began to despair and reject the very little food and comfort she was offered. She grew pale and silent, shed weight and refused even to converse with Errin. It seemed she was preparing herself for an early death, an easy escape from the shattered grey prison of her existence. At times she was stoical and almost indifferent to the pain inflicted upon her. Heaton found no delight in torturing her and gave up abusing her entirely, turning his fiendish attentions to Errin who reacted with fear and trembling.

After another few autumnal days a visitor arrived at Westerdale upon the back of a chestnut horse which he tied up in the yard in order to gain admittance to the house. He was tall, good looking in an angelic sort of way and scarce more than twenty years of age. His blonde hair curled crisply about his face in a pleasing but slightly ethereal manner. He walked like a gentleman and had a well to do manner. Arriving at the main door he tapped upon it with his riding crop. His request for admittance was speedily answered and he was shown in with strained politeness and relieved of the bundle he carried. After this he was taken through to the kitchen where the womenfolk of the house sat, one employed in paring vegetables and the other in sewing. Only one looked up as the gentleman entered, the other continued listlessly with her needlework.

The man removed his hat, sat down upon one of the wooden stools encircling the table and murmured , a little awkwardly,

"Well, Rachel, I am come at last!"

This statement brought forth no response and the sewer stitched on. Only the cook gazed, in awe, at the blonde gentleman.

"Rachel," pleaded he. "Are you not glad to see me?"

"Yes, Gerald," replied she briefly, raising her eyes to his face then dropping them again to her work.

"That is good," replied her brother. "For I've argued long and fiercely with Papa in order to get permission to come! Your situation has caused many bitter quarrels between us although, at length, he relented and so I am here."

"Then I'm very sorry for it!" returned she, gazing up at him. "You should not have come if Papa was against it. Indeed I would rather you had remained at Garstang to where you must return immediately and patch up your rift. You should not have come on my account."

Gerald made no comment on this but rose and went over to the fire to warm his hands.

"Where is Mr Grimshaw?" asked he. "Your husband answered the door in his usual surly manner although I own he was tolerably polite, if not indifferent."

"Father is gone to Scarshead on business," replied Errin, seeing her sister-in-law made no answer.

"Ah ha!" said Gerald. "Then Hardy is your grim jailer today. I heard him lock the door as soon as I was through it and mention he would come for me in half an hour."

"The door ia always locked," replied Rachel. "My husband fears I would desert him! He has grown tired of humouring me and I, too, am sick of him!"

An uneasy silence fell during which the workers resumed their half-finished tasks and the guest wandered back to the table.

"I suppose it is pure folly to ask how you survive under such a roof?" queried Gerald, bending over his sister.

"You may ask me many things, Gerald," replied she, without looking up. "But I am not at liberty to answer them. If I did my answers would give you nightmares. There is one matter that I would speak to you about though. Errin, tap upon the door and ask Hardy to remove you so I may have some privacy to discuss family matters with my brother."

"Hardy will never allow it," replied Errin, directly.

"I believe he would for just a minute or two now that the tyrannical master is not here to hawk eye him. Please try."

Errin rose and did as she was asked and after three or four appeals Hardy allowed her through for a few minutes.

"Well, sister," murmured Gerald when they were alone. "Of what would you converse with me that cannot be spoken of in front of your sister-in-law?"

"It is of her that I would speak," whispered Rachel. "Draw nearer, brother, and listen to me for we have but a minute or so before Hardy throws Errin back in. Now answer me quickly. Do you like Errin?"

"Like her?" enquired he. "Why....yes...I suppose so. She is my cousin after all."

"Good but in what way do you like her?"

"I do not fully comprehend your meaning?"

"Do you like her well enough to love her. Well enough to marry her? O Gerald she leads a ghastly life here! This misery she suffers is not of her own making as mine is. She suffers far more than I do for Heaton believes I am now immune to his torture as I hide my fear! But Errin! She shows her fear in every minute of her waking existence. Hardy and Heaton constantly abuse her and by and large I am left free of cruelty. Of course I am unhappy and desperate but I am immured by my marriage. Spiritually I try to rise above it but Errin sinks into her misery. O Gerald how wonderful if you could somehow remove her from all this!"

"Your unselfish nature does you great credit, sister," replied he, kissing her. "But you do not know what you ask! Do you believe Heaton will give me her hand with his blessing? O Rachel

– if Errin was not sired by such a man I would marry her. Last time I was here and saw the suffering in her eyes I could not forget it for days and days and I am aware this time will be no exception."

"Then, listen," cried she, grasping his hand earnestly. "For myself I have hopes I will withstand this place and these tyrants. I wean myself daily from the comforts of life – from food, from warmth, from love but for Errin I have deep-grounded fears. Gerald, she has not my cunning nature and my strong will. I will survive this. I will! Think no more of me, think of Errin! You must come and see me whenever you can and in doing so pay attention to Errin and so gain her confidence. After that the time is yours to spring the trap and ensure you both get away safely."

She had scarce finished speaking when the door was flung open and Errin was pushed through with a verbal interjection that Heaton had now clattered round to the yard and demanded to know whose horse was tied up there.

"I will stay no longer, sister," cried Gerald, rising swiftly and putting on his hat. "Heaton is back and probably furious enough to put a few punches about my ears. Goodbye, darling, goodbye, Errin – I will come again soon!" He hurried out through the door and was on the point of crossing the hall when the very figure he sought to avoid entered the passageway and spying the guest barred his path.

"Mr Drayton," sneered Heaton, tossing his tousled black hair from his even blacker eyes. "I am overjoyed to see you in my house. What? Are you preparing to leave already? Hardy – we cannot allow this!"

"I have been to see my sister, sir," murmured Gerald, withdrawing from the tyrants path. "And now I must return to my waiting father for I promised I'd not be long and I like to keep my word."

"Of course, of course!" replied Heaton in a condescending way. "You must come and go as you like here. You will come again will you not? Hardy – fetch Mr Drayton's horse if you've locked the door."

150

Hardy did as he was told, Heaton meanwhile surveying the fair visitor who positively trembled in his presence.

"I trust you find your sister well?" enquired Heaton.

"She appears to be a little out of spirits!" replied Gerald, suddenly growing bold. "Her husband seems to be tired of her already. In fact she seems to be neglected."

"Oh really? There I must disagree with you Mr Drayton for I believe you are quite mistaken and the truth is the situation is totally reversed. Rachel has grown tired of pleasing Hardy. She cries very loudly at times when he wishes to sleep and a less patient man, such as myself would have resorted to violence to silence her. But not my Hardy! Well, Mr Drayton, here comes your horse. I trust we will see you again soon. Goodbye!"

"Hypocrite!" snarled Gerald as he mounted and tightened the girth. "You dare to speak to me in that tone do you Heaton? Well – my sister is right. Her plans speak to me of revenge. I will marry Errin without your permission and take her away from this hell hole!"

His whisper did not penetrate the walls of Westerdale but floated, unheard, into the cold, clear air.

The autumnal days drew on, each one significantly shortening the daylight hours. The face of the moorland was changing. Tight bells of heather unfurled themselves, purpled for days and finally died upon stiff, brownish stalks amidst black frosts. Huge oppressive clouds rolled eastwards, caught the rising sun and became translucent pink silk that darkened over time and gave vent to heavy down pours. Westerdale shivered in its elevated position at the head of the ridge, looking deep into the open moorland. Garstang Hall, at the opposing end nestled further into the greening valley and seemed to take refuge from the icy winds.

Gerald came thrice more to Westerdale, his attention now firmly fixed upon his cousin, Errin, almost to the exclusion of his sister. She frequently sat sewing quietly whilst Gerald and Errin conversed in whispers. On days when he was absent Errin was restless and sad, her conduct soon noticeable to Heaton, who attributed it to the frequent guest. From that moment he swore the visits should come to an end and chancing upon Rachel and Errin whispering together in the kitchen his resolve to ban Gerald took a tighter hold on him.

Stepping up to them he spat savagely,

"There! Put an end to your infernal secrecy! I have had enough of it. These past weeks I have been leniency itself and allowed your brother to waltz in and out of here like he owned Westerdale!And now, you sluttish pair, Hardy tells me that Errin is becoming powerfully attached to that fair ass! Is that not so daughter? Ah, do not turn away so bashfully! Do you think I am stupid? Yes, those puny golden locks have charmed you. God, what a choice! More lass then lad as Hardy would say. Well, it has gone far enough I say. When your admirer comes next time you must inform him it will be his last visit. He will not be tolerated within these walls again. And if he should chance to return Hardy will greet him with a shotgun and you, Rachel, will find yourself an only child! What will Papa do then? Both his darlings distanced from him."

He moved to the window and gazed out upon the dying moorland from which arose the sharp outline of the granite stone erected to the memory of his wife. His eyes narrowed upon the stark, black earth upon which nothing had grown even though many months had passed. As he watched the powerful muscles in his neck went into spasms, he gave a short cry and fell back, one hand endeavouring to hide his eyes.

Rachel grabbed him as he reeled backwards and held him until the fit passed and his feet were steady enough to support him again. Then she gently released her hold and moved over to the window.

"Heaton!" cried she. "What ails you? There is nothing out there save your wife's grave. Why are your eyes so tortured?"

"It – is – nothing," panted he, struggling to control his breath. "I thought I saw – never mind, it is no matter. I am myself again. Why did you touch me? Yon lady there would have let me fall to the ground. She'd not lift a finger to help me. And I can't blame her." He wiped his face with trembling hands.

"You are still a human being, Heaton, whatever you do," replied Rachel, evenly.

Heaton appeared much troubled by this but he recovered himself, gave a small bow and left the room.

Next day came the first powdery fall of snow whitening the moorland and freezing the water in the drinking troughs. Rachel and Errin drew closer to the kitchen fire eagerly and warmed their chilled limbs.

Towards midday Heaton came in, shaking his boots free of snow and heaping more logs on the fire. He had no sooner done so when the heavy tramp, tramp of horse's hooves announced the arrival of a visitor. The rider came boldly past the kitchen window and went round to the yard. Heaton jumped up and went to the door, dragging on his coat as he went.

"Hardy is back early from Scarshead," announced Heaton sullenly. "Errin – lay out the food. I believe we can eat now. Come, look lively! Do I have to raise my hand against you again?"

"'Tis not Hardy," replied Rachel who had identified the tall figure on the chestnut horse.

"O God," groaned Heaton. "Then it must be your dolt of a brother come to bid you farewell and leave you to your fate. Ah, Errin, that caused a flash of feeling! You must say goodbye today for he's no mate for you. I am resolved you shall die a spinster. This wench shall bear my grandchildren whilst I live and see they are raised to be a model of their father. Now, I am resolved to be merciful today. Here comes the idiot, yes, he approaches the back door. I will leave you alone for about fifteen minutes or so." He jerked the door open at just the right moment to admit the visitor and ushering Gerald in he let himself out and relocked the door.

Gerald stepped into the room and took his sister's proffered hand.

"I hardly thought to see snow in September," murmured he.

"It is October tomorrow," replied she. "How time stagnates here. We have all winter before us and months of mind-numbing cold to live through. O, Gerald, Heaton has discovered the mutual regard you and Errin share and he instructs me to inform you that after today you are welcome here no longer!"

Gerald released her hand and drew off a little, fixing his eyes on Errin, who sat dry eyed and silent amidst the dishes, her face turned to the fire.

"Well, Errin," murmured he quietly, worried lest Heaton should be listening. "It seems the time has come for me to prove the deep regard I have for you. Trust me or else you must live out your life here, in the shadow of your tyrant father. I would understand if you wanted to throw in your lot with my sister and remain here rather than go with one who is almost a stranger to you."

"How can you even think I would stay here after being offered such a proposal?" cried Errin. She became conscious of her loud tones and dropped her voice. "You offer me life, Gerald, and if I stay here all I will experience is existence and slavery. And THAT is all I would have until the annihilating forces of death come for me. True, I have not known you for very long but I trust you and to me you are an angel. My angel. If you will have me I will come with you and be a good and loyal wife."

"Then we shall fly!" enthused he, kneeling down by her and kissing her hand.

"We must travel by darkness, Errin. I will come for you tomorrow night. If I could I'd take you away tonight but there are things to be done and plans to be made. As yet Papa knows nothing of my going away and I must pack and get some money."

"Yes," whispered Errin, gazing anxiously over at her sister-in-law outlined against the window. "But Rachel must think me a totally self-centred soul who plans her own escape and leaves her sister immured in the very prison she seeks to break out of. No, I cannot be so selfish, Gerald. Rachel must come with us."

"No!" cried Rachel, immediately, coming over to the fireside to join them. "No, I cannot go! How can Gerald take two of us and where would I go? If I went to Garstang Papa would send me back and Hardy, as my lawful husband, would come looking for me."

"But we'll not go to Garstang will we?" pleaded Errin, anxiously.

"No, indeed!" replied Gerald. "Even Papa will not know where we are going. We will head for Scotland and there attain our union. We'll only return after the passage of time has softened the blow to Heaton. I have already planned your escape but you must work on distracting your jailer's attention. Now I need to know all of the household's whereabouts by night. Rachel, you can come with us and must. We can't leave you here and Hardy will not find you in Scotland!"

Rachel sat down by her sister and put an arm about her shoulders. They both gazed deep into the spitting fire.

"I will," affirmed she. "And we can all be together. Whether I can ever return to Garstang Hall.....well we will see. We must gain our freedom first."

And the three fell to planning and whispering for the few minutes remaining they had together.

That night a fresh sprinkling of snow graced the frozen moorland and reflected a cloud-strewn sky speckled with winking stars. Garstang Hall was warm and lamp lit yet strangely empty although a huge blaze graced the hearth. High shadows flickered on the walls and Joseph watched them as he sat, bitter and silent since the loss of his daughter. At the other end sat a restless and nervous Gerald, his brain running over and over his ambitious plan.

The servants had cleared away the scarcely touched supper and had drawn the shutters together. All doors were locked and bolted against the bitter flakes and a wailing gale flung its fingers over the house front. The parlour grew warm and Joseph dozed in his chair, almost unaware of his jittery son who got up frequently to walk about the room, his arms folded behind his back.

At length the constant wandering stirred Joseph and he looked up at the agitated form of his son.

"What's the matter?" asked he.

"Papa," replied Gerald earnestly. "I am going to leave you tomorrow and may, in truth, be away for a considerable time."

"But where are you going?" asked his father, pulling himself upright and appearing shocked.

"Papa, I cannot say," continued Gerald."All I can tell you is that my going away may be the means of saving Rachel and bringing her back into your life. Yes, I knew you would shake your head and doubt me but you may, as yet, be reconciled with your daughter. Hear me out at least! In the weeks that follow you may have cause to rebuke me but have faith, dear Papa, and see things through. Yes, I know you'll feel deserted and lonely but it won't be forever and, in less than a year, I'll be back."

"When are you going?" asked the old man, dejectedly. "And more important how shall I manage without you?"

"I leave tomorrow night. Papa – please do not question me any further. My lips must keep silence or I may doom my plans and jinx my journey."

"If I have displeased you," cried Joseph. "Or driven you away I'm sorry for it! Please forgive me and stay. Do not go away on my account I beg you. Say it is not me that is sending you forth!"

"Papa," pleaded Gerald rising and taking his father's trembling hand. "Papa, it is not because of you. One day very soon you'll understand why but until then wish me god speed and good luck!"

"I do, son, of course I do!" replied his Father.

They wished each other good night and Gerald withdrew to his room. His heart ached. He began to throw a few belongings together. The flickering candles spun high shadows on the dove coloured walls of his chamber. Going over to the window he regarded the wild moorland scenery in the distance and the gentler green valley nearer at hand. Would this be the last night he stood here listening to the wind moan around Garstang?

He stood his packed saddle bags by the wardrobe and gazed at the rows of coats, jerkins and trousers he had to leave. Throwing off his clothes and putting on his nightshirt he wondered if she he loved was sleeping or if she, too, lay awake with a fearful heart.

In bed he tossed and turned and went over his plans till they seemed to jumble into one long tragedy. Could he succeed? Could Heaton and Hardy be fooled? And what would happen if he failed? Life would be intolerable for him but for the girls.....He dared not think of that.

A few minutes later he heard his father ascend the stairs and pause, uneasily, by his door with a deep sigh. Then his heavy footsteps died away and the door of Joseph's bedchamber shut. A tense silence fell over the house. Even the wind stopped its restless crying. Midnight rang out. Gerald was suddenly weary of his emotionally unprofitable life and turning his face to the wall he closed his eyes and slept.

CHAPTER 15

The next morning a heavy and persistent spell of rain moving across Heldon from the west effectively dissolved the frozen wastes of white that clung to the bleak hillocks. Ere nine o'clock rung out every trace of snow had disappeared and the world ran with melt water which poured through the stable yards of Westerdale and Garstang Hall. The latter dwelling appeared empty and the yards echoed with the consistent drip, drip, drip of thaw. The windows were sightlessly bleak and silent and the servants moved about quietly, conscious of the great sorrow in the house. Meals were served punctually only to be cleared away hours later untouched as neither Joseph nor Gerald could swallow a morsel. Gerald took to his room after lunch and wandered fitfully about his chamber, gazing at the things he was forced to leave behind. At length he sat upon the windowsill and scanned the bleak view that had trapped him since birth. To the left of the house rose a huge, black crag of granite stone, studded with shiny particles of grit that caught the sinking sun in refulgence long after the house front was in darkness. Nearer rose the swell of a green hill, much softer than the contours of the moorland which peered over its shoulder. Heather grew profusely at the bottom of the hill and had spread into the tiny valley wherein Garstang raised its time worn head, sheltered partially from the tempest of wind and rain that assailed the moor itself. Beyond the crag desolation reigned and the miles of wild, tangled heath fell away until it backed onto the house front of Westerdale.

Gerald wondered if the girls sat as idly and silently as he did or if they suffered cruel blows from the tyrant men who would soon be forced to do their own housekeeping. If his plan succeeded, of course. He prayed aloud for help, eager to show his

Errin the love and tenderness he felt for her. Her life had been devoid of such care until now and he ached to show her kindness and respect. Rachel had tasted such goodness so she did not move him to pity. Indeed curiosity had thrown Rachel into her present life and she must learn to curb her wild spirit in the future. If he was honest he had derived this plan for Errin and for her he was prepared to risk life and limb.

Towards the afternoon he became calmer. Everything was done, every item packed and his horse ready. He threw himself into a chair and was content to wait until the hues of darkness crept across the evening skies.

Dusk came. Anxious eyes traced the rapid progress of the moon ascending to her zenith, clear and bright with the promise of a late frost. At Westerdale, once supper was over and the fires tended to for the long cold evening Hardy escorted his females into the kitchen and flinging on his worsted jacket took down the key to the tack room.

"Where are you going, Hardy?" asked his wife, leaving her stool and approaching him.

"Lay off!" cried he, backing away. "I can't stand yer wheedling – you know where I am going so why ask? If I beat you later it's the work of the bottle – I'll not lift a hand against you!"

"Then it's a good thing your horse is conversant with your bouts of drinking and knows the road home else you could end up drowned in some bog."

"Hah! That is right!" goaded he, sneering in her face. "Curse me, damn me! Your oaths don't mean a fig! They are worthless! Do you imagine the God you speak so much of will appear like a will'o' the wisp and lure me to my doom? Sit and contemplate, my lady, on YOUR doom. Cos when I return I'll be just about ready to carve my name on your pretty face!"

He snatched up his hat, unlocked the door and let himself out. They heard his footsteps echoing in the yard and were thankful. After a couple of minutes he passed the window astride his black stallion and Rachel, out of habit, tried the door religiously but it was locked.

"I am resolved one day they will grow careless and forget," murmured she, returning to her seat by the fire. "If only Gerald would come now. Hardy is gone and he would have no trouble in forcing the door. I feel impatient enough to force one of the windows."

"Patience!" cried Errin. "For though Hardy is gone Father wanders about somewhere I'm sure."

"Yes. He is a Daniel when it comes to darkness is he not? He reminds me of some vampire or werewolf, some sort of ghoul that by day retains a human shape but by night is transformed into some blood lusting beast!"

"He is certainly possessed by a strange fixation," acknowledged Errin, letting her gaze wander into the hot eddies of the fire. "Exactly what troubles him I cannot comprehend. Sometimes, at evening, his face twitches with a strong passion and his mouth contracts as though in pain. He stares too, not at anything in this world but rather OUT of it. In such a mood he recognises no one!"

"Well, what it is leading to we are not at liberty to pursue, thank God! We shall be gone from this fireside in a few hours," replied Rachel calmly.

"Aye. And Father will be alone with just Hardy to do his frantic bidding. Does it not inspire you, sister? How will it feel to taste freedom? I've never known it. It will go to my head like wine."

Rachel rose and wandered gracefully around the room, pondering upon Errin's words.

"It is strange," murmured she, pausing in her walk. "But in all I have been through – pain, humiliation, persecution – I still feel some sympathy, nay, empathy, with Heaton. Some part of me dreads leaving him. Hardy, yes, he is an ignorant boor but Heaton...... I know my flesh revolts his but we have some sort of bond I cannot break. Something links us......here," she put a hand on her heart, "Something links our soul. O yes, I've sweated fear at his approach, trembled when he's beaten me but when I've looked into those black eyes I've seen things no one else has. And sometimes when I hear him sighing at night I sigh too! I feel his tormented wanderings, I feel his night terrors! They are mine too. God forgive me but I feel a twisted admiration for his doomed black soul!"

Errin smiled at this but did not condemn her sister-in-law. "Have you not been pushed to the very borders of sanity by Hardy's infernal conduct?" she replied soothingly. "You have not been raised in such brutality as I have. I am used to it. God knows, it's all I have ever known! Heaton is a man of granite, never forget that. Yet even granite has its flaws and time will widen those cracks and fissures. Heaton mellowed? I think not but maybe you have picked up an honest feeling in that seething mass of cruelty! Certainly you affect Father. He cannot look at you lately without trembling. But, unlike you, I feel nothing for this place or anyone in it save you. And when we leave here the stream at Heldon may rise up and flood Westerdale! I'll not care! I'll not shed a tear! Heaton is not my true father but a black demon sent to destroy me. And if I escape from him then good is victorious over evil."

"Then will you never feel the urge to come back?" asked Rachel.

"Never! Nor waste one thought on its occupants."

"In truth I am not sure how long I can stay away!" cried Rachel. "Something in this grim house stirs my blood. And then there is Papa too. I yearn to see him." She spoke earnestly and a few tears fell.

The minutes ticked by and the kitchen fire was almost extinguished. The intense cold crept up and the girls searched for spare fuel but found none. No wood had been chopped for days and the peat buckets were empty. They drew their shawls tightly around their shoulders and closed tired eyes. O that eleven o'clock would strike and bring their winged Mercury to rescue them!

A low noise outside the window aroused them and Rachel spied her father-in-law coming in from his labours. However no key sounded in the lock and, returning to the window she saw, by the light of the moon, he had left the house front and was approaching the grave where he suddenly knelt down and then disappeared.

"There!" cried she, returning to her seat. "Your father has spread eagled himself over his wife's grave and rests there in silent adoration. May he sleep there all night! The house is empty now – O Gerald where are you? Well, he will not come yet. Errin – if you are tired you may sleep and I will wake you."

"And you?"

"I am too restless to sleep!" replied Rachel. "The moon has a strange gleam about her but the night is omniously still. Do you not notice that, for once, no wind buffets the house front?"

Errin lay back and slept, but Rachel wandered nervously around her tiny prison, the only sounds audible being the scratch of her skirts over stone.

Eventually Rachel discerned the approaching gallop of hooves. Her heart beating wildly, she shook Errin and bid her get up and stand by the back door.

"Hark!" cried she. "Hardy comes in!" She dropped her voice to a whisper. "Gerald will be waiting the other side of the stable block. You must be attentive to the key Errin – 'tis the largest, heaviest one! Godspeed, angel. I will follow. Now – silence, my husband approaches."

They heard the awkward stumbling of drunken feet, a muffled curse and shout, then the click of a key in the door. Rachel braced herself; Errin, pulling up her skirt with one hand, fixed nervous eyes upon the grim form that almost fell into the room.

"Well, Rachel," murmured Hardy, when he had righted himself and shut but not locked the door. "I shall not murder you tonight – no – well, maybe just a little. Your good brother has filled my belly with beer and even escorted me home! O, he's gone now – I saw him off! He knows better than to trespass here after Father's threats. Still, I am nicely drunk. Come here and let me escort you upstairs. Damn Errin – she can wait. It's YOU I want!"

He staggered over to his wife and laid heavy hands upon her, dragging her roughly by the waist. Rachel raised her arms and put them round his neck then commenced kissing him. Then she slid one hand inside his jacket pocket until her fingers tightened on a bunch of keys.

"What are ye doing?" cried he, stopping the kiss as he felt her lift the keys out. "Give 'em here, you slut!" He made a wild grab for them but missed and fell heavily to the ground.

"Here! Quick, Errin!" cried Rachel, throwing her prize. Errin caught them, discovered Hardy had forgotten to lock the door anyway and ran out into the yard, gazing around for Gerald. His horse was just coming up the aisle between the stable blocks and she was about to rush up and greet him when a loud scream from the kitchen turned her head. Running back she beheld, through the open door, Rachel held down by one leg which her monstrous husband had fast in a strong grip. His nails had sunk through her stocking and were crescenting her white flesh with blood which ran onto the floor.

"Go, go!" screamed the victim wildly when she beheld her sister-in-law hesitating on the threshold. "Go, Errin! He has just screamed for Heaton and that fiend will be here in a second. I cannot escape! Hardy holds me fast!" She gave a great cry of pain and collapsed on the floor.

Gerald drew up behind Errin and urged them to be quick as a ghostly form was rising from the grave.

"In God's name – GO!" screamed Rachel." Go and Godspeed!"

Gerald grabbed his bride to be and threw her up onto his horse, vaulting on behind her. Clutching each other tightly Gerald urged his horse to a gallop and the couple passed into the darkness around Westerdale.

A scurrying form traversed the grass in time to catch a moonlit glimpse of the two riders. Then they were gone and the echoing earth swallowed up the pounding hooves.

Heaton bolted into the kitchen and slammed the door. He grasped his daughter-in-law by the neck and aimed a kick at his son who rolled over and released his hold on Rachel.

"Get up! Get up, you fool!" yelled Heaton. "If I were not here yer wife would have been off too! Is it not enough that Errin is gone off with Joseph's lad? Get up, Hardy! Get up! I was a dolt to trust the keys to a drunkard. Why was the door left unlocked? Damn you, boy! Get up!"

He pulled the half sensible form to his feet and thrust him out of the house with instructions not to return till he had secured the runaways.

Then he slammed and relocked the door, coming back into the kitchen. Perspiration covered his face and his eyes were dilated whilst a pulse raged at his temple and neck. His breath came in rapid gasps and he leant heavily upon the wall to recover. Ere long his black eyes fell upon his daughter-in-law who huddled in the hearth. A gleam of firelight fell upon her white, strained face.

"You thought to go then too did you?" sneered he, showing his cruel teeth. "Well, your plan has failed. Do not think another such opportunity will arise. Hardy will watch you like a hawk from now on and one small disobedience will feel the weight of my hand too!"

"On the contrary, Mr Grimshaw," murmured she spiritedly. She picked herself up and righted her torn skirt. "My plan has worked to perfection. I knew I would never get away as well as Errin. Why do you think Gerald had only ONE horse? No, I was the diversion – I made the Judas kiss and sealed Hardy's fate. He can't resist me! He might be a tyrant but he is a man too. Ah! You start and roll your eyes. Have you ever known anyone do an unselfish act? I sacrificed my freedom for Errin's. You will not apprehend them. Errin is gone forever. Yes, you may hit me, yes you may torture me but you'll never behold your daughter anymore. Think on that!"

"Speak no more!" cried he, furiously but he trembled and leant against the wall again for support. "Hardy has gone out on his horse and will soon bring them back."

"Hardy is blind drunk," replied she. "Face it, Mr Grimshaw, you have lost your daughter and your son was never worth finding in the first place."

"Now you have said enough!" yelled he. A peculiar look came over his face, causing his nostrils to dilate and the muscles in his throat to ripple powerfully. He tried to raise his hand against her but she drew herself up to full height and stared at him. Faced with those eyes Heaton could only cover his face uselessly.

"Get out, get out," whimpered he. He struggled to the door and unlocked it with difficulty, motioning her through. When her steps had faded on the stairs he relocked the door and collapsed by the fire, holding his aching head.

"Be gone," breathed he painfully. "This was YOUR work. Yes, your hand was here and at the end of it I don't even have the strength left to enjoy torturing her! O you are killing me so slowly. When I eat my throat muscles contract and I can't swallow. I hate the night – I dread it! It's gone twelve and you are almost through." He broke down and wept copiously, then, starting up he ran out into the uniform darkness and screamed,

"O God, if you exist in this infernal world – take her! Take her! Take her to your bosom! If you have the power Elizabeth then show yourself! Show yourself! I can't quite see you. I can't! Yes, I can feel you – I can almost touch you! In Christ's name if you exist appear to me tonight!"

His words ended in a wild sob but nothing else came back to him save the rising wind sweeping the firmaments. Then, suddenly, he convulsed heavily, his face changed and he fell to the ground.

When the light returned to the sky Rachel, who had slept very little upon her sister-in-law's bed, rose and put on her dress. Gazing out of the window vague, conflicting thoughts raced in her head – desires to be free from this earthly condition, desires to be reconciled with her father and a desire to pay Hardy back for his unspeakable cruelty. Her leg ached spasmodically but it had stopped bleeding and the wounds were drawing together. When her tired eyes were able to focus on the world outside she was surprised to see her father-in-law lying as if dead on the grass, only a few feet from his wife's grave. She ran out of the room, hurried down the stairs and finding Hardy's room still locked she concluded he had not yet returned. This gave her new hope as it proved the couple were still free. Descending to the ground floor she found the kitchen locked and silent. However the front door was only bolted and slipping out she ran round to the stables where Heaton's stallion pulled at hay and her own pony lazed in the next box. The box where Hardy's horse was stabled was empty.

A wild plan came into her head and she returned to the house front where she crept up to Heaton and observed he breathed, if shallowly. Relieved, she drew off, reached the pony's box and allowed him to clatter out whereupon she vaulted onto his back, hitching her skirts up. Urging him onwards they left Westerdale and headed out onto the moorland track.

Zephyr sped along as though he recognised the path to Garstang and Rachel's spirits rose with every mile. Soon she would be with Papa again. He would be overjoyed to see her! Ere long the valley she sought came into sight and she saw the twisted chimneys of home. Home! Such a sweet word and her heart leapt with delight. She clattered into the deserted stable yard, dismounted and tied her pony to a ring in the wall with a halter that she found lying by the drinking trough. Running up the steps to the back door she rapped for admittance while her heart raced and danced. In a few moments the door swung open and her father's youngest servant stood before her.

"Why, Miss Drayton!" exclaimed she, surprised but overjoyed at Rachel's appearance. "Why, Miss, have you come back to us?"

"Yes, Harriet, it is I but alas, Miss Drayton no more! Is Papa within?"

"Yes, Miss, he is. He'll be out of his head to see you again. But how pale and thin you are. Obviously food is not plentiful in that place!"

"No – I've been starved in every way since I entered Westerdale. Now – where is Papa?"

"He's in the parlour looking over some papers, Miss."

"And he's well?"

"Tolerable, Miss, tolerable. Now come in properly. Welcome home!" And Harriet kissed her warmly.

Rachel pressed her hand and ran along the familiar passage way before tapping at the parlour door.

A tired, low voice called out, "Come in!"

Rachel entered and threw herself at her father's feet as he sat at his desk. She hugged his legs then jumped up and kissed him fondly. Joseph did not respond but stared at her warily so she drew off and regarded him with startled eyes.

"What now Papa?" cried she, her heart sinking. "Do you not perceive who I am? I've come home, Papa, I've come home to you. I may stay? Please say I may stay!" She tried to take his hand but he eluded her and turned his face away.

"So, Rachel – you've come back! You've crept back at last. But where is your husband? He is your keeper now – not I!"

Rachel stood up and her eyes filled with tears.

"Papa," wept she. "Don't spurn me like that – don't! I can't bear it! I'm still your own flesh and blood. If I've done wrong then please forgive me! Come, look at me! I'm still your daughter! O Papa! I've been to hell and back since I last beheld you! Do you not care how I've suffered? How I still will suffer if I have to go back – there. I cannot go back! I can't! Papa – Hardy may come looking for me soon so please hide me! I need to put my pony out of sight so he thinks I've gone off with Errin and Gerald!"

"What nonsense is this?" cried Joseph, getting up and pushing her imploring hands away. "Errin and Gerald together? Are you insane child?"

"No," replied Rachel earnestly. "They have run off to save Errin from her fate – a lifelong sentence to Westerdale and Heaton's cruelty! It was draining every ounce of youthful sap from her. Papa, you must have known Gerald visited me at Westerdale. It was my only joy in an empty life since you would not answer my letter or come and see me! And on his visits he and Errin fell in love and made a plan to run off together. I was supposed to accompany them but my husband had other plans and stopped me in his usual cruel fashion of brute force!"

"Yes, I knew Gerald had gone away but not under those circumstances. Does he know whose offspring he has rescued? What evil force begot her and nourished her for many years? Ah, what children I have raised! What fools to let themselves be tricked by that black-hearted villain Heaton! That devil exudes mischief and misery and attracts it like a magnet. He revels in it."

"Then help ME to end MY misery concerning Heaton!" cried she. "Let me leave that house of horrors and come here!"

"No!" shouted he, angrily. "I cannot hold onto something that is not mine and bring the wrath of the owner upon my head! Rachel, I am old and frail. This very morning I have been looking over my will. You made your decision when you said "Yes" to that man's son. He possesses you now. You must go back."

Rachel gave a groan of despair and sunk to her knees. She covered her face and shook her head uncomprehendingly. Joseph commenced turning over his papers and avoided looking at his daughter. Although his heart ached his terrible fear of Heaton could not overcome his paternal love. Rachel was Hardy's wife. His hands shook as he digested this. Would he ever see any grandchildren from this unsuitable union? And would these children inherit Heaton's evil streak? He shuddered at the thought.

An unearthly silence reigned. All that was audible was Rachel's sobs that she tried hard to stifle and the rustling paper.

After a few minutes a knock came at the door. Both people roused themselves and fear crossed Rachel's face. The same servant that had ushered her in entered now wringing her hands in anxiety. She gazed at Rachel's prostrate form and her glance said a thousand words.

"Well, Harriet?" asked Joseph, looking up.

"Pardon me, sir, but the young gentleman from Westerdale is here, looking for his wife...."

Rachel jumped up in horror.

"No, no, no! Send him away Papa. Say I'm not here! O God I must hide!" She looked round fearfully for somewhere to run to. "Papa, do not give me up to Hardy. Heaton, I could bear but not Hardy!"

"Bid him enter," said Joseph, quietly. "Say his wife is here and he must take her back with him. I have no further claim upon her and neither did I entice her here. She is his."

At this Rachel gave a great cry of resignation and as she did so her lord and master burst into the room.

"Good day, Mr Drayton," sneered Hardy, casting his eyes furiously on his cowering wife. "I had a notion the good for nothing slut would crawl back here! After all, where else would she go? A pity she continues to trouble you after she has signed herself over to me, body and soul. I trust you do not hold any wild ideas of keeping her here? I could not bear to be parted from her, even for one night!"

"Get up, Rachel and go with your husband," replied Joseph, averting his eyes from the pair.

"Yes, come, madam," cried Hardy, holding out his hand. "Mr Drayton has no further use for you and I'm waiting!"

Rachel never moved but her body trembled powerfully

"Come here at once!" shouted her husband, losing his temper. "Rachel – I am getting angry and you'll be sorry later if you make a scene. You know what I am capable of and Father is in a black humour too!"

Wearily Rachel drew her pleading hands away from her father and, standing up, backed away from him towards Hardy, who grabbed her arm roughly and twisted it.

"Papa," cried she, pointing a trembling finger at him. "Papa – I pray you remember this when sleepless nights overcome you! I pray you'll remember that I tried – I tried to make my peace with you! I threw myself on your mercy – ah what mercy! I am still your daughter – your blood runs in my veins! And yet you sentence me to this! See how he treats me. I'll die if I go back to Westerdale. I'll die!"

Hardy yanked her out of the room crying furiously,

"Right – you have said enough now! Shut up! Can't you see no one gives a damn for you here?"

"No!" screamed she, holding on to the door frame and pulling herself back into the room. Hardy temporarily lost hold of her and she ran back to Joseph's side and stared in his face.

"Listen to me, Papa, listen! I condemn you – God condemns you for abandoning me! My blood is on your hands and my soul hangs heavy around your neck!"

Joseph moved violently away, upsetting his chair as he did so.

"Get her out," he stuttered, turning his back on her.

Hardy grabbed her and propelled her, kicking and screaming, out of the room. In a few minutes the outer door banged and silence reigned once more. A clatter of horse hooves and a muffled curse sounded from the yard and then just a cry of wind shaking the parlour windows.

Joseph turned from the fireplace and his face twitched uncontrollably. Tears cascaded from his eyes and sobs came thick and fast from his chest. He fell upon his knees and lifted his hands in prayer but though his lips moved no words came out. Several hours later he was still sitting there in a waking trance and though the tears fell thick and fast nothing could ease the pain of his aching heart.

CHAPTER 16

And thus the weary winter drew onwards. Days turned to weeks and weeks into cold, depressing months that eventually gave way to the warm radiance of springtime. No news was heard from the runaways and every means of tracing them adopted by Heaton failed. At length he was forced to conclude he had lost his daughter for good. He turned away from the search and became fixated by the stealthy night when he wandered abroad, ragged, haggard and unkempt – fast becoming a walking skeleton. But as his frame shrunk his eyes became huge dilated portals that were almost painful to behold. The people of Scarshead were convinced he had taken to opium to ease the mental anguish of losing both his wife and daughter. Others, of a darker hue, believed he had sold his soul to the Devil for a fortune and it was pay back time.

Rachel regarded her life at Westerdale as a life sentence. Only death, she believed, would remove her from her present location and at times she almost wished for it. Heaton shunned her, as he shunned all human company since Errin went, but Hardy frequently abused and tortured her for his own amusement. At first, sunk deep into despair by her father's rejection, she found it difficult to rally against the cold, the cruelty and the meagre rations but with the lighter mornings and evenings mental strength reasserted itself. Her mind and body both grew sharp and hard and she could bear Hardy's slaps and pinches without a tear. Latterly Hardy was forced to regard himself as possessing the weaker faculties.

Joseph, meanwhile, began to sink into a consumptive decline. As he lay bedridden, racked by coughs, his daughter's words haunted him. His appetite failed and he grew thin and wasted. He began to regard death as imminent. The doctor spoke of new hope with the coming spring but even in June's gentle warmth Joseph failed to blossom. He wondered a hundred times a day where his son was and why he had never written. The doctor told him to prepare for the worst and write to his daughter but his stubborn mind refused. His will had been put in order and he had remembered Rachel in it but he would not send for her.

"She was dead the moment she crossed the threshold of that place," he wheezed. "And she did it of her own free will. She has chosen Hardy over me and she must keep to him. AH! To have the old Rachel back – but no – she is gone and buried and it seems I die childless!"

The summer drew on in heat and sun and soon passed away to allow September to purple the moors. With the return of frost and fire Joseph knew he had only weeks, maybe days to live. Still the servants pleaded with him to see his daughter that they might be reconciled before he died. Finally he agreed to send a message to Heaton beseeching him to let Rachel come for just an hour so he might die content. He felt sure such a request would be refused but on the last day of September an answer was received to the effect that Rachel would be with him about four o'clock on the morrow. She would remain about two hours and at six Heaton would return for her. He would also escort her over to Garstang.

The first of October dawned with a hoar frost gracing the dying heather and a pale weak sun rising over Heldon. Joseph had slept spasmodically, his rest punctuated by fits of coughing and pictures of his dear wife who seemed next to him, helping him breathe. Rachel was there, too, as a little girl with stars in her eyes and his blonde haired son at five or six years of age, playing with his wooden train. He had a feeling Gerald was now very happy and safe, too. He was filled with a state of calmness and contentment, and a sense of floating above the frail body he was now about to leave.

The day drew on and to Rachel, sitting in silent contemplation by the kitchen fire, paring vegetables, it seemed endless. She stirred the simple stew and longed for four o'clock to come. She knew now that her father was dying and the last precious link with her true home would be lost. Westerdale was her prison and could never be her home. And where was Gerald? Over a year now and no word! Would he come back when their father died? Was he dead too? Were he and Errin at the bottom of a peat bog? Her head raced.

At one o'clock Heaton came in from the stables and asked for a large portion of the meal which he always took alone in the parlour. Invariably, most of the food came back congealed on the plate.

"Are you ready to ride over to Garstang Hall this afternoon?" asked she as Heaton washed his hands in a bowl prior to eating.

"What?" cried he, starting from his constant preoccupation and turning to face her with pain twisted eyes. "Ride? Aye, what else? Would you walk?" asked he.

He slouched at the table whilst she served up the lunch and rubbing his head he set up a low moaning.

At this Rachel put down the stew pot and going up to Heaton touched him upon the arm and asked him what the matter was. As soon as he felt her fingers upon him he leapt up with a scream and hiding behind the table cried,

"No! NO! No! Keep back Elizabeth! I saw your eyes start from her face and oh your icy fingers were in that touch which burnt into my flesh!"

"Heaton" replied Rachel. "Heaton, it is only I – Rachel – your daughter-in-law! Why do you talk of Elizabeth and stare at me as if you saw the Devil himself?"

"Ah, yes, Rachel," murmured he, coming out from behind the table."Yes, yes, I thought you were – well it is of no importance. Serve the lunch. No, don't put mine on a tray. I don't want it. You might as well give mine to the fairies for I can't eat it. I thought I saw her poisoning it."

He pulled himself up and stumbled to the door where she heard him ascend the stairs and recommence his sighing.

She sat down at the table and began to eat her portion whereupon Hardy kicked the door open and entered, casting her an evil glance.

"Where's Father?" asked he, sitting down to his steaming plate.

"Upstairs," replied she. "He needs to rest. You'll not disturb him will you, Hardy?"

"'Tis no concern of yours if I do!" sneered he, nastily. "He is not your father. Now be quiet or I'll punch you black and blue if I hear any more of your whining. If he'll not eat your cooking, I will!" and reaching out he emptied the third plate of stew upon his own.

At this Rachel rose and went over to the fire where she sat down with her back to her husband. Hardy ate rapidly, wiped his mouth on the back of his hand and went over to her. Still she ignored him so he nipped her shoulder cruelly. Accustomed to his blows, Rachel did not flinch, nor turn her eyes towards him.

"Well!" cried he, furiously. "You think yourself so high and mighty don't you? Let me tell you, Rachel, you'll not be worth a penny soon! When your father dies everything bequeathed to you will fall into my hands. So everything Joseph owns is as good as mine already. He'll soon be stark and cold Father says and then we can take it all!"

"I won't hear you talk of my father like that!" snapped she, her eyes blazing furiously. "Do you not realise he will have left all his money to Gerald and you won't get a penny!"

"A runaway son," sneered Hardy. "Pah! I have no fear of him. He's probably dead and Errin along with him. Do not pin any hopes of him coming back and rescuing you!"

"Get away from me!" screamed she, turning away in anger. "I've seen enough of your ugly face today."

"Do not give me orders, madam!" replied he. "Have you forgotten who I am? As your husband I can demand anything from you I like. Now, kiss me!"

"I will NOT!" affirmed she loudly, folding her arms. "You are all dirt from the stables. Even clean you revolt me."

"You WILL kiss me!" screamed he, dragging her roughly up by her hair. Rachel managed to evade him at the expense of a lock of her tresses and darted to the other side of the table but to her horror, he lifted up the furniture and threw it, plates and all, into the hearth. Reaching her easily now he pressed her up against the wall and tried to dip his lips down upon hers. Rachel used her sharp, white teeth and bit him hard, drawing blood. Furious, he let go for a second.

"You slut, you bitch! You'll pay for this!" he yelled, grabbing her again.

As he tried to crush her in his arms rapid footsteps descended the stairs and the kitchen door was unlocked and flung open to admit the shaking form of Heaton.

Hardy turned to face him and Rachel slipped gently to the ground and out of his cruel embrace.

Heaton took a few steps into the room and cast his son an icy stare.

"In Christ's name what is all this noise?" shouted he, fair spitting out his words. "Can't I sleep in peace by day now? At night I am subject to infernal torture but to be awoken by your tempestuous passions!!Well, are ye playing cat and dog with my furniture? Hardy, as you've finished your meal, put on yer jacket and get back to the stables. I shall punish you later!" He watched his son go sullenly and silently with clenched fists and a brooding countenance.

"Aye," mused he. "That was me – what? Twenty years ago or something like it. Sullen, morose and ready to fight the world. Well, well, and I am come to this!"

Rachel watched him questioningly, half moved by his musings and half revolted by his latent brutality. His handsome face was twisted and lined with pain but his eyes blazed.

At length he recovered himself and turned to her.

"And you, you useless bitch. Clear up what has been spilt and right the table. You and Hardy will pay dearly for this! There will be no supper tonight. Huh! You think I punish myself by starving you both? Not at all since I live on memories and fresh

175

air! Now I am going back to sleep and I trust, for your sake, I shall not be woken again!"

"It is nearly a quarter to four, Hardy!" said his grim master, meeting him several hours later in the stable yard. "You may saddle my horse and Rachel's pony and bring them round to the front door for our journey. Come – do not sulk with me! Don't you see I am off to secure you a fortune? Doesn't that mean anything? In future keep your lovemaking to the bedroom. You may smash that up but I won't have chaos in my kitchen."

"I'd be glad if the duffer left it to Rachel but if Joseph's lot falls to Gerald I won't get a penny!" fumed Hardy.

"How so? Has the brother returned? Has anyone heard anything from him? He'll have plunged off Edel's Crag or be drowned in Pedlar's Bog and my daughter with him. Why could we find no trace of them? They're with the Devil and he's welcome to them!"

"What if he does come back tho'?"

"Well, well, we shall have to see. He's nowt but a man, Hardy, and as such can fall to any blow!"

At this Heaton withdrew and throwing on his worsted cloak he unlocked the kitchen door and bade Rachel hurry up. After a minute or two she appeared with her long dark hair tied back and partially concealed beneath her coat which Gerald had brought from Garstang on one of his visits.

"See – I am ready!" cried she, her eyes flickering nervously over Heaton's face. He leant back against the partially open door and appeared to be stifling a sob. Eventually he recovered himself, drew breath and called to Hardy to bring up the horses.

"Now," said he, turning to his daughter-in-law with wild and dilated eyes. "Can I trust you at the Hall for two hours? You'll not run off or attempt to leave? A year ago I'd not have even acknowledged such a request but...well...circumstances have altered and I fear repercussions if I do not comply."

"Repercussions?" echoed she, in surprise. "Why? From whom? Do you think I would rebuke you for refusing to let me go? No – I wouldn't! You need fear no angry words from me! From Papa? Well – I pray he'll soon be safe in the arms of God."

At this the black figure gave a hoarse laugh.

"Hah!" cried he. "I fear no retribution from you. Even if you curse me what can you do? You're nothing! No, I fear nothing from the living but O, the powers from beyond the grave! Do I not tremble every night at their intensity to keep up for nine hours what no man could bear for nine seconds? Still – I will survive it! If my act of kindness in letting you see your father does not lessen the torture then my only choice is to take refuge in the grave itself. But it is useless to talk further. Here are the horses. Let us go!"

He vaulted onto his stallion, waited till Rachel was comfortably seated on her pony and then set his horse's head in the direction of Garstang and cantered off.

When they arrived one solitary light shone out against the gathering gloom of a rainy afternoon, but the Hall was strangely silent and still. Rachel dismounted and found her legs weak and trembly at the prospect of seeing her father again. Their last meeting was indelibly etched on her memory and even now caused her pain. She waited till Heaton had tethered the horses, then together they climbed the steps and Heaton knocked briskly. Receiving no immediate reply he let himself in and Rachel followed. Brushing aside the arriving servant, he took his daughter-in-law's arm and they mounted the stairs, crossed the landing and found the chamber where the solitary light burnt. Heaton threw back his cloak and approached the bed.

"Mr Drayton," he murmured. "I have kept my word to you – do you hear?"

The figure in the bed stirred slightly and raised his grey head.

"Who is there?" he whispered, faintly. "Is it Rachel? Come nearer, child. Come into the light."

Heaton took a step or two closer and revealed himself.

"Well, Mr Drayton? Do you recognise me now? See – I'm no stranger though many times in your life you've no doubt prayed to be rid of me!"

"Aye," murmured Joseph. "But where is my Rachel? Mr Grimshaw, my breath is almost gone and I would keep a measure of it for my daughter. But I do thank you for bringing her. Ah, soon I can die in peace."

At this moment Rachel, who had been conversing with the servant, stepped closer and looked up questioningly at her father-in-law. Heaton refastened his cloak and laying his hands on her shoulders searched her face for any signs of deceit.

"Now Rachel," warned he. "Do not listen too keenly to the words of the dying for they may urge you to do things you will be paying for long after they are gone. Well – I am forced to trust you. I will return in two hours and I expect to find you ready!" He hurried out and descended the stairs, pushed aside the servant and went out to find his horse.

In the candlelit chamber Rachel approached the reclining figure and smoothing back the crumpled coverlet turned to the ashen face supported on several snowy white pillows. Her heart was heavy and her eyes full and in vain did she suppress the sobs that bubbled up like volcanic lava. Finally she gave into them and lay her head on her father's chest. It was a touching scene and surely moved the angels in heaven to tears. Ere long she lifted her head and gazed at his rheumy eyes, then sought his feeble hand that felt it had lost its grip on life.

"O Papa!" breathed she. "Why could you not send for me before? To be silent a whole year and leave me in painful ignorance of you. I knew not if you lived or lay neglected in your grave and I had no way of gleaning knowledge. Yes, I have suffered greatly at Hardy's hands but that is nothing to the suffering I am going through now, seeing you like this. Where is the Papa I once knew? The kind, gentle force that raised me? Are you come to this?"

"I wished you would forget me," whispered he.

"Forget you?" cried she, starting up with eyes full of horror. "How could I ever do that? Can a tree forget the warmth of a summer's day in winter chill?"

"Aye – for many a month when the ground lies deep in snow."

"O no, Papa," wept she. "If you had sent word before, Heaton would have brought me. He is almost reformed. No longer actively cruel but greatly preoccupied with nocturnal apparitions that craze his mind and dispel sleep and appetite."

"Heaton suffers does he?" murmured Joseph, forcing a smile. "Why – I can die content now knowing he's unhappy."

"No, Papa," rebuked she, gently. "Do not curse him. When you are gone he'll be all the father I shall ever have. Of course he'll never be you but only this morning he stopped Hardy torturing me. For some time now he is unable to raise his hand against me."

"I would tremble, indeed," replied Joseph, breathlessly, "If fate decreed I must submit your soul to his evil clutches. Beware him, Rachel. A man such as he can never change. He may hide his hatred well – aye – but it seethes, nevertheless, beneath a feigned air of indifference."

"Do not speak of Heaton," pleaded she, taking his trembling hand. "O, Papa say you forgive me and ease the guilt I feel. God seems to frown on me and I cannot bear that you think ill of me. Don't let my hands be stained with the innocent blood of my father. Papa – you are the dearest thing in the world to me."

"Child, child," murmured her father. "With all my heart and soul I forgive you. I have for many days been aware of your suffering and I feel for you. Well, my time is almost up. I can nearly see the angels and I shall be glad to go."

Rachel sat up and wiped her face.

"But I shall always blame myself for causing you this pain and hastening your end," she cried.

"No, no," whispered he, struggling to raise his head. "It is God's will, not ours, that I go. I cannot stand that my death brings you yet more grief. You had no hand here. It is wonderful to behold you again. I can die happy. Rachel - my breath is fading. Hold my hand and sing me to sleep as you used to sing when a child. Ah, the years slip away and I have my Emily at my side. Both my children are here too – I see Gerald's face. I wish he were here in body but I hold him in my heart."

He closed his eyes and was silent whilst she sang a lullaby of her youth in a small but sweet voice that rose above the sound of the wind outside.

"I am at peace," whispered he when she had finished. "My last picture is of you kneeling by my bedside, holding my hand. I am going to be with my brother and your mother too. Stay with me Rachel. I see a bright light approaching! Ah, it's Death. She's come for me." His breath came in gasps and his hands shook. Rachel lay by him, their heads touching and their arms entwined.

The light departed rapidly from the sky and a wet dusk descended onto the moorland. Curlews and lapwings cried into the gathering darkness and from out of the night a black horse came galloping up to Garstang Hall. The clocks were chiming six as the rider dismounted in the stable yard and tethered his mount. Entering the house without knocking he strode into the hallway.

"Well?" demanded he angrily of the servant. "Where is she? Six o'clock is rung and gone. If you've persuaded her to leave you shall pay dearly for it! Do not bother lying to me – I'll not hear your excuses – I'll search for her myself."

He mounted the stairs and, crossing the landing, flung open the door of the sickroom and stepped boldly inside.

His daughter-in-law knelt on the floor by the bed, her hands folded in prayer. She looked up as he approached and her eyes blazed to be left alone.

"What is the meaning of this, madam?" snarled he, choosing to ignore her silent entreaties. "I told you to be ready at six sharp and here it is ten past and still you sit!"

"Mr Grimshaw," begged she, fixing her wet eyes on his face. "I beg you – if you are a human being – be merciful and do not separate us now! Not at his last moments!" Her gaze dropped to the floor and then up to the unconscious form in the bed.

Heaton regarded her coolly, then stepped up to the figure and finally put his hand on Joseph's chest and mouth.

"Dead and cold!" sneered he. "Gone this last hour. Yes, you do right to drop his hand. 'Tis the hand of a corpse!"

Rachel drew close, called her father's name and kissed him but one glance at his face told her he had gone from this world. At this she began to wail and dropped to her knees, covering her face.

"Come away!" cried Heaton, angrily. "Do you not see how he grins at you? He's beyond it all now. Get up you fool – the servants will be in soon and I shun human company! Come quickly or I'll send Hardy for you and his temper is much worse than mine!" He grasped her hand and pulled her to her feet but her legs would not support her so he threw her over his shoulder.

Descending the dark stairs unseen Heaton hurried through the door and out into the yard to the waiting horses. A light, soft drizzle fell and revived Rachel. The breeze caressed her hair from the temples and brought her back to reality. Somehow she got onto Zephyr and gathered up the reins. Heaton vaulted onto his mount and giving him his head they clattered out of the stable yard and onto the moorland track.

Within a few minutes Rachel felt composed and peaceful and soon the lights of Westerdale glinted out. Hardy had lit the lamps and was waiting to take the horses. Nothing was said to her but that night Hardy left her alone and Heaton did not curse her for breaking her word.

Two days later there followed the simplistic funeral of Joseph Drayton, his wasted corpse being carried to church at dawn in the company of his servants and daughter. Rachel was escorted by her father-in-law, who gazed in envy at the yawning depths of the grave as though he, too, wanted to be swallowed up by the swart earth. The service took place in pouring rain and grey mist swirled up to the church door, wetting the mourners and tangling their hair with gossamer. During the service Rachel sat dry-eyed but subdued, her attention on the oak coffin and plumes of autumn flowers. Heaton, she observed, was not listening to the service but was muttering to himself low, fervid words that she could not quite hear. His black head shook and his white teeth showed in a ghastly smile from time to time and he twitched too, as though someone touched him. When he felt her gaze upon him he cursed and ground his teeth furiously. Outside, by the grave, the wind blew his long black locks about and the rain washed him but his eyes were on other elements.

The day after the funeral brought a message that Rachel would be required to attend the reading of the will at Laxby Hall, the dwelling of her father's solicitors. Heaton affirmed she would be there and slammed the door brutally in the messenger's face with a loud curse. Rachel, hearing this, hung over the bannisters and stared quizzically at her father-in-law.

"For Christ's sake why do you persist in staring at me like that?" shouted Heaton, gazing up at her. "If I was not so sure it was HER I would have murdered you months ago for yer gawking! Aye – and stained the flagstones of Westerdale wi' yer blood. Damn you! Why do you still stare? Who gave you those eyes? What do you see before you? An evil caricature? A demon? Or the decaying body and soul of a once great man? Come down, come down, you have things to face!" Rachel descended the stairs and stood trembling in the hallway, certain she was going to be the victim of one of Heaton's blackest humours. As he approached her she flinched and jumped back into the shadows of the stairway and he, perceiving this, stopped himself and, striking his forehead, gave a loud laugh.

"Well," jeered he. "You are afraid of me now are you? Now, when I cannot lift a finger against you! It seems years since I beat and abused you and you did not even tremble then! Yet now you shake and blanch!" A new light came into his eyes and he gazed past her and mumbled words too low for her to hear. Not wishing to witness another outburst of passion Rachel turned and went back up the stairs but he called her name and seemed recovered.

"Rachel, tomorrow we must go to Scarshead to hear about your father's will. Yes, I am back here now. I remember that he died!"

"Why do you persist in gloating over it?" cried she tearfully. "Do you not remember his body was committed to the ground only yesterday and you stood and watched it?"

"Watched it?" breathed he. "Watched it? I wanted to pull off the lid of that coffin and get in there. I wanted to be buried in that earth and covered in that peat. My God! I'd be safe then from HER. Yes, I envied Joseph! ME! Me, who has life! But of what value is it? Nowt, nowt! She has taken it from me. Ah, Rachel, your father is the lucky one."

"Do not talk so, Mr Grimshaw," replied she, shaking her head at him. "I'll not listen to your ramblings. If you carry on I'll side with the half of Scarshead that say you are mad or the other half who say you are in league with the Devil!"

At this he gave a dreary laugh and raised his eyes to hers.

"No, Rachel," murmured he sadly. "I am in league with a far more tormented soul than the Devil. I'd welcome Lucifer's advances but HERS! O my God! She never rests! I put a gravestone over her but that won't keep her down. She has to be pick, pick, picking over me. How long is it since I have eaten a proper meal, or slept in a proper bed for that matter or – God damn me – uttered a decent word. Why am I so tormented? I have done no more than any man would do given my opportunities. Am I to be punished for wanting to better myself? What is wealth to me now? Now when I do not have the faculties to enjoy even basic comforts. Go your way, Rachel, but be ready by nine o'clock tomorrow and we'll go see if you're worth a fortune." He turned abruptly and shut himself into the parlour where he fell upon his knees. Rachel continued, somewhat perplexed, to her chamber.

Next morning she rose very early and descended the stairs to perform her customary duties in the kitchen. As she passed the parlour she was horrified to hear a string of deep groans. Grasping the door handle she attempted to gain admittance but it was locked and her knocks and entreaties brought no answer or cessation of the groaning. At last she ran upstairs and roused her still sleeping husband, begging him to force open the parlour door.

"Will yer cease yer row!" snarled Hardy angrily, pushing her away. "I wish to sleep. If Father wishes to lock himself away that is his decision and I'll not be the one to break down a perfectly good door."

Rachel was fraught with anxiety and begged Hardy come quick, for she believed Heaton was dying.

"Dying!" sneered her husband. "Aye – that's a good one! He'll never die. The only reason he skips meals is because of your diabolical cooking."

"But he groans hideously!" cried Rachel, shivering.

"Aye, and so will you in a minute if I am subject to any more of yer nonsense. Why keep on? I'm not breaking down the door and if I did what reception would I receive from Father? An uncouth blow and a mouthful of curses! No, I'll not do yer bidding. If you believe it necessary then break the door down yerself or coax yer way in with soft words. God knows you wheedle your way with me for favours!" He kicked her off the bed and pulling up the bedclothes sunk once again into slumber.

Rachel descended the stairs unabashed. The dreadful noise had not ceased and at length, when she could stand it no longer, she went to the kitchen for a sturdy knife. After several minutes of struggling she bent the lock and throwing her weight against it repeatedly the door at last gave way.

It was quite dark in the room but the hideous moaning was even louder. Rachel returned to the kitchen and lit a candle which she took back to the parlour. The light flared and dipped as she directed it upon her sleeping father-in-law.

He lay spread eagled upon the sofa, his head restlessly turning from side to side whilst the tortured groans escaped from his quivering lips. Sweat beaded his forehead, his shirt was torn open to reveal his hirsute chest and his hair fell in untidy locks over the cushions. He blew out his breath with difficulty and white foam frothed at his lips.

Rachel went up to him, called his name and then touched his arm, shaking him gently, whereupon he let out a hideous scream and leapt up, raising his hand as if to strike his rouser. When his dilated eyes had recognised his daughter-in-law he sank back onto the sofa and turned his head away.

"Father," murmured she, in concern. "Why do you groan so hideously in your sleep? I feared for your safety and your sanity."

No answer came from the frothing lips but his blood flecked eyes were upon her.

"What is it, Father?" asked she. "Why do you stare as if you see a divine being? Or do you see a devil?"

"Father?" echoed he. "Why do you call me that? I should be no more to you than a creeping insect!"

"You are my father, now," Rachel replied. "My blood father I have delivered up to God and now I have you. Why shouldn't I call you Father? Don't you like it?"

She began wiping his face and neck with her handkerchief whilst his lips twitched with the ghost of a smile.

"There," soothed she, "You are almost beautiful again." And carried away with benevolent feelings she bent and kissed him.

At this he leapt up and tearing her handkerchief in two he flung it aside, his hand covering the area she had kissed.

"Now," snarled he. "That is enough. Yes, you do right to look shocked. What a vile, ungrateful creature you have just kissed. Well – let that be a lesson to you to lavish your affection on your husband in future!"

"I would rather kiss my pony than Hardy!" pouted she.

"You mean you would rather kiss me. Damn you! I see the lock is rent in two and quite useless. However you did the rest out of charity and I cannot rebuke you. There – I am quite myself. Go and fix me some breakfast whilst I change and pull my good for nothing son from his bed!"

"Of what were you dreaming when I woke you?" mused she but one glance at his face made her regret her words. His temple pulsed and his eyes flashed with horror.

"Dreaming?" echoed he. "O, to dream! No, this was a living nightmare that came to me in warm flesh. I was sitting by this fireside all alone and I knew both you and Hardy had deserted me as no doubt you will soon. There was a strange tapping all around me but I could not discover the source of it as there was no one at the door and, at last, in a frenzy, I pulled back the curtains and there – O God! There was the sight to provoke my groans! There was the sight that wrung sweat and even blood from me! It was HER. But, O Rachel, she was a creature transformed. She was shackled in chains and mutilated by deep cuts and lacerations. She seemed to call to me and beckon and it moved me so much that I broke the window and stretched out my hands to her. But she rebuffed me, saying, "See these wounds? You did this to me! YES, you! And on your death they will come to you. I carry them for you. But not for long. O, no! Not for long. Then I will be free!" 'Come in,' I called to her. 'Come in and get warm!' but she shunned me and drew off. I could hear her but she had vanished and then the sound dimmed and there was the night, the moon and the tangled heath. And the heavens seemed to laugh at me and cry," Do not die! Do not die!" and so frantic was I to survive that I joined in their chorus and sweated blood to live, live, live! I fell to my knees and begged them to give me life and then...and then... O God, that monster with the candle was not death as I thought but YOU!"

He dripped sweat and shook but his look was reproachful and when he had recovered he climbed the stairs and locked himself into his chamber.

At eight o'clock Heaton reappeared and dragged his son out from his late breakfast and set him saddling the horses. Returning to the kitchen he attempted to drink a basin of coffee, swearing furiously when he could only swallow a mouthful or two. He flung the offending article against the opposite wall and grimaced wildly.

"No!" screamed he, when Rachel moved to gather up the pieces. "No – let them rest there. God damn it! Fetch me a glass of water and at least let me have the tasteless pleasure of drinking that." Rachel did as she was asked, observing how his hand shook and how his hungry eye fixed upon the bread on the table.

"Shall I cut you a slice?" asked she when, after several minutes, he had succeeded in swallowing the water and had flung down the empty tumbler on the table.

"Cut me a slice?" mocked he. "Aye, crumble it over my head and curse me for it'll not get to my stomach. Yes, I could take it in my hand, I could even bite and chew it but my throat had lost the fundamental principle of gaping with appetite. My stomach is perpetually full of over-fed sorrow and pain that swells up and stifles all physical feeling. There, I have said enough. Your waxen face inspires me to spew secrets but who do you see? They are well kept, no doubt. Fetch your cloak. Do you not hear the horses coming round to the front door?"

A little before nine they arrived at Laxby Hall which was a tall, imposing building on the outskirts of Scarshead. From the hall the countryside fell away to mixed fields of pasture and uncultivated moorland. The day was fine and clear, remarkably clear for October and only a slight frost chilled the air. The atmosphere was fresher and drier than at Westerdale, more vigorous and lighter as though it luxuriated in space and time.

The offices of Smith and Bradley comprised the lower storey, where it could be seen many feet had entered and left black, unyielding marks on the scrubbed floor.

Heaton paused at the door and gazed about him, evidently uneasy at the atmosphere the impressive exterior exuded.

"Well?" asked he. "Have you been here before?"

"No," replied Rachel. "I have passed here with Papa once. I believe he left me and went in but I was very young and my nurse walked on with me to amuse me. I remember asking where Papa had gone but nurse told me he was sorting out business."

"Ha! What you have come down to now!" sneered he, nastily, looking as though he saw the spent grandeur of her past hanging heavily in the air. "To be raised with a nurse and a brother and a Papa too. Now you don't even have a maid to dress you. In fact you have become our maid. You are the mate of a

187

worthless union – a penniless traveller bequeathed to a gentleman's daughter in order to raise a bastard. Well, your heart has born it well! That I must say. And soon you will have only Hardy's cruelty to face. Mine is spent. Rachel – I am entering a strange, sedentary phase of my life. Let us go in. They expect us."

They passed under the impressive gateway and tethered their mounts in the yard. At Heaton's knock and rattle of the chained door a matronly woman from the back apartment admitted them and showed them into a lofty chamber that glowed with a well heaped fire. Rachel sat down at once and warmed her hands by the genial blaze but Heaton kept watch by the partially open door.

The heavy tramp of feet announced the arrival of two gentlemen who entered silently and cast their eyes over the unlikely pair. One man was very tall and thin with a ragged moustache and the other was shorter but thickset with small, gimlet eyes that darted from one visage to the other. Both men were in their fifties and were dressed as respectable councillors in dark worsted suits.

The fatter one turned to the thinner and murmured in surprise,

"I see Miss Drayton is here, Mr Bradley but I am not sure why this man is present."

The grim figure stepped forward and tapped his heels warningly.

"I am Heaton Grimshaw," snarled he, fiercely.

"O I am aware of who you are, sir," replied Smith with sarcasm. "But I regret to say you were not invited. This matter does not concern you – only Miss Drayton."

"Then you would do well to remember that I am Rachel's father-in-law and that her surname is now Grimshaw. Her other name is gone to the Devil with her father."

"Mr Drayton chose not to recognise the union, sir," replied Bradley intervening.

"Recognise it or not, it exists," snapped Heaton. "The eye that was blind to it is gone and that is why I am here. My dealings were honest. The marriage was legal so do you deny its validity?

Come, let us hear the will. We've travelled a long way for the reading and cannot remain long."

"The will, sir, was altered in the final hours of Drayton's life as he became reconciled to his daughter. But he also provided for his son."

"His son?" cried Heaton, in anger. "Why he's fifty feet under in a peat bog and my daughter with him. Am I to be compensated for such loss?"

"Mr Grimshaw, nothing is certain concerning Mr Gerald. He is at present absent but we are trying to contact him-"

"So as a missing son he will lose the right to anything that fool has left him!" shouted Heaton.

"Not so, sir. The time limit to the inheritance that Drayton added is a month. A full thirty-one day month. Hardly a week has gone yet. You must be patient, Mr Grimshaw. The full clause states that should Gerald return within a month of Drayton's death he shall have the right to inherit Garstang Hall and all the land and monies. But if after thirty-one days he does not return it shall fall to his sister, Rachel. If Gerald dies the same applies; Rachel inherits it all. So, beware, Mr Grimshaw, that pretty head could die as penniless and impoverished as her cousin before her."

"What do you know of her cousin?" spat Heaton, a furious light flashing in his eyes. "My wife was no concern of yours. Come, Rachel, we have heard enough. Mark my words, we'll be back in a month to claim our inheritance and we go now merely to bide our time. Gerald Drayton will never return!"

He pulled the door open wide and called his daughter-in-law forth. She came willingly enough and remained impassive as he threw her up on her pony. Pulling his own mount's rein roughly he vaulted on and urged Zephyr ahead of him through the gates of Laxby. There he stopped and turned to the house front, mumbling a string of curses and spitting vociferously at the building. Avoiding his daughter-in-law's eye he set a track for Westerdale, pulling Zephyr by his lead rein and breaking into a gallop. Scarshead vanished behind them and the stark moorland swallowed them up.

CHAPTER 17

A few more dreary days passed, robed in wet weather, each one marking clearly the approaching hostility of winter. Rachel's hopes were now at their lowest ebb and the kitchen, where she spent most of her time, felt like a cold, damp prison. For a few hours she escaped but it was all work, work, work. Heaton remained silent and withdrawn but Hardy revelled in his power over Rachel and exercised his reign of cruelty relentlessly. With each passing hour her fortune came closer but she knew it was an inheritance she would never be free to enjoy. At times Rachel thought Heaton a being insane as he often slept during the day, shunning all company and scarcely eating, only to emerge at night to wander round the passageways uttering horrific sounds. Yet try as she might she could not stifle that mixed feeling of pity and love he evoked in her. In vain did she encourage him to eat and drink, although she shrank from encountering him during the hours of darkness. Many a night she heard him quit the house for the moorland and she wondered where he went and what he did. Some mornings he would crawl into the kitchen and sit by the fire robed in wet and muddy garments that she tried to persuade him to change. He spurned her attempts at kindness promptly but not violently so she was moved to keep trying.

After a week of being housebound she almost wept for a ride out and sighed so plaintively at breakfast that Heaton was shaken from his own inner preoccupations to ask what ailed her.

"O I'm weary of always being inside!" cried she, flinging up her hands. "My appetite seems wasted by constant yearning to be on the moorland again! Father – it is only October! Could I not take my pony out? You have no fear I'll not return for I have nowhere to go now!"

"Hardy shall take you out after breakfast," replied her father-in-law. "The day is tolerably bright although the rain poured all night and a tiresome wind blew, not strong nor cold yet persistent and relentless. Well – Hardy? Will ye not give your wife a gallop or two over Heldon?"

"If you make me," snarled his son, sullenly. "And because I shall get some peace tonight instead of listening to her moaning. Do you know, Father, she was crying all last night and even though I beat her black and blue she wouldn't stop! I half-thought to join you and sleep on the turf but at last she gave over, well after midnight."

"Well, Hardy, you are quite failing in the command of yer wife! If she had squealed around me so I could not sleep I should have ripped out her tongue and left the tears to roll in silence. There! She views me with distaste again. I cannot control these satanic urges, Rachel. They have been with me too long and are impregnated into my heart. There, get out of my sight for an hour or two. She is becoming intoxicated with my company and knows not what to think of me!"

He rose from the table and went out of the room, Hardy following shortly to commence saddling their mounts.

The day was tolerably bright, a little damp and misty in places where the dying heather gave way to black bog holes. But the air tasted so sweet to Rachel she was moved to tears of gratitude for her release.

They took the track that led to Scarshead and had only cantered a short way over the turf when Rachel, who was leading, spotted two riders descending the long rocky track from the next tor. Immediately she turned her pony round to observe her husband, who had also marked the approach of the pair and forced his horse ahead of his wife's mount. Turning his horse's head to face the riders he ordered Rachel to get behind him and waited for the two to meet them.

The horses the couple rode, one grey, the other chestnut, seemed spiritless and tired in the way that they stumbled down the slope and white steam blew freely from their nostrils. Rachel had noticed the yellow shine of the gentleman's hair and the lady's familiar vermilion riding snood. She trembled and attempted to get ahead of her husband but he blocked her path.

"Keep back," snarled he, grabbing Zephyr's rein and pulling Rachel close to his stallion. "Stay where you are! They will be here soon enough though at the moment I would wish them elsewhere, yes, in hell or worse!" His face was furious.

"Ah," murmured she. "So you know them too, do you?"

He did not reply to this but turned to face the pair, still keeping tight hold of Zephyr.

Ere long the travellers reached them and Gerald, who led, reined in his horse and dismounted. He ran to Rachel and lifted her bodily from her mount and kissed her.

"O, angel!" cried he, tears appearing on his cheeks as he hugged her. "O, angel! You are still alive, thank God! I feared to return and find two corpses."

"Ah, so you know about poor Papa, then," said his sister, lifting herself from his shoulder. "O Gerald! I am so glad to see you. I have had a year of hell since you left."

Errin dismounted, too, and holding out her hand to her brother, murmured she was glad to see him. Hardy stared insolently at her, twiddled with a lock of his stallion's mane and asked her why she had come back after all this time.

"This is a strange greeting," mused Errin, approaching him and laying her hands upon his horse. "Are you not glad to see me? Come – don't look away – let us at least shake hands seeing you will not kiss me." She took his arm in hers but he furiously shook her off and turning his horse round to face her cried,

"Lay off me, Errin! If you touch me again I'll give you a taste of this whip. Don't fawn upon me after all these months. Huh – glad to see me. You were wild enough to leave me."

Gerald let go of his sister and returned to his mount.

"I very much fear, Hardy," said he angrily to his brother-in-law. "That although we are now related you and I will come to blows, or worse, if I catch you threatening my wife again!"

"Well," sneered Hardy, contemptuously. "This is domestic bliss, is it not? Are ye listening, Rachel? He has married her! Come, get on yer horses and get out of our way! Rachel – you had better mount immediately – or else.."

"We are bound for Westerdale," replied Gerald, assisting his sister onto Zephyr and then turning to his wife.

"Can we not ride back with you then?" asked Rachel, gathering up the reins.

"Go back?" fumed Hardy. "By Christ – you screamed enough for a breath of freedom and cried hour upon hour for a gallop so God damn you – I am going to give you one now!"

"You forget, sir," interrupted Gerald. "That you are now outnumbered in desire. We all wish to go to Westerdale and you alone wish to ride on. Perhaps we had best leave you to your gallop since you so desire it?"

"What business have you got at Westerdale?" snapped Hardy. "Father would rather take supper with the Devil himself than you!"

"I wish to see my father," replied Errin. "And if the tales we hear of him are true then he is wasting away and is much mellowed by the passage of time."

"Do you honestly believe that?" asked Hardy. "Father is the same and any man who says otherwise is a liar and a maniac! Have you forgotten, Errin, how you suffered at his hands? Do you really desire a reunion with a black soul who hates you? He told me he cursed the day you were born and he curses you still!"

"He is no worse than you!" replied Rachel, angrily. "Brother, do not listen to him. Heaton HAS changed, so much that I fear you'll not recognise him. The source of all my torment lies before you. Heaton has not struck me since you left. The strange preoccupation that asserted itself a little while before you went has now taken over Heaton's life. I truly believe he has little time left on earth."

"Well," murmured Gerald, fixing his eyes upon his brother-in-law. "Let us return to Westerdale. Hardy – you may come ahead with me and the womenfolk can ride behind."

They set off slowly, Hardy furiously averting his gaze from his brother-in-law and taking his anger out on his powerful horse in a series of kicks and cuts from his whip.

Errin allowed her husband and brother to edge ahead a little and then, riding close to her sister-in-law's pony she proceeded to question her.

"How is it," asked she, "that these rumours concerning Father circulate so freely about the district? We only stopped at the Anvil in Scarshead to water the horses when three different people accosted Gerald with queer stories of Heaton; tales that left him silent so powerfully did they impress upon his mind."

"Did he disclose them to you?" quizzed Rachel. "For, in truth, those that name him as insane might be correct at certain hours of the night. He is clearly distracted and neither eats nor sleeps. His large frame has suffered considerably. Errin – you know I never hated Heaton even after his diabolical acts of cruelty but now....now I positively pity him. If you view me as foolish then I'm sorry for it but I believed I had lost you and he seemed the only thing in the world to cling to. I could not cling to my husband – one might as well embrace a poisonous snake and be done with it! But Heaton! He is almost gentle now. Brooding, yes, and silent but he locks no doors and frequently rescues me from Hardy's tyrannical cruelty. Yet you will see Father soon enough so I shall talk about you. How did you come to hear of poor Papa's death?"

"O Gerald met someone he was casually acquainted with from Scarshead and in asking him for news of you he told my husband of his father's death. That was at Grievesborn and we have ridden hard ever since but we are come too late for the funeral."

"And how have you lived through all these dreary months?"

"Ah – you forget, Rachel, the days were never drear for me as each was filled with love and kindness. I have never known such affection and am almost drunk on it, intoxicated on a heady wine! Gerald and I fled for days and never stopped, for even Scotland did not seem far enough away from Heaton's clutches.

After a week we were married and since then have lived in many counties in plain lodgings, my husband labouring by day to keep us. I think we both knew some day we would return. I must own I desired it; I wished to write to you but Gerald said no, as Heaton would intercept it and you, for whom it was meant, would never see it. Secrecy was our main objective and in such secrecy we lived for many days but I thought of you constantly. That terrible picture of you impaled on Hardy's nails troubled my sleep for many a long night but you seem bonny enough! You have neither grown sick nor pale or thin."

"No, and you likewise are radiant."

This conversation lasted until they entered the stable yard at Westerdale, whereupon Hardy dismounted and led his beast forward to drink. As he did so Heaton came out of the further most box and beheld the gathering with widened eyes and trembling lips. The bucket he carried he flung carelessly to the ground and approaching his daughter he murmured, breathlessly,

"What! Is it really you I see before me and not some vision come to haunt me? I thought you were cold in your grave and that man along with you. Ah – Errin, what a perfect silence you preserved. If I had the strength I would damn you for coming back when my happiness was almost secured. You have blasted it into pieces now!"

"I did not come back to pain you, Father," replied she. "And I have no shame in returning as we are man and wife."

At this Heaton drew closer and cast his dilated eyes upon her husband; then his survey complete he turned away.

"Ye Gods! What a son -in-law!" cried he, with an indignant laugh. "What a pale-faced wimp she's chosen. I see in the golden contours of his face a lass's beauty coupled with the fleetness of Mercury! O, Errin, you have chosen well. Do we not make a good pair? Why, I am as black and grim as death and he is the golden, pallid light of life! It makes me realise how far I am from the path of humanity. Damn me! This will never do. Get inside until I am composed and can bring myself to exude some manners. Hardy – see them in. I'll tarry just a minute and then follow you!"

The horses were tethered and the four people moved inside whereupon their grim observer knelt down in the mire of the yard and covered his face.

"O God," snarled he, through clenched teeth."O God, gouge out my eyes that I may never see them again. By Jesu, what an awakening. What a dream-filled existence I've led. Yet, it must be faced – it really is them come back after all these months of silence. I can't get it. I can't get it. It pours through my hands like water. The whole inheritance will fall to him and Hardy will become a beggar before Gerald suffers to lose a penny. A cruel blow – yet – I have got through worse and my mind is not yet stalled. Yes, I am composed. I shall go in."

He rose from his knees and entering the house found the little group settled in the fire lit parlour.

"Forgive me," murmured he, gazing at their anxious faces. "My reception of you was anything but cordial – you must excuse me. I am a man confused and divided by preoccupations too deep to overthrow. Hardy – take the cellar key and fetch some wine. I am disposed to be hospitable to my guests even though their sudden appearance has shocked me." He threw the rusty object to his son and flung himself down upon the nearest settle.

"How can I speak of my daughter any more?" mused he. "When she is that no longer – no – she is your wife, Gerald, and she can never be both. I entrust her to your care and hope you will be a firm and unyielding master."

"Aye," replied Gerald dryly, choosing not to look at his morose interrogator. "I've been as fair to her as you ever were and I shall attempt to match your kindness."

"O that is a good joke!" cried Heaton, raising his lip in hauteur and parting his animal-like teeth. "Ha – I see your plan – you meant to pierce my heart and instead pierced my humour. God damn you! I vowed days ago never to laugh again and now you have beaten down my resolve in one sentence. It'll be hard enough to leave this life as it is." He gazed taciturnly into the glowing embers of the fire as if to seek out the very truths that eluded him.

The wine arrived and was distributed but Heaton could hardly swallow a drop and seemed strangely agitated by the company. After a while he leapt up and commenced prowling the room like a caged animal, his eye darting from face to face and back again as though he strove to recognise them.

At length Gerald rose, buttoned his jacket and stooped to kiss his sister, whom he hated leaving to Hardy's cruelty. Errin rose too and kissed Rachel, then she approached her father and attempted a similar embrace. Heaton recoiled in horror and flung her encircling arms away, pleading desperately that she keep such caresses for her husband.

"But why, Father?" questioned she. "I felt heartened by the earnestness of your words. You seemed tolerably content to see us. Come – can we not be friends? If I am not permitted to kiss you let us at least shake hands. I can't bear you to be so cold and distant." At this she moved closer and extented her hand.

"NO, no, there is no need," panted Heaton, pressing himself against the wall as though in fear of physical damage. "No – I'll say it – there – I'm glad to see ye. There, is not that enough? Hardy, be attentive to the horses and Rachel – take yer sister-in-law outside. I would talk to yer husband alone."

The others departed at his words and presently Gerald found himself facing his father-in-law alone.

"Do not alarm yourself," murmured Heaton, searching his son-in-law's fair features for any trace of fear. "I mean you no harm. Do you not perceive I am a changed man and that time has altered this once ruthless countenance to a feeble shadow of his former self? You are bound for Garstang now I suppose?"

"Aye, we called there on our way across the moors and arranged for a room to be prepared for our return." "Aye, you are master there, sure enough. Will you do me the honour of coming shooting tomorrow on my land? Sadly I am no longer able to find any pleasure in such sport but my son is a crack shot and will bag you a few pretty birds to grace your table."

"Very well, Mr Grimshaw – I will accept. Your generosity does you credit. Shall I call at two? Unless you dine late?"

"Not as a rule. No, I, in fact, do not dine at all. Do you not see a change in my contours? I am only half the man I was. Yes, a miserable, wasted wreck, and worse to come! I firmly believe before the north wind blows across those purpling moors again I will be laid to rest beneath her blossoms. Well, that is for the future. Let me live what life I have left and see my children happy. You must go to your wife now. She will be harbouring fears that I am murdering you slowly and tearing out your heart with my bare hands." He strode over to the door and, opening it, allowed Gerald to pass through, blind as to the sinister curl of the dark lips and flash of power from the black eyes.

In the yard's dim light Errin mounted her horse, turned him to face the shadowy front of Westerdale and looked in vain for her husband.

"Hardy!" cried she, riding forward a little way to where her brother sat adjusting the straps of a bridle. "Hardy, go and see what has occurred to keep my husband. What can Father want with him that demands solitude? Come – you must know? No one but you is acquainted with that man's heart."

"If you wish to eavesdrop on their conversation then you go in," snarled Hardy, carrying on with his work. "And if you don't wish to interrupt them then shut yer mouth!"

"But Father may be threatening or harming him!"

"Nay – he'll not hit a man that looks more like a lass. But why should you care? I don't give a damn."

"I am well aware of that!" cried she, thoroughly vexed. "I still cannot completely trust Father, much as I want to."

"Well, he didn't shed a tear at your departure," sneered her brother. "But don't forget what he did to you and what he is still capable of. If you think a heart like his can ever change then you'd believe the rocks beneath our feet are made of paper! Bah!

Go home without Gerald. Maybe Heaton has devoured him. He eats precious little human food!"

Just at that moment the outside door opened and the man himself appeared much to Errin's relief. He fastened his jacket and looked for his horse which his sister held for him. Gerald mounted easily, nodded to his wife and led the way from Westerdale onto the moorland track.

"Why did Father wish to see you?" asked Errin, as she drew level with him. "He seemed in a strange mood, Gerald, and although I tried to be friendly I don't think we should associate with him any more."

"It was an act of kindness to hear him out," replied Gerald calmly, checking his horse. "He's invited me to make up a shooting party tomorrow and it's years since I had any such sport so I thanked him and accepted."

"No, no, you cannot go! I wish you had declined. I don't trust him, Gerald. I can't. Send notice you are indisposed."

"Whatever for, my love? If the man is really sorry for past events and wishes to make amends who am I to place obstacles in his way? He seeks to right wrongs and I would meet him halfway."

"Heaton righting wrongs?" echoed she, aghast. "I do not think so. Do not let his front of physical sickness fool you."

"But he seemed both calm and earnest in his requests. I could hardly refuse him. Besides he is far from well and too ill for any trickery. He is on a path to the grave unless nature intervenes and I doubt he will see a doctor."

"Huh! Heaton is at his most dangerous when his deep undercurrent of passion is covered by a calm untroubled surface. Yes, he's lost weight, yes he seems weak and tortured but it could all be an act," replied she knowingly. "Don't go, Gerald. He schemes some wild plan to take your Father's fortune for his son, I'm sure."

"I have quite reconciled my soul to forgiveness," said Gerald quietly. "And so has he. Hardy is a boorish lout but he only wants to lord it over me with his gun skills. I shall enjoy out shooting

199

him and bagging my dinner into the bargain. I'll only go once but it'll keep the peace and then you and I, my love, can settle into Garstang."

CHAPTER 18

That evening, in the gloomy atmosphere of Westerdale, vague whisperings haunted the corridors, crept up the stairways and whistled into the lofty rooms. Rachel was banished to the kitchen where she lit a taper from the dying fire and sat, silently poring over the events of the day and her brother's sudden reappearance. The evening was cold and damp with a depressing wind that howled around the crannies and blew smoke rings down the chimney. It forced icy fingers into unsealed cracks and vibrated the glass in the windows.

Rachel remained undaunted, even after her husband's rough treatment and a gentle inner warmth sustained her after the company of the day. She felt certain neither Gerald nor Errin would neglect her or leave her to Hardy's cruel advances and that Westerdale would ring again with their voices. Even Heaton seemed to encourage their company as though his darkness was receding and he wanted to bring light and life back to his house. The future looked rosier for her.

So, when Hardy came in at ten o'clock to beat her up to bed she felt reconciled to his sadistic caresses and remained unmoved by his cruelty. Afterwards she slept peacefully with the comfort of a clear conscience and woke briefly to Heaton's groans as he stumbled about the corridors. She sent a mixture of sympathy and love to him and drifted back to sleep.

The next day she rose later than usual and discovered her bedfellow was already about his work. Kindling the fire she went into the parlour where she discovered Heaton loading his gun with distracted eyes.

"Do you mean to shoot today, Father?" she asked.

"Aye," replied he, languidly, not choosing to look up. "Hardy can go to the summit of Heldon and bag me a flock of birds to keep you busy. I mentioned that your brother might go with him and he seemed delighted with the opportunity. I'll pick off the stragglers but they'll see the main sport."

"Well!" cried she, in amazement. "Are you suddenly reconciled to Gerald's company? A week ago you would have cursed him for even breathing! In fact you hoped for months he was at the bottom of a peat bog."

"Ah ha, Rachel," mused he. "That was yesterday and today is today. I am prepared to be generous and have my children around me before this old black carcass rots into oblivion. Indeed I desire it. Gerald as Errin's husband cannot be any worse than Gerald as your brother. Besides what do I gain by harbouring hate? Maybe if I was hale and hearty – aye, but I shall very likely die soon and then where will such abhorrence be? I cannot bury it with me!"

"Your role as a peacemaker is a strange one, Father," said she. "Not in keeping with your nature – or at least the nature you have shown to others. It seems pure gold is come from dross at last."

"You do me credit," replied he, lovingly stroking his gun. "Now I am off to my room. I've wandered these corridors all night and shall sleep till past noon. They can start shooting at two and I'll wander up after then to finish off the stragglers but the main sport I leave to them!"

"Aye, you should sleep," scolded Rachel. "I heard your heavy footsteps and deep sighs echoing round Westerdale for the last few nights and the tale still goes round Scarshead of your insanity."

"Then let it," retorted Heaton, rising and tucking the weapon under his arm. "If you believe them then so be it. It does not affect me. It will not help me leave the path I am forced to tread – that path leads to death and damnation I am sure. You can cuss me then and call me mad – I'll not hear, I'll not care!" He left the room and climbed the stairs with heavy steps, then reached his chamber and slammed the door. Rachel heard him turn the keys as if to blot out all humanity from his silent lair.

At Garstang Hall Errin was still far from reconciled to her husband's rendezvous. Indeed, the nature of it brought back pictures of her father's cruel behaviour to her. But every argument she threw at her husband only succeeded in annoying him, causing him to dig in his heels even further.

In the end Errin begged him that if he must go he should take a servant with him.

"I have dreadful premonitions of disaster," murmured she, rising from the table. "Fears rise up and choke my words so I can hardly speak with anxiety. And you will not listen."

"Your memory plays tricks on you," replied Gerald, calmly. "You remember only the cruel, black figure that imprisoned you. That figure is gone now. Can a man not change? Why do you find it so hard to believe Heaton has?"

"Hard!" cried she, hitting her fist on the table. "No, I don't find it hard – I find it impossible! How can a demon ever possess the virtues of an angel? Yes, he might not be quite as evil as he was. Yes, illness may have mellowed him but it can never change him. Well – I beseech you no longer and go prepare for widowhood."

"Your imagination runs riot," snapped he. "That is enough. Plead no more – it is nearly time for me to leave but if it eases your mind my father's servant shall accompany me to Westerdale."

"No," replied she. "No, let me come with you rather than him."

"Impossible! I will not have you exposed to bloodsports! My mind is settled. Brownlow shall accompany me and you, my queen, shall remain here." He kissed her gently to show he was no longer vexed and throwing on his cloak he departed to the servant's quarter to organise his guide.

Errin moved to the window that framed the misty outline of the moors, culminating in the rough scar of Ravenscrag, many feet above the house. A few minutes later she watched her husband ride off, followed by an elderly man on a grey horse. Her heart still raced within her despite Gerald's escort and she flung herself down upon the settle to wait.

"You'll not be needing yer beast from now on, Mr Drayton," murmured his grim host nearly half an hour later. "You must leave him round the back. And this person – I see no reason why he should attend."

"Nevertheless he shall," replied Gerald, dismounting and fixing Hardy with an icy stare. "As my valet he is paid to accompany me everywhere."

"Very well," replied his brother-in-law. "My father sends wishes for a good afternoon's sport. He is indisposed, as he frequently is of late, and sleeps in his chamber to make up for his midnight excursions."

"Very well. Let him keep to his bed. I am come for the sport, not the company." Gerald handed the reins to his valet and watched the man lead the two horses round to the stable yard.

"While your servant is thus employed we'll get the guns," murmured Hardy. "You may take one of Father's – he'll not be up to shooting today."

The two men stepped into the scullery and Hardy took down two objects, handing one to Gerald while he split and loaded the other.

"Well?" asked Hardy, watching his brother-in-law check and test the weapon. "We'll begin shall we? 'Tis only a walk of a mile or so – your man can catch up. He can hardly miss us on such terrain." He shouldered his weapon, observed Gerald did the same and led the way onto the moorland.

A chill little breeze blew and flapped the dark edges of the men's cloaks as they walked in single file, silently and morosely through the dying heather. Occasionally lapwings rose at their approach, screaming eerily and circling over them before flying off. The men continued until they ascended a steep, rocky path which ran round the side of a lofty crag and led to a flat topped plateau of mingled gorse and heather much favoured by game birds. A number of these flew off as the men climbed but more still remained hidden in the undergrowth. Hardy beckoned to his brother-in-law to come forward and the two men cast their eyes over the scene, one a little warily.

"I'll just commence a survey of the land that falls away from this plateau to see no moorland ponies throw off our aim. Then I'll beat these bushes and you may load and fire. Has your man reached us?"

"Not yet," replied Gerald, turning round to look for him.

Hardy strolled over to the plateau edge and gazed below him where he winked at a dark form crouched in the shadows who lifted a gun butt as signal and moved forward. Hardy returned to his shooting companion and observing the valet to be approaching he stood away from Gerald and let the man catch up.

The three men moved forward onto the plateau and the valet began to beat the bushes for game. Heaton crept onto the far side of the plateau where he was hidden by boulders. He pointed his gun and waited for his son to step to the side which was the signal. Gerald stood, gun ready, his eyes on the bushes.

And suddenly, as Heaton took aim there appeared to him a leering figure, elusive as mist yet as real as the ground he knelt upon. The figure was familiar to him and she beckoned mysteriously and laughed silently at the horror on his face. Soon she stood before him.

"No," whispered he. "No – it can't be. By Christ she's risen from the grave and vowed to torture me. I'll put an end to it now and save my soul from the eternal burning she promises."

"Come, shoot me then," teased she, opening her arms wide and embracing the whole of his view. "Kill me and I swear I will rest in the earth and haunt you no more."

He pressed his finger on the trigger, moved the rifle so its sight was level with her face and fired. As he did so, Hardy, who wondered why the sniper was so silent, walked forward to the area where he knew his father hid. Gerald and his beater were left behind him.

The shot hit Heaton's ears and filled him with such terror that he was on his feet and running back along the path and away under cover of the crag. He never paused or turned his head, his ears assailed by the high pitched scream of a woman that turned into the deeper, stronger tones of a man. Then, silence.

Heaton continued to run blindly back to Westerdale, his heart sobbing in his ears and his breath shuddering in his lungs. He gained the front door, flung himself in, threw his weapon into the far extremities of the cellar and ascended the stairs, throwing off his cloak as he climbed. Locking the door of his chamber he fell upon his knees by his bed and clasped his hands together in silent prayer.

Upon the moorland plateau of Heldon no one spoke. The gentle breeze that had haunted the stony outcrops all day now broke out in a loud wail and gained strength and power. A few stray sheep, huddled under the leeward projection of the crag, bleated loudly and regarded the two standing figures with suspicion.

Gerald Drayton strode forward and knelt down beside the spread eagled figure, unmarked save for a small hole in his chest from which a stream of blood flowed. The same fluid had stained the rocks and heather beneath the fallen figure.

"O my God!" cried he, covering his eyes and shuddering at the gory picture he confronted. "O God! What is to be done?"

The valet stepped forward and kneeling down besides his white faced master stretched out his hand and drawing away shook his head.

"There is nothing to be done for him," murmured he. "Mr Drayton, sir, your brother-in-law is dead."

"Dead?" screamed Drayton, leaping up and trembling at the words his servant uttered. "O God – they will hound me and Heaton will shoot me down like the very birds we sought to slaughter. But, wait, my gun though loaded is unfired. I saw no one approaching or fleeing and no sound save that single shot."

"No, there was none," replied the servant. "Yet we are easy targets on this ridge. Any man could hide in the rocks and fire. Master – we must go as the murderer may still be here."

"What? And leave him?" cried Gerald."His blood has stained my hands and cloak and only you are witness to my innocence. What must I do? Aye, I know it. I will run back to Westerdale and fetch assistance. You remain here with poor Hardy. God give me strength to attain those grim walls!"

He turned swiftly and ran fleetly back along the rocky path scattering lumps of grit and shale as he went.

Arriving at his goal some breathless minutes later he burst into the kitchen, which was unlocked, where he discovered Rachel paring some vegetables with such a sweet contentment that he shuddered from the nature of his mission. She had been singing softly to herself but at his abrupt entry she stopped and rose to approach him.

His face was running wet, partly with half spent tears and partly with perspiration, his eyes dilated wildly and his breath came in short gasps. Rachel touched his arm and her gaze fell upon the drying blood that had soaked into his cloak and stained his hands.

"O my God!" cried she. "Gerald – what....?"

"Where is Heaton?" interrupted he. "I must see him without delay."

"He is confined to his room as usual by day. Shall I run up and call him? You are trembling, brother. Here, sit by the fire and calm yourself."

He did as she bade but, catching her eye, he knew he could conceal his secret no longer.

"O Gerald!" exclaimed she. "What is it? Why can't you tell me?"

"Fetch your father first," replied he, gazing into the fire. "You shall know soon enough."

She approached the door, turned back and asked gently,

"It's Hardy isn't it? I can see by your face what has happened. You always were very transparent, Gerald! Your whole heart is contained within the contours of your visage."

"Go fetch Heaton, sister," repeated he. "I'll not do or say anything till he is here."

She mounted the stairs, approached Heaton's chamber and knocked. She waited patiently then knocked again. From within came a low, persistent moaning and then muted words as though he held a conversation with someone. Rachel listened then grasped the handle and finding it locked called out to him. There was no reply and her entreaties brought forth no answer that she could understand. After another few minutes she returned to her brother and begged him to go up and try. Gerald's attempts produced no results either although the muttering grew louder, tinged with crying. They both stood before the kitchen fire unsure of what to do next.

"Have you no servant?" asked he, at length. "No work boy who could help me? Rachel – Brownlow is waiting – I must go back."

"There is no one here but Father and myself," replied his sister. "O Gerald, what are you going to? Is it a corpse lying in the moorland wind?"

"There was -an – accident," murmured he, choosing not to face her. "You must understand that, Rachel, 'twas not my gun that fired but that of a stranger's hidden from our view. We saw nothing. I was struggling to load my weapon and Brownlow was raising birds a few yards from me. Hardy was – Hardy was oh hell curse where Hardy was – but he stood apart from us. We heard a single shot and he fell – he fell – and will rise no more." He bit back a fit of passion and stifled a sob but turning to her he observed she stared at him quizzically, dry-eyed and calm.

"What?" breathed he. "No laments – no sobs – no wails? Your husband is dead, Rachel – your husband is dead!" He shook her gently as if to instil his news into her but she broke from his grip and turned away.

"What would you have me do?" asked she, hiding her face. "Should I fling myself from the top of Ravenscrag and be reunited with his black soul? Yes, you look at me in wonder. Why do I not cry and wail? Gerald – I have for so long been exposed to mindless cruelty that every trace of emotion in me is stifled, strangled. Do you think I could feel any love or even liking for my husband? He is dead – aye – I am relieved – or could be if my sufferings had not left my heart stony and cold. The hand that beat me is stilled and the voice that cursed me is silenced. How can I be sad?" She moved over to the door and took down her cloak.

"Come," she murmured. "I am not yet helpless. Let us go. Heaton has a trailer round the back and beasts to pull it. Do not look so shocked. What can you expect from me after months immured here?"

She opened the door and went out, Gerald presently following whereupon he found her in the stable harnessing up her father's carriage pony in readiness for hitching him to the trailer. After this was done they set off, Rachel remaining unmoved by proceedings, and leaving the pony tethered to a bush at the mouth of the crag they performed the latter part of the journey on foot.

As they neared the top Gerald took his sister's hand and bade her prepare herself for what she was to see.

"I would have come alone," murmured he. "But for your words. Are you still so indifferent Rachel?"

"Yes," replied she. "You have no fears of me fainting. So what if he is bloody? He has drawn my blood many a time and now, in death, he bares his own. Let us go on. Your man is waiting. Poor Brownlow – he has had a strange vigil!"

They proceeded slowly and crossing the rocks came upon the brooding figure of the valet who stood outlined darkly against the shifting sky.

"Well, Brownlow," called Gerald. "I am sorry to have left you for so long but Mr Grimshaw – even after considerable effort – could not be raised. This lady is Hardy's wife. You remember Rachel do you not?"

"Aye, of course," replied Brownlow. "I shouldna' come too close ma'am. Tis' not a pretty sight and one calculated to give you nightmares."

"I am quite prepared for that," murmured Rachel. "Else I should have stayed at home and thrown on mourning. He had a black heart and now – well – it is at peace and - " she caught sight of the pallor of her husband's face and the blue tinge that illuminated his skin. He lay stretched upon the heather, one leg slightly drawn up as if he were sleeping and his lips apart, ready it seemed to utter obscenities against the world at his feet. From the corner of his mouth and his nostrils blood had run and dried as a vermilion stain. His long, black hair lay matted upon his shoulder and apart from the wound in his chest he seemed perfect and almost beautiful. Rachel was reminded of the nights when he lay beside her and she woke and regarding his face by moonlight, wondered how so much cruelty could come from such a physically attractive frame. She fell upon her knees and stretched out her hand to touch him but Gerald pulled her back.

"We must carry him to the cart between us and you, sister, can guide us," he said.

"But he seems transformed into the loving child he once was,"breathed she. "All the evil has drained away. He seems so much a part of the scenery that could we not leave him here? But, no, I suppose not. The birds will spoil his beauty and the worms consume him. I almost envy his sleep – I've never tasted such a fine rest since I came here."

"Hush!" cried Gerald. "Brownlow – seize his legs and I'll take his shoulders. Rachel – you can escort us. Pick up the guns, sister, they can go in the cart."

Slowly the procession descended the slope, moved to the wooden trailer and laid the body on it, Rachel depositing the guns beside him. She climbed in and sat on the other side of her husband. Gerald insisted she sit up the front but she shook her head and murmured there was barely room for two.

"And go slowly on the way home," begged she. "For this shall be the only funeral procession he'll ever receive. Poor

Hardy! He did not deserve this, even if he laughed at my fear and abused me with his strength." They set off at a walk, Rachel stroking her husband's hair gently, as though she feared waking him.

They made very slow progress. Once the pony broke into a trot but Hardy's head was seriously jolted about and Rachel scolded. At length, in spite of the blood, she lifted him up and put her arms around him.

"Alas, for what I could never do in life!" cried she. "I cannot weep for you, Hardy! I cannot! You deserve your fate. Yes, you do if death is a gentle dream and life was a painful struggle. It leaves me free. Freedom! How can I taste what is alien and unknown to me....." She continued to caress him and her tender eyes filled with the tears that she had sworn not to shed.

They reached Westerdale and drove silently through the stable yard until they drew up at the open barn. Gerald leapt down and approached the back of the trailer murmuring that he and Brownlow would transport the body up to Hardy's room. Rachel relinquished her husband, laid him down and dismounted. She entered the back door of the house and proceeded the sad procession upstairs. They found the key in Hardy's breeches pocket and laid him on the bed, his wife turning to her brother with steady eyes.

"Gerald – I think you should go now. Errin has been waiting for your return and worrying too, I've no doubt. There is nothing more to do here."

"I will see the magistrate for you," replied her brother. "Brownlow can stand witness for me. When your father knows there will be trouble as he is unlikely to believe me innocent."

"He will be brought round to that way of thinking, never fear," said Rachel. "Please do as you say, brother, and I thank you for all the help but I need no further aid. Heaton can hear the story from my own lips." She touched Gerald's hand and her fingers felt like ice whilst her whole body trembled with either shock or cold. Kissing her gently on one cheek he murmured he would call again tomorrow and bring Errin, too. He withdrew with his valet and moments later she heard their horses leaving.

Time passed by. Rachel, feeling lonely and in despair, sat by the side of her dead husband and kept a cheerless vigil. Soon she heard sounds from the chamber next door and when the first vestiges of darkness crept over the walls she heard her father-in-law unlock the door and step out. He did not at first come into the death chamber but after stumbling down the stairs and finding the kitchen empty she heard him come up again. He paused outside Hardy's chamber and after a minute or two he entered. She saw by the damp shine of his face he had been weeping and in his hand he carried a candle that shook with every rasp of his breath.

"Why do you sit so silently in the twilight?" demanded he. "Your eyes are full of unspent tears. What has happened here?"

"Why did you not let me in earlier?" cried she, reproachfully. "Why did you lock the door and ignore me?"

"I was – asleep," lied he.

"The noises I heard were not the products of slumber!" cried she, angrily. "No man would sleep and utter such groans."

"Ah," murmured he. "If you slept as I slept, always with her frozen dead flesh pressed against you YOU would groan and cry out! You would not pass a night without yearning aloud for release. But there is no release and so I writhe in unconcealed torment."

"Do not speak so," rebuked she. "Heaton – your son is dead. Do you not perceive it is his corpse I keep wake over?"

"Hardy?" cried he, flinging the candle onto the dressing table and falling to his knees. "No – no -oh God – it cannot be!"

"He has been gone four hours and more, pierced by a bullet from a stranger's gun. Gerald brought him home and he fears you will point the finger of suspicion at him. But sitting here this past hour my mind has been busy and I've had visions of a murderous plot that does not leave you innocent!"

"How can you cast your accusing eyes on me?" cried he, turning to her in astonishment. "Was I not locked in my room when you called? What, would you have me cut in two and half of me wandering on the moor with my gun?"

"Aye, you were in your room then but when I called Hardy was already dead and cold. And you were proposing to shoot, Father, as I saw your gun earlier. I sat peacefully by the kitchen fire whilst Hardy met his death but did I not hear footsteps on the stairs at one time? Did I not hear a door slam and a man running? How can that be, Heaton?"

Heaton covered his face and shook his head.

"Do not trick me," begged he. "It is not as you have said. Yes, Hardy was killed by a stranger's gun. In that you are right!"

"And Gerald, Father?"

"He is innocent, of course. Do not question me further. Is it not enough that I have lost my son? The man that did it must be miles away by now." He covered his face and commenced weeping loudly. Rachel's tender heart was touched and she approached him softly, bidding him compose himself as she meant no harm with her questions.

"Come!" cried she, picking up the candle and raising it till it illuminated the face of her dead husband. "Come, rise, look at the peaceful form of your son. He seeks no revenge for the loss of his life. In dying he has gained a new life, one far superior to his existence here."

Heaton raised himself on one knee and stared at Hardy with streaming eyes. Upon glimpsing the chest wound, now dried and blackened, he broke into a terrified sobbing and hid his face in his daughter-in-law's skirts.

"No – no – don't show me!" screamed he. "Cover him up! Don't let me see him, Rachel, his blood is on my hands. Are they red? Yes?" And he held them up to look. "This – this is my death bell. I can hear it! This is the final act of my life! The road from here can only lead to eternal damnation and death. O what is that light? Tis' my corpse candle for sure!"

"Do not be so desperate," whispered she. "I see nothing to instil such panic in you. How can the dead torture you now? They are beyond such passions. Here – rise up and be a man. Don't grovel at my feet like a coward!"

"Have pity upon me, God. O have pity upon me!" sobbed he. "For God's sake, Rachel, and for Hardy, show me some mercy!"

"You talk to me of mercy," cried she, furiously, jerking away. "What mercy did you or your son show me? What pity did you have for my innocent soul? No, you sought to blacken it until it was as twisted as your own! And yet you ask ME to be merciful!"

"I am only a man," implored he, holding out his hands to her beseechingly. "A weak man who has now lost both his son and his daughter. I have only you. Don't turn away from me, Rachel, don't!"

She felt the power of his eyes and feeling herself weakening she hurried from the room and sought the refuge of the kitchen and the comfort of the fire.

As soon as he was alone Heaton flung away the last of his tears and forced himself to look at his son. He knelt down by Hardy and took his hand which he kissed many times. Mingled feelings of love, revulsion and fear convulsed his frame and he shook violently. He bowed his head in reverence.

Minutes later his daughter-in-law mounted the stairs and tapped on the door.

"Father!" she cried, entering. "Father – I've prepared you some supper. Will ye not come down and eat?"

"O -you are still here then are you?" replied he, without looking up.

"Why do you ask that?" cried she, almost angrily. "You know I will never leave you. Now Papa is gone you are the only father I'll ever know. It is my duty to look after you, even though my husband is gone."

"Duty?" cried he, in horror. "Duty? You stay here with me for – duty? Rachel, if only duty ties you then begone this instant! I'll not call upon you any further. Why are you still here?"

"I am here because, despite your past cruelties, I love you," replied she gently, bending down and kissing him. "If I was angry then forgive me. I forgive you all your past indiscretions."

"Don't talk to me like that," growled he. "Love? I spurn love! Tell me you hate me, fear me, abhor me. Never tell me that you love me. I cannot take it, I cannot take it!" He shook his head as though in pain and stumbled wearily out of the room.

CHAPTER 20

During the next few days Rachel learnt the true meaning of the word freedom. Hardy had been a cruel and tyrannical master and from his oppression she was now released. Heaton remained sullen and silent, keeping to his room by day and emerging at night to haunt the passage ways of Westerdale.

Errin had been deeply shocked by the news of her brother's death but she could shed no tears over it. Her one emotion was relief that Rachel was now free.

"Heaton can have no further hold over her," stated Errin gleefully. "After the funeral, Gerald, we must bring her back to Garstang. Tis' her rightful home after all!" To this Gerald agreed at once as it meant Heaton would reside alone at Westerdale. No longer would any one suffer from his pollution.

The day of the funeral was a wild, wet day of torrential rain with a cold gale force wind that flew across the moorland, scattering uprooted vegetation in its wake. Westerdale remained cold even after the igniting of several large fires, the largest composed of coal, peat and wood roared up the parlour chimney but left the room icy and empty.

About midday Heaton emerged from his room and slunk downstairs to the roaring blaze, his weak limbs stiff and frozen from their nightly trails around the draughty passages. In aspect he appeared an old man though he was only a little over forty, his hair still retaining its strong black colour, peppered here and there with grey. It hung matted almost to his waist and his shadowy bloodshot eyes stared beyond this world to hidden spheres where dark forces moved and breathed. He still attained his massive height but his broad chest was sunken and his bones stuck out pitifully. The rasp of air in his throat to his corrupted lungs was frequently audible and blue lips framed his mouth and covered his sharp yellowing teeth. In short his restless soul seemed to have killed his body and taken possession of an empty, decaying shell.

As he sat brooding in the fire's glow Rachel came in bearing a tray upon which sat a basin of coffee and a bowl of porridge. She set the tray gently at his feet.

"Father," murmured she. "Will you not try and eat for tis' two days since you tasted food."

There was no reply to this entreaty and no hint of recognition in his dilated eyes. In fact they seemed to look right through her.

"Father!" cried she, a little louder, seeking to distract him from his inner reflections. "Father!"

"What?" mumbled he, still not recognising her. "Who calls me? Who is it?"

"Father – stop this nonsense!" snapped she, touching him. "Do you not know me? Tis' your daughter-in-law who bids you return to reality and eat the food she has prepared for you."

"Daughter-in-law?" echoed he, in surprise. "Ah – yes – now I know it. You must excuse me. I thought for a moment that you were my wife back from her peaty grave."

She handed him the dish of porridge but he set it upon his knee and continued to stare at the rain-soaked window his lips occasionally moving as though in prayer.

"Must I feed you?" cried Rachel, in exasperation. "Why do you stare like a man possessed by demons? Give over now and eat your breakfast, though tis' late enough to be your lunch." She handed him a spoonful but although he grasped it his hand shook so much that white globules flew over the floor and into the hearth.

"There!" exclaimed she, truly vexed. "Now see what you have done. Father, what distracts you so much at the window?"

She walked over there and looked out at the wild scenery drenched with heavy rain. The oppressive mauve sky – almost black in one corner – reflected a mass of glistening raindrops from the glass and though she scanned the moorland she saw nothing but a few storm tossed birds trying to fly against the gale. Turning towards him she shrugged her shoulders and drawing one curtain over the spot where his restless eye fell she returned to his side.

"It will soon be time to change," she murmured.

"Change?" echoed he, hollowly.

"Aye," replied Rachel. "Have you forgotten the funeral is at two o'clock, Father?"

"Funeral?" cried he, in shock."Funeral! Then tell me who has died? Tis' not you – no, you feel as solid as a rock! There is living blood there."

"Heaton, tis' your son who is dead. My husband. Why do you look so amazed?"

"Ah-ha," whispered he, as if to himself. "Then you are not who I thought you were. I'll not eat this mess. Take it away."

In despair she snatched up the food and tray and marched angrily from the room, slamming the door.

Soon after one o'clock she changed into her shabby black dress and put on her black silk hat, drawing down the veil over her eyes. As she did so the parlour door opened and her father-in-law stumbled out.

"I'm ready!" cried he. "I'm reconciled to the fact that Hardy is dead and we must bury him. This draught is wearing off – reality is coming back and with what horror I can hardly tell. O, I sought to escape for a few hours and now I am back with a deafening blow! Is my face bloody – any of it?"

"Give over!" replied she, turning away from him. "You are as sane as I am now. What have you been drinking, Heaton? Your breath has a queer sweetish smell that I cannot attribute to alcohol."

He gave an odious grin at her words and flung his black, mud stained cloak over his clothes, clapping upon his head his ragged, broad brimmed hat.

"There," cried he. "I am done. Do not look at me with such reproachful eyes. What would you have me do? Hardy was never such a dutiful son to me. Why do you waste your time upon him?

Did he not treat you infernally? Rachel – you are free to go. Walk out of here this minute and know that I have no further claim upon you."

"I have no wish to do that," replied she, directly. "My mate is dead – aye – but I shall honour his memory and attend his funeral. Few enough will be there anyway. It is not for me to punish him by staying away – God will do that!"

"How can you be so generous to him?" grimaced Heaton. "He has ruined you – desecrated you. Why don't you curse him and bless the man who ended your agony by killing him?"

"Do not speak of that, Heaton," begged she. "I do not wish to remember.....if you understand me....think of the mercy you entreated me to feel...well I do and it extends to the dead as well as the living. There – I have said enough. Let us go. Will you harness the horse or am I forced to do it?"

Heaton said nothing but brushing past her stormed through the kitchen and she followed slowly in his wake. She heard him cursing as he harnessed the horse.

"Infernal, infernal rest," snarled he. "Always I am plagued by women that take the form of witches. One is at my side now and her glassy eye rolls so persuasively I am forced to regard myself as a paragon of a father. Climb aboard, angel, and see what transpires. My spirits are elated – I feel fit for a marriage, not a funeral!"

"Mr Grimshaw!" begged Rachel. "Do not smile so! I do not like that queer light that fills your eye."

"What?" sneered he. "Would you have me grim and brooding then? No – that phase shall return but for now and until we reach Scarshead's worn outline I am jovial!" He whipped up the horse and setting his lips in a grim smile he guided the carriage past the house front and onto the moorland track.

Ere they reached the churchyard Heaton, who had professed himself jubilant, sank into a depression brought on by the silent row upon row of grey tomb stones rising up with scarcely a blade of grass between them. Some were sculptured as pillars, others standing as grim tables under whose enveloping cloth their masters lay. At once Heaton began to tremble, his eyes assumed a haunted aspect and drawing away from his surroundings he cowered petrified on the floor of the stationary vehicle. Rachel attempted to help him but he merely whimpered, animal-like, and shutting his eyes pressed his burning forehead against the sides.

"Whatever is the matter now?" asked she, perplexedly stretching out her hand to him once more.

"O God!" cried he, through bloodless lips. "To think I have a wife imprisoned, a son soon to join her and as for me!!!...... Well, in a little while I must lie as still in unhallowed ground which is the only earth that will take me. I cannot bear it! There is no place for Hardy here. The funeral shall not go on. No, no, I'll not permit it and come eventide we shall carry him back to Westerdale." He descended slowly and surveyed the mouldering mounds that fell around him with eyes no less dark nor haunted.

"What nonsense is this, Father?" murmured she. "The rector is already here and the other mourners. Do you not wish to see your daughter again?"

"Don't mention her to me!" cried he, furiously, his dark eyes sparkling with ire. "Go on, go on. I'll wait a while and then follow."

He turned away and Rachel left the shelter of the carriage and made her way up the gravelled path and into the tiny church. She sat down in a front pew and sorrowfully marked the passing moments until the big doors fell open once more and the solemn funeral procession passed through.

The words of the parson became a monotonous drone in her ears. They seemed to belong to another world. She was unable to sit still; strange tensions pulled her outside and in the bleak graveyard, with its wild winds caressing the grey stones, she raised her eyes and saw the carriage was no longer there.

The simple coffin was lowered into the black earth. Not a tear was shed save it was squeezed out by the north-easterly gale. Errin was quiet but composed, her husband sombre and pale-faced. The rest of the company consisted of a couple of servants from Garstang.

At the end of the service her brother led Rachel down the path and stopping at the lych gate murmured he must speak to her as he was deeply troubled.

"Sister," said he. "You are now a widow and though it cannot comfort you to know black suits you still it must cheer you to know that your connection with the Grimshaw family is over."

"How can that be?" mused she. "I still bear the name Grimshaw, even in the eyes of the law. Tell me how am I to escape it?"

"Your mate is dead," replied Gerald. "And no such bonds tie you to the father-in-law. His hold upon you is gone! Rachel – Westerdale is no longer your home. Whilst your tyrant husband lived no one could scale the walls there and free you. But fortune has smiled on you. She knew your sufferings and saw your bruises so today you can quit the dark delights of that grim mansion for the pleasures of another dwelling where love and happiness live!"

"Of where do you speak, brother?" murmured she, searching his face with uneasy eyes.

"Why, of Garstang!" echoed he, taking her hand. "You have only to say the word and my servant will collect all your possessions from that evil place and never more will you cross the threshold of that hell! Come away today, Rachel! He has no hold upon you and I, as your brother, are all the kin you have in the world now!"

"I have a father-in-law," replied she, gravely, lowering her eyes.

"And what a man! Not a man but more of a devil that spawns black magic. Rachel – you owe him nothing – leave that place today!"

"Leave Westerdale?" cried she, in horror, turning her shocked face to his. "Desert Heaton and forsake him? Brother – you do not know what you ask!"

"I only ask for your happiness," replied he, calmly. "It is pure folly to continue an existence with....that man. He cannot rebuke you...no...you were a good and faithful daughter-in-law, but the chain that binds you is broken and thrown off."

"No, Gerald," insisted she, becoming annoyed. "I cannot come to Garstang. I cannot! It is no more my home than Westerdale is yours. I have no use now for refinements and luxuries. I have struggled so long without them that they are now unnecessary burdens. My abuser is cold in the earth and his Father is not the cruel demon you believe him to be. Gerald – if I leave Heaton now I am certain he will die."

"Then let him," snapped her brother, angrily. "Has he not performed enough wicked deeds?" But seeing he vexed her he checked his feelings and pleaded,

"Rachel, I am concerned only for you! After the misery you have endured are you not entitled to some contentment? Do not turn away from it. Come, surely you are humouring me with such talk!"

"I am by no means disposed to be humorous," replied she warmly. "If you care about my happiness then think less harshly of my father-in-law and believe me when I utter the sincerest words I have ever spoken."

"You were always blind to that man's faults, Rachel," murmured Gerald, sadly. "Did I not warn you before of his true character? Aye, but still you persisted in seeing good in him and accordingly have suffered for these views at his hands."

"Yes," acknowledged she. "For a time I was very wretched and miserable, but after a while I knew my unhappiness lay solely within the hands of my husband. Heaton scarcely lifted a finger against me. Brother – he is preoccupied by a powerful obsession that threatens to engulf him. He neither eats nor drinks save I feed him. I really believe he is dying."

"Then your presence will be of no consequence. Do not prolong his agony. Let him go. Let this obsession take him and much good may it do his black soul!"

"You must learn to be more charitable," murmured she, sadly.

"Rachel!" snapped Gerald. "I am quite out of patience with your blindness and my offer may soon be withdrawn unless you act upon it. Come, I'll not repeat it again."

"Then I'll say good day, brother," replied she, disengaging her hand and moving off.

"Yes," cried he as she walked out of earshot. "And you'll be back sobbing and begging at my feet – but I'll not hear you! I'll not harken to your lamentations, Rachel. You're finished if you go back with – that man. Finished!" Averting his eyes from the vanishing figure he turned back to the church and rejoined his wife.

When Rachel arrived back at Westerdale she was dampened from a heavy shower and muddied from the over flowing tracks of Heldon. Her dress dripped water upon the kitchen floor and hanging her cloak upon a peg she sat down by the dying fire and began to rub her wetted hair.

After a moment or two she heard her father-in-law descending the stairs. His deep sighs pierced the kitchen's gloom and presently he entered and came forward to the fire.

"Father," murmured she, raising her eyes to his face. "Father – I am back. Did you have to go and leave me? What? Why do you stare at me so wildly?"

"What?" echoed he. "Is it really you. Rachel? No, no it cannot be. Tis' some weird dream raised out of opium and tinged with bitter memories. O yes – I never thought to see you again – yes, I did. Fain would I have given you to another!" His eyes filled with tears and reaching out his hand he stroked her hair gently.

"Why did you come back?" sobbed he, turning away from her and fixing his bleary eyes on the walls, lit by flickering firelight. "I could have borne it – yes, I was prepared to. By Christ!" screamed he, striking his forehead against the wall. "Rachel – you are a fool. Can you deny you wanted to leave?"

"Leave you?" cried she. "O no Father! That I was asked to I will not deny. But I thought of you and declined it."

"Me?" gasped he, turning his bloodshot eyes towards her. "Why did you think of me? Haven't I done enough to repel you? Haven't I done enough to revolt you by my cruelty?"

He walked about the shady room, his lips twitching uncontrollably whilst his daughter-in-law watched him with anxious eyes.

At length he seemed composed and returning to the fireside he stood on the hearth and fixed his eyes on the flames.

"O God," breathed he, his face convulsing in sudden horror. "O God, Rachel, the light is going and withdrawing her welcome face and no, no ,no, I am not ready for darkness!"

She bid him compose himself as he was not likely to die and she had returned to raise his flagging spirits by every conceivable means.

"Ah!" sneered he. "So you do not mark this strange derangement in me? This marked sinking of my countenance – this bleary eye, this sunken cheek. I am at times convinced my hair is on the point of turning white and my heart of bursting out of my body, so full of fire it seems. I have not tasted food for days. My throat is parched but fain would I drink! I cannot raise the cup to my lips before I shiver and shake and cannot remember why I raised it. No, perhaps I am hungry for only one thing which it seems I've set my eyes but not my heart on. But, ready or not it will come! I see it as a wolf waiting to spring and you, not even you, can prevent it!"

"Are you ill then?" asked she. "If so I'll gladly fetch a doctor."

"A doctor?" mocked he. "No – I have no feelings of physical pain – no bodily agony racks me. My death comes from mental torture and from a heart that cannot rest till she has stopped mine. Till she's torn it out and drunk my blood! Her spirit seeks to pull my nerve ends till they're taut as catgut whereupon she'll proceed to snap them like the wind breaks the reeds!"

The long, cold winter evening drew on and Rachel sat alone by the dying fire. A harsh wind roared about the chimney breast and Heaton moaned from the icy interior of his room. More than once had she mounted the stairs and shook the door handle, in order to beg him to come down to supper. He did not even reply except in incomprehensible groans that scared her by their intensity and volume. Each time she was forced to descend alone and eventually she kindled a candle and fetching pen, paper and ink she commenced a letter to her brother at Garstang Hall.

Dear Gerald, wrote she,

There is scarce a more drear location than the kitchen of Westerdale upon an autumnal eve. The wind howls so fiercely down the chimney and Heaton groans so infernally from his lair that I can hardly think! You, I dare say, spend your evenings in the fragrant warmth of a huge fire with Errin by your side and a whole wealth of love unfolding before you. Yes, you may pity me and uphold the foolishness of my refusal to change locations but I, too, uphold my vow that Westerdale is still my home and that I desire no other.

Brother – that does not mean that I do not love you and neither does it mean I reject your friendship but just as you have vowed to care for your wife I have promised to look after my Father-in-law. If it pleases you to know that Heaton suffers – far greater than I have suffered – then be assured of it. A more tortured and wasted figure you could not imagine! He has, so far today, swallowed neither bread nor water and now has locked the door of his room where he groans in his isolation. Be charitable, Gerald. No man lived who gained anything by rueful actions. Let us leave to God any reproach that is due. Heaton suffers continually now and at present neither sleep nor food can refresh him. Sleep or rest of any kind has deserted him entirely for his face wears a haggard, hollow expression and my words fail to reach him. He regards me as a mystery or else he likens my face to another's that taunts him in that infernal world he is trapped in.

Brother – if you still think it is sheer folly to devote my time to helping such a man then we must be as strangers to one

another. My heart hopes that, upon reflection, you will cling to
our kinship, if only for our papa's sake. Please, please Gerald
remember me in kindness and light the heart of your ever
affectionate sister
                            Rachel.

She blew lightly upon her work and perceiving the ink had
dried she folded it with a trembling hand. After this she left the
last few embers to their fate and took herself to bed. The letter
was taken the next day and in a couple of days a reply was
received. Recognising the familiar hand Rachel took it into the
kitchen and broke the seal. Her father-in-law sat opposite her, his
lips twitching constantly, as though with pain or amusement. He
had been quiet for a couple of days now and apart from the
uneven rasp of his breathing he seemed tranquil. Occasionally he
rolled his bloodshot eyes or sucked in his cheeks but he seemed
content to watch the fire and the growing shadows on the wall.

With trembling hands Rachel spread out the letter and read -

Dear Sister,
I was, on the whole, surprised though pleased to receive a
letter from you and have furnished a reply that I hope you will
find suitable.
If I was angry and ill-tempered when we last met you must
forgive me. If I still sound somewhat irate believe it comes from
the loss of your company and not through hate or indifference. I
was cool as soon as you left and bitterly regretting my harsh
words would have called to see you, but fear of meeting Heaton
put that scheme out of my head. Errin is likewise anxious to avoid
her father. If you think us cruel please forgive us. Maybe love has
made us selfish but do not mistake my feelings, Rachel. I have no
bitter hate for Heaton such as he once held for me. Yes, I dislike
him but mostly for the hold he has over you, my dear sister. Were
he dead and buried you would no longer be required at
Westerdale. I desire to see you – yes, but not at the expense of

Heaton's life. Tell him I wish him well and pray for the renewal of his health. Folks in the town believe he is dying. Can you not summon a doctor to help you deal with him?

I await your further communication.

Your loving brother,

    Gerald.

"Heaton," murmured she when she had finished reading. "Heaton, I have a letter here from my brother, Gerald. You do not mind us communicating do you? It does not mean I have any plans to leave you. Gerald feels no resentment nor utters any reproaches."

"You may do as you please," gasped he. "I no longer have any strength to oppose you."

"But if you could would you still keep me prisoner here and watch my every move?"

"No – no – your presence fades into insignificance besides the visions I am forced to behold! Every decent thing has left me and this haunting throws your face into shadows." He gritted his teeth as he said this and laying his fist upon the table began to whimper softly.

"Father," murmured she gently after an interval of silence."Father, Gerald wishes you no ill. He sends wishes for your recovery and begs me to obtain a doctor for you."

"Tell him I am past caring about my health. It will soon be beyond my care. Pain? Surely I can decline no more once I have crossed the threshold of hell. I mean to be swallowed up into the jaws of death and expire with a blessing for all except HER. Her I curse for so infernally disturbing me this past year! Never a night has gone by when I have not been forced to look into her face. If I laid down to rest her head would be on the very same pillow. If I stumbled along in the darkness always her visage would float at my side and even with my eyes closed she would still disturb me, still leap at me, leer at me, sneer, laugh and destroy my spirit! And I am now, as you see me – a broken man!" He drew a long, sad breath and fixing his glazed eyes on some invisible force a few feet away from him he rose shakily and put out a hand.

"She wears a venomous leer tonight and has come to inform me that my death day is nowt but a week away. Prepare yourself exults she, plucking at my soul as if she would rather take it than the Devil. By Christ! I'd rather surrender myself to Jesu than to you!"

He stumbled out of the door and she heard his heavy tread echoing up the stairway. Reaching his room he slammed the door and became enveloped in a temporary silence that often preceded his hours of groans and laughs. At night she knew he walked abroad, although the location of his nocturnal wanderings completely eluded her. She had, once or twice, descended in time to observe him dragging his wrecked frame in ; his coat torn and muddied, his hair wet and in his eyes a look of unbearable sorrow and torture. He never told her where he had been but for hours afterwards he was restless and violent, his face twitching constantly and his lips moving with frenzied curses. Yet even in his wildest passions she evinced no fear of him and took no trouble to keep out of his way. Indeed, she often sought his company as if by being with him she could instil a sense of sanity into his infernal world.

Two or three days of dark, cold followed each one marking its passing clearly upon Heaton's physiology. Rachel, who felt the long hours more keenly than her house mate, commenced writing in a small leather bound book she discovered in one of the chambers. It was empty apart from some handwritten dates from a year more than a decade ago. This she took considerable trouble to conceal in a small niche to the right hand side of the fire place. After the duration of a fortnight events occurred to allow Rachel to reveal its contents to her brother, the very person to whom it had been secretly addressed through the long, dark hours that saw its birth.

CHAPTER 20

NOVEMBER 19TH.

Today dawned bright and clear, with a sharp hoar frost that has only now – at eleven o'clock – released its hold upon the moorland. How I long to be up there! As I descended the stairs I chanced to look out across that sparkling landscape and recall the days of my childhood when I wandered at will across those stark plains. How I drank the balmy air as though it were wine. Alas! That sweet, careless spirit of youth no longer possesses me. It fled years ago, it seems, betrayed and worn out by the trouble that has fallen on me. And yet in my deepest misery I am content at Westerdale. I cannot ever contemplate leaving it.

It is now evening and as I sit writing this by a roaring fire, that spits with the fall of frost, Heaton sits opposite me, sighing with the same intensity as the wind that haunts the crannies of Westerdale. He has, all day, nourished a venomous temper within that black brow of his and has scarce spoken a word to me. In vain have I entreated him to take a sip of water or eat a slice of bread. It is to no avail – he will have none of it and falls deeper into illness that I can only describe as being self-inflicted – painful though I find this to admit. He looks up every now and then as though distracted by the scratching of my pen but his eyes, when I meet them, are vague and hazy. It seems he is bleeding with a pain that goes too deep for tears. How can I aid him? My usefulness is past and he appears to wait for death much as the trees await winter; that is, he knows it is approaching but as to the exact time of its coming he is as ignorant as I. At times I think he will wake from this tortured sleep but at other times I am saddened to believe he will not see Christmas or the birth of a New Year.

It is almost eleven o'clock and he has just left me. As his custom he has gone to his room. I thought his breath more audible tonight and it seemed to echo throughout the house and cause him a considerable struggle to attain ere he reached the landing. But I have many times witnessed him clinging feebly to the bannister rail, struggling to regain his wasted breath. I can do nothing more for him. He will not even permit talk of a doctor, much less agree to one being summoned. Once he murmured it was his wish to have it this way and, in truth, I dare not and would not change this.

NOVEMBER 20TH.

As this morning was reasonably fine I descended early (a little before seven o'clock) and observed the door to Heaton's chamber to be wide open. Accordingly I looked in and found it empty but in such a state of disrepair as made me wonder how many people inhabited it. Odd piles of clothes – most of them wet and muddied – lay all over the floor. The dresser was strewn with small slips of torn paper adorned with strange symbols and upon his bed lay a slim phial of pills. These I took the trouble to remove, fearing them to be harmful – I would have him no worse than he is. On closer examination they hold a strange colour and odour; this perfume I have smelt before on Heaton's breath late at night. After locking them in my trunk I descended and had just raked through the fire when my father-in-law stumbled in, coughing abysmally and dressed in clothes that had become mere tatters through which his wasted body showed as a confusion of bruised skin and staring bones. His hands and face were covered in mud and the stickiness of peat adhered to his trousers as though he had been digging for some reason. My curiosity was aroused and I am planning to follow him tonight that I might keep him in on future nights by locked doors and windows if his nightly excursions are likely to harm his health further. In truth how can I doubt this? Today he was drenched and trembling, almost hysterical in his restlessness, whereupon he began pacing the floor like a caged animal.

"Mr Grimshaw!" cried I. "What is the matter with you and what business takes you out so late every night so you only come home in the morning?"

He did not answer me but rather stared as though he did not know who I was or what my business was in his house. Gradually his eyes became less dilated and urging him forward to sit by the flaring fire I observed he now saw me in a softer light.

"Do you know me?" asked I, turning my face to the healthy glare.

"Aye," murmured he, breathing shallowly but very fast.

After that I could wring from him no further communication. He neither replied nor acknowledged my questions and merely dropped the steaming bowl of gruel I thrust into his hands. The entire meal was consumed by the two house dogs who were exceedingly grateful for his accident. The coffee I sat beside him until it had grown cold, whereupon I threw it away. His lunch and dinner received similar treatment. I do not know how much longer he can go on and once again I am forced to contemplate his death. How my heart aches with sorrow to commit him to the earth – a sorrow too deep for tears. It leaves me not only saddened but numb too – a powerful emotion that I have never previously experienced.

NOVEMBER 21ST.

As last night appeared, upon retiring, to be fine and dry I did not change into my night attire but remained dressed and lay down upon the bed. My plan was to wait until Heaton commenced his night prowling and then follow him. At times it seemed I was wide awake and at others I appeared to doze and even fell into a light sleep. My cloak lay ready upon the chair and very thankful I was for a glimpse of moonlight in the black sky.

After several hours of alternate listening and dozing I heard the click of a door and instantly rose and flung on my cloak. The hour I guessed to be about one or two (we had retired slightly earlier that evening) and when I finally quit the room he I followed had already left the house. Silently I descended, slipped into the shadowy night and saw by the silver moonlight a lonesome figure approaching the grave clinging to the swart heathland on the boundaries of Westerdale. The wind blew fiercely, as though it endeavoured to force back the faded form but he, with supernatural strength, pressed on at great expense to his corrupted lungs. Slow and steady he pursued his goal; called by an exacting force and I, half in fear and half in curiosity, pressed onwards, even running a step or two when the wind lulled. Very soon I felt a sprinkling of rain in the air and drawing my hood up I observed Heaton had reached the grave. He stood like a statue and murmured words that the wind whipped away from him. I drew as near as I dare and spreading my cloak on the ground I knelt down and observed the strange antics of my father-in-law.

At first he seemed content to look down upon the weather beaten grey stone in silent admiration but after a few minutes he flung himself to the earth and appeared to be digging, feverishly, in the peaty soil. His breath came in grating rasps under such exertion. For a time I watched, horrified, as he flung away the earth with his bare hands and presently his form disappeared. Hastily I rose, edged closer and observed him to have stepped down into the hollow he had laboriously created. Hearing the crack of wood I realised he had reached the coffin of his wife.

A loud groan rang out, then the wind whipped it away and flung it out over the dark moorland. My heart beat loudly and all the blood in my body became chilled with the horror being acted out before me. The silver moonlight lit up the open grave and illuminated the scene which my eyes seemed unable to leave. Peering down into the open grave I saw Heaton struggling with the coffin lid. I felt faint and was glad of the boisterous wind, bringing me to my senses. The lid, I observed , was not riveted on; the long nails had been removed, presumably by the very hands that now pulled at the tomb. Ere long Heaton succeeded and flinging the wooden barrier aside he drew a deep, painful sob of breath and cried,

"I am come as promised, Elizabeth, I am come! How cold are your lips. Ah well, there is a bitter wind tonight, my darling! It brings strange pictures to me and tells me there cannot be many more nights like this. Ah – you smile. The peat has embalmed you perfectly and you – yes – you are like a tiny child gone to sleep. Yes, you are silent but I know you dream vividly enough. Yes, you are shrunken but you've been here, starved of my love, for many a year. As such I've been starved too – starved long, weary decades for a cheek such as this and a silent heart. Come to me – come to me! I can't go on much longer – I can't!" he sobbed. "Why do you taunt me to death? There is no need – I am content to surrender up my life to you!" There followed a long paroxysm of coughing and finally I observed Heaton had laid himself down in the grave, his arms round the decaying corpse, his cheek laid against hers, their forms entwining. A shaft of moonlight fell upon her silent face, the face that bore a strong resemblance to my own. Heaton lay so still that I thought for a moment he had expired and the two lay safe in death, whereupon I could have shovelled the earth in upon them and disturbed them no more. But his lips twitched yet and as jealously overtook him he pulled her closer so the air became soaked with the stench of decaying flesh and I fell back, covering my face. Nausea overtook me and the full horror of what I had witnessed sent me running back through the silver night to reach the safety of the house front. Desperately I clutched at the solid walls and tried, fruitlessly, to dispel the terrible pictures flashing through my head. I sought the safety of my chamber but even there I could get no peace. How bitterly I wept, how I shook and covered my eyes as if to blot out the painful images. What I had seen convinced me that Heaton was mad and eventually, exhausted, and distraught, I slept.

At six o'clock I woke, hearing Heaton enter the house, and jumping up I put a fresh gown on and descended. Heaton sat grimly by a dying fire, his visage almost as sad and low as my own, his clothes torn and muddied, long wheels of white in brown flesh revealing his tears. His eyes, when they fell upon mine, were ghastly – I shuddered from their gaze and looking away shed salt water of my own which he, at last, became sensible of.

Gently he reached out a hand and turning my face towards him he murmured, almost kindly,

"Why, lass, you have been crying, have you not? Are you so very unhappy? There is no necessity for your staying any longer if you are set to go? At the cessation of another week I hope to be beyond help and safe in the earth where I may sleep as long as I will!"

I bade him not to talk so, there was no truth in it.

"Come," begged I. "Come, Mr Grimshaw, renounce your self propelled path to the grave! Come – you do have something to live for. I will never desert you – never – unless you turn me out. There! Let me stoke up the fire and obtain some clean clothing for you after which I can prepare breakfast and bring health and sanity back to your fading form, which is crying out for care! Do let me, Father, do! How can I aid you? How? I will not give you up to the jaws of death – I will not! Tell me what I must do or say to save you?"

"There is only one thing I desire from you," replied he slowly, fixing his bleary eyes on mine. "Rachel – do not leave me. I beseech you. I find vestiges of comfort in the knowledge that I shall not die alone!"

"You do not have to die at all, Father," cried I. "Listen to me. Renounce this self-extermination. I must not lose you!"

"No," avowed he, a strange gleam entering his eye. "No, I have no choice in the fulfilment of my destiny. I am – that –

close. It must be as fate decrees and though I weep and gnash my teeth and pray till the world goes black – it will not change!"

"How can you say that?" rebuked I, angrily. "Are you not a man? Have you the power invested only in God to chose – to will – whether to live or die?"

There was a long silence whereupon he lowered his head and letting it fall forward onto his breast he whispered,

"Last night, Rachel, I did a very wicked thing, that will forever damn me. I hesitate to tell you. I have not, of late, been able to sleep – indeed I have scarcely been able to breathe without the most speechless agony and she, who is responsible for all my pain – SHE – she lies beyond my reach in a decaying grave. Last night I suffered as never before and hurrying out into the moonlight night where I could scream at will I was summoned, as usual, to that queer grey stone that rises above the moorland. Many is the night I have yearned to stretch myself over her grave and force her spirit to remain there, instead of escaping to torture me. But that was not enough tonight and so I did what I have only done once or twice before – I DUG UP HER COFFIN!! It was not concealed very deep and neither was it securely fastened. I took care to pull out the long nails with my bare hands that she might do her duty by me. Last night I struck her coffin, grappled with the lid and forcing it open felt myself again in those arms that have tortured me for so many months. But she was cold, dreadfully cold, and though the face was still hers the stench of death was upon her and she was alien to me. I beseeched her to come – I implored the very air and was, at last I believed, answered. A sudden pulsing warmth went through her, her face was renewed and I could nearly feel her beating heart. Nearly, nearly – and yet I could NOT! I grew wild to touch some proof of her human form – I affirm she lives yet – and as I lay there cheek to cheek I dreamt an odious nightmare.

I remember it was very dark and I appeared to be climbing up a steep track, covered in treacherous boulders and rocks. Once or twice I fell but I was driven on by a compelling fear of what came behind me. How I sweated and toiled! Round a bend I came across a bright form who beckoned to me.

It was HER. Almost before she came I knew her. Her dress was the same tattered robe which lay on her in the grave only now it was sleek and new as in life. Her face shone pallid and perfect, her figure lithe and full. She continued to beckon to me and ere long I perceived I was nearing the top of the track. I threw myself up, lost my footing and rolled among the crushed stems of vegetation that smelt like heather. Swiftly I rose; my wife asked me if I knew where I was. I affirmed it directly – I was on the moors at Westerdale and behind me was the imposing front of the house, just as I had left it not two hours ago. But no moon shone now and the track below me seemed to melt away into nothing. I stepped forward and she took my hand in her icy fingers and led me onto the path that snaked its way to Scarshead. I cast my eyes about me and at length observed two objects, where I knew in reality there was only one.

"Stop!" cried I. "Take me over there so I may see for myself what grave lies beside that of my wife."

"We have come forward in life," murmured she. "Come – we must hurry or it will all melt into dust!"

I did as she bid and as I drew near a terrible fear came over me and I shook but she pulled me onwards until I stood next to that clean, white stone." He paused here and let a tear escape amidst a deep, searing sob.

"It was my own grave," continued he. "The earth was freshly dug, the stone unstained by time or weather – the name upon it mine – the dates those of my birth and, as she told me, my death. I asked what day it was and she mentioned one not so very far distant.

"I cannot bear the place," wept I, endeavouring to close my eyes and block out the image."There is a feeling of desolation here, a strong emotion present in the air. Tis' not love – no 'tis too bitter for that – it tastes like neglect – almost hate! O let us go – I can't bear it!"

Accordingly she took my hand and led me to the house front where I hoped to find warmth and habitation but – O God – the doors and windows were all locked and when I looked in it was silent, cold and empty. No candles graced the windowsills, no fires brightened the grates and no forms flitted across the rooms. The curtains were torn down and the air was so foul and stale, so fetid that I cried aloud for deliverance and then I woke to find myself lying by – HER. And the stench of her decaying body filling my nostrils was the reason for the putrid air in my dream. Dream! No, never a dream. A nightmare!

Dawn was barely an hour away and I rose swiftly and covered my desecration. Believing myself an enlightened man I stumbled in here – and beheld your face!" He gasped for breath again and giving a prolonged shudder that shook his entire frame he stammered, "It shall all come to pass!"

I could not believe it. His story so shocked and affected me I was unable to furnish a reply. Presently he rose and ascended to his room where he remained for the rest of the day.

It is evening. Heaton has just descended to find me writing this and demanded his tablets back. In affirming I do not have them I know I lie but I cannot risk them damaging his already failing health. My question as to what they are produce no response and on examining them closely I suspect opium or some hallucinate. I shall destroy them nevertheless.

NOVEMBER 22ND.

Heaton has fallen into a decline which he affirms to be due to the loss of his tablets. I found him on his knees this morning in the kitchen, quite grovelling for their return (he still believes I have them). When I questioned him about them I received the same response as last night – a hostile silence. He then begged in such a heartfelt way that I felt tempted to fetch them for I have not yet thought of how I can destroy them. Since yesterday evening he has watched me like a hawk and though he does not accuse me verbally his eyes speak volumes and I blush and tremble before them.

This evening he seems very much worse. He lays languidly upon the hearthstone and gnashes his teeth, frequently allowing his spittle to ooze over the grate until it causes the fire to sizzle. He groans hideously and his body becomes violated with strange tremors, twitches and pulses so neither of us get any peace. He beseeches constantly for mercy and seems unable to exert any control over his limbs. In truth I fear he will not last another night.

Alas! How can I mount the stairs tonight knowing he cannot do so? How can I leave him to a lingering death? His eyes forever seek mine, his weak hands clutch at my skirts if I even shift in my seat and in truth I can bear it no longer. I cannot be sure that the tablets are harming him and he can surely not be any worse than he is at present for he borders on insanity and approaches the very threshold of death! O God – I cannot leave him to suffer so and believing I have now done the best I can under such tragic circumstances I close now to fetch the tablets and so give him either his life back – or death.

NOVEMBER 23RD.

He is better! Last night, as soon as I gave him the tablets, he pulled himself upright and focusing his rheumy eyes on the phial I handed him he bade me fetch some water and having swallowed a couple of the pills he seemed content, and stretched out over the hearth, preparing for sleep. I tiptoed out and having securely locked and fastened all doors and windows I ascended to bed in vain hope to sleep.

It was a bitter night and the wind howled so fiercely that at first I could get no rest. The room seemed icily cold, draughty and haunted by strange noises that played on my over strung nerve ends. In vain did I close my eyes a hundred times; it seemed I must open them again at the incessant howl of wind against my lattice or the rattle of my ill-fitting door. Ere midnight struck I began to feel easier and lying down again dropped into a light doze. Suddenly an appalling frenzy of sound assailed my ears and I woke. It seemed like the crashing of glass and was followed by a horrendous scream. Believing Westerdale besieged I jumped up, threw on my gown and descended the stairs at a rapid pace.

From the kitchen came a repetitive sobbing, the dull moan of anguish I had often heard Heaton emit. To this room I now repaired – the faint yet pulsing light from the fire enabling me to see into the far corners of the place. He stood there transfixed, whimpering quietly now and as I approached I could see the stain of blood upon his forearm and face, some of this liquid already crimsoning his clothing. The small window opposite the fireplace had been completely shattered and irregular pieces of glass were scattered across the kitchen floor, a few of which I crunched between my feet.

"O, my God," breathed I, turning towards him. "Mr Grimshaw – Father – you are covered in blood! What can be the meaning of it?"

"Why did you lock the door, Elizabeth?" snarled he. "Why did you imprison me? I must get out – I must – I must! I have tried every handle, every knob! Do you not hear the wind rising? It's her voice from the lonely grave. She calls me!" And fleeing from the room I heard him battering against the front door. I lit a candle from the remnants of the fire and followed him into the hallway where I saw he had given up his struggle and reclined, drunkenly, against the wall. Long wheals of blood scoured the door, great splashes of red, darkening as it dried. I raised my candle to the pallid framework of his face, offset by drops of crimson that ran from an open wound on his forehead. I became almost faint with all the gore and begged him to let me dress his cuts and take him upstairs to his bed.

"I require no assistance from you, Eliza!" moaned he, twisting his face this way and that as though in agony. "I thought you were out there in the darkness – I thought you were in your grave. By Christ, I'd like to be in mine – now – safe from all this witchery I see about me!"

"Stop this nonsense, Father!" cried I. "It is way past midnight and I'm tired!"

"Then go to bed," shouted he. "No! Wait! Have you the key to this door?"

"Yes," I replied, hesitantly.

"Good – then unfasten it for me and withdraw from my sight."

I dithered for several minutes and at length deemed it better to leave him where he was for tonight. At least the biting cold could not reach his wounds and the rain would not soak his shrunken frame. I drew off slowly and had reached the bottom of the stairs when he rose and stepping after me, asked why I had not done as he bid.

"I will not do it!" I cried, defiantly. "Father – it pours out there and an icy wind blows. I'll not give you your death of cold."

"Then you deny me any chance of life!" screamed he, dragging me down from the stairs roughly by my shoulders. "In God's name, if I ever implored you for release it is – NOW! Come – I cannot wait. Agony makes me desperate and soon it will make me cruel. Do not tangle with me – not tonight – I am in no mood for gentleness!"

He leered at me with such an evil sneer that I believed his sentiments true and fetched the key from its hiding place. His eyes lightened considerably, he closed his hand upon it and after freeing the door he ran out into the night.

I followed him to the threshold, gazed out into the darkness and after a minute or two called his name. No response, save for a mammoth blast of wind and a tumult of rain that flung itself in upon me. I felt certain I would never see my father-in-law alive again and accordingly shut the door and retired to bed.

In vain did I try to sleep but my eyes would not close and at six o'clock I rose and, descending to the kitchen, found Heaton had not returned. In truth I did not expect him to and when the dreary day was half over and the rain had departed I threw on my cloak and went out onto the moorland.

I journeyed first to the grave but, although there were clear signs it had been recently disturbed, no form lay recumbent in the long grass around it. I went a little way onto the path to Scarshead but could see no trace of life, save for a couple of wild ponies who moved off as soon as they saw me and some flocks of birds, moving from bush to bush in search of food.

"O God!" cried I, anxiously scanning the misty scenery. "What if he should have fallen into a bog hole and drowned?" There were several such traps between here and Scarshead. I could scarcely believe it for he knew the moors as no other man living and every step of every path he could traverse without light.

It began to rain again and not desiring a soaking I hurried indoors and called his name aloud in case he had crawled in and lay, prostrate, in the shadows. There was no answer. I searched the out buildings, which were mostly empty, Heaton's stock having all been sold to free up money for his debts. Again, I found no trace of him.

It is now evening. He has not come back and as I listen to the wind howling and the rain lashing the house front I fear he will never return in person. My mind is in utter despair; never since Papa's death has anything so dear to me departed from my life. I can bring myself to make no decisions save that the doors shall be left open all night and I will wait at least another day before I inform my brother.

NOVEMBER 24TH

Alas! What a miserable night I spent surrounded by despair and sorrow and unvisited by that most welcome stranger, sleep! The night seemed eternal and though I did not retire till midnight the dawn seemed no nearer at five than it did at one. If I could be certain that Heaton was dead then I could allow my grief to swallow me up but there is room for doubt and a little for hope that he will come home. I am wary of journeying to Garstang or Scarshead for fear of infuriating Heaton – if he is alive – and driving him off. It haunts me that because I caged him in like an animal he has gone. Yes, it may not be a reason for his departure but I cannot feel blameless in this affair. So I shall keep vigil here and leave the doors open, despite the risk to my personal safety. How could I live with myself were he to return and find Westerdale empty? It smacks too well of the dream he told me. I shall wait another two days notwithstanding.

NOVEMBER 25TH.

I was much grieved to receive a letter this morning from my brother, enquiring into the minutiae of Heaton's condition and proposing, if allowed, to call upon me tomorrow afternoon. I can do nothing but write lies and that I did so, detaining the post boy, after he had brought some milk, by cooking him a second breakfast, I must admit.

To all outsiders I affirm steadfastly that Heaton is no better, that he keeps to his room, and that he is not a troublesome patient – perhaps the greatest lie I have ever told. He troubles me unceasingly, day and night, waking and sleeping – and when I do sleep he haunts my dreams. I have told Gerald that I could not possibly receive him at Westerdale while Heaton's health is so poor. The slightest change in routine, the slightest echo of excitement upsets him. I have written that I am fearful he will only last another few days. I know Gerald will press me to leave Westerdale after Heaton's demise and go to Garstang Hall, and I will gladly comply with this if such a situation arises. But how can I vacate the only home my father-in-law has ever known and may return to very soon? No, until fate clarifies his death I will remain and Gerald must think what he likes.

NOVEMBER 26TH.

It is now three days since Heaton left and with every passing hour my hopes diminish and my heartache increases. This morning I woke to a squally snow shower which I believed would do more to bring him home than anything but when the flakes ceased and a watery sun broke through I was still alone. In spite of this the snow has settled and the moorland is studded with white in the first fall of the winter. Seeing this reminds me of childhood winters and I wish with all my heart that Gerald, Papa and I were settled at Garstang with Mama singing to us, as she used to before the consumption took her from us. How she coughed in the evenings and how pale her cheeks were, her hair at the temples soaked in sweat from her constant hacking. It is the same pallor and the same harsh, barking cough I have seen and heard in Heaton, his, brought on by neglect and the burning torment of his mind.

I half thought to go out this afternoon but the snow seemed so deep and my heart so sad I should probably get lost on the heath and sinking down under a drift be quite content to die. I must lift myself out of this apathy into which I have fallen and so I have opened a book and attempted to read. This occupation I gave up after ten minutes of sighing for the words meant nothing and at every crackle of flames or blast of wind I felt compelled to raise my head and distort the noises into footsteps.

How much longer I can conceal the truth from not only my brother's eyes but from my own too I know not. Still, I will not bar the windows or lock the doors; reason affirms he will not return but hope, optimism and every positive emotion in my soul deem it possible I shall wake up one morning and find he is home.

NOVEMBER 27TH.

Last night I was blessed by the mind numbing forces of fatigue and being convinced I could and would sleep I lit a taper and retired to bed early. A fresh covering of snow graced the landscape and as I pulled down the shutters it was still falling in resolute flakes that hit the glass with a muffled thud. Strangely that soothed and lulled me as I lay in bed and ere long I slept and began to dream vividly of him who haunted my inner self.

I remember I was lying in my old room at Garstang and though I could not see him I knew Papa slept peacefully in the next room and my brother in the room opposite mine. It was a bitter, blustery night and heavy flakes of snow hurled themselves at my window, falling faster and faster until they obscured the glass. A cold wind blew under the door and rattled the lattice so that for a time sleep eluded me. Then, slowly, I drifted into a light doze from which I was aroused by a plaintive but repetitive sound. I sat up, suddenly wide awake. There – it came again. A light, gentle tapping at my window, slowly getting louder and more urgent. Then, at last, a voice wailed,

"Let me in! Let me in! I am Heaton Grimshaw and I've lost my way on the moor in all this snow!"

"Wait a minute then!" cried I, swiftly rising.

Heaton began to bang on the window and ere long I heard the glass cracking under his blows. Throwing open the curtains and lattice I was blown back by the huge tumult of wind and snow that whirled in and around me.

Out of the darkness Heaton's face appeared, pale and trembling with a little blood trickling from the corner of his mouth. He clung to my windowsill and cried,

"Let me in! Let me in! I've been lost on the moors for three days! Three days – and oh what nights and now – this!"

I grabbed Heaton's arm and attempted to pull him up but he was far too heavy and I cried aloud for help. At last my screams brought Papa in and also my brother.

"It's Heaton Grimshaw!" I yelled. "Help me save him. He's been wandering in the snow for days."

But Papa and Gerald stared at me in horror and refused to help.

"Mr Grimshaw," shouted Papa, whilst I struggled still to pull Heaton up. "What is your business here and what in the Devil's name do you mean by waking us at this hour? Rachel – I order you to release his arm! Let him go!"

"No, no!" yelled Heaton. "Do not release me. Help me! Let me in! I've not eaten for three days or drunk!"

"I won't let him go!" I cried to Papa as he tried to pull me away from the window. "Do you not perceive he is dying and that his blood will taint you if you persist in this heartlessness? Leave me alone if you will not help me. I'll do it alone!" And I pulled with all my might.

But Gerald stepped forward and began wrenching Heaton's hand from mine and between him and Papa slowly but surely Heaton's grasp loosened. He began screaming for mercy but Papa was adamant and pushed him brutally off the windowsill. I heard the thud of his body falling and I began screaming and screaming until everything whirled round in a blur of blood and snow and white faces.

I sat up in my own room in Westerdale, shivering and sweating with fear at my dream. Lying down I endeavoured to still my violently beating heart but to no avail. It would not be silenced and after a few minutes I rose and dressed myself though I knew the hour to be but three or four.

Downstairs all was as silent and cold as the grave. I rekindled the fire and sitting down by it I attempted to read in order to suppress further reflections on my dream but the same line of words stayed before my eyes and my mind was far away.

Dawn at length crept in silently, revealing a cloud filled sky from which the snow continued to fall in heavy flakes. The ground was deeply covered and the thick carpet was disturbed only by the tracks of birds and small animals.

About midday it grew very quiet; the wind dropped and the snow, which had melted into sleet, ceased completely. A small break appeared in the universal grey sky through which a weird violet light shone, veiling the moorland in a mauve splendour. I believed it was a warning of further inclement weather; the onset of a blizzard or great storm possibly. But gradually the purple light faded and by two o'clock the air was once more alive with white flakes, whirling madly in the rising wind. How far away did that midday lull seem now! I shivered and placed another log on the shifting fire, trying to dispel pictures of Heaton lying, stark and cold, in the deepening snow. Not even my favourite novels could win me, so sick and sad did I find their characters!

This evening finds me indulging in the same joyless preoccupations. How weary I am, not only of loneliness, books and cold but of life too! Would that I were safe in the next world where there is no grief or tears and certainly no books to lie to us about the sweetness of life!

NOVEMBER 28TH.

He is back! I cannot fully comprehend this as yet as he is such an altered man that I am all amazement at his newly found goodness. He has spoken freely in kind tones but nothing will induce him to tell me where he has been and how he has spent his time.

Last night I felt myself falling into a morbidly low mood with depressed spirits and pounding head. This state I attributed to poor diet, biting cold and the all pervading loneliness of my situation. By seven o'clock I was worn out, sickly and peeved by my throbbing head that luckily prevented further inward reflections. Scarcely knowing what I did, I slipped into a restless doze which turned into a much longer sleep.

The first thing I became aware of was a prolonged banging, then the click of doors and finally the unsteady ring of footsteps approaching me. A hand reached out in the darkness to touch me and starting up instantly, in the apprehension of it being a thief or vagabond, I seized a candle and thrust it into the fading fire. A comforting refulgence spread through the air, revealing dark satanic features that were not unknown to me.

"What?" cried I, my throat almost strangled with the swell of my heart. "Is it really you, Father and not your wretched ghost sent here to haunt me for my wickedness?"

I placed the candle upon the table as my hand was shaking considerably and drops of wax beaded my gown. Turning to face him I put out my hand but he grabbed me and flung his arms about me, crushing me so intensely I could hardly breathe.

"O Rachel – O my God! I have been a fool and the suffering I metered out is nothing to the suffering I have been through since I left you!"

"Where have you been?" cried I, struggling for air. "You have been gone for days."

He let me go upon hearing this and stared in surprise, his lips twitching. Snow covered his hair and clothes, thick white flakes starting to melt in the gentle heat from the dying fire. Water ran like tears down his grimy face and his cheeks were hollow and wasted. His eyes were dull and bloodshot, black stubble covered his chin but his thick, dark hair was as profuse as ever and fell over his face in matted confusion. He half turned away as though my words had wounded him.

"Can you tell me where you have been?" cried I, again.

"No, no," shuddered he, taking my arm and drawing me to a seat by the fire. "O Rachel – why are you still here? After all I have put you through? Yet, you are not lost to me. I scarcely knew the passage of time – the transformation of day to night – it seemed perpetual darkness to me, inhabited by shadows of men I had once wronged! I cannot tell you where I went or what I did – God, that I drive you away now! It's too much! My sole reason for returning was because I knew Westerdale lay as empty and idle as in my dream. A desolate wind told me all hope was extinguished and there was no chance I would ever behold you in this life. I have given you more than enough reason to hate me. No, said the zephyr, she has left you. She has gone. And the gale

247

rose up and taunted me; "She will return no more in your lifetime which is nearly over!" At this I fell into the snow and sweated tears of blood. I felt composed. "Ah! If she is gone," I told the wind, "'then I'll have reason enough for dying'."

"I don't understand you!" cried I, mystified. "Father – is it that you wish me to leave?"

"No, no," sobbed he, drawing me closer. "For myself I would always have you near me; more so now that the shadow of what is approaching creeps closer. But to you and your brother I am an evil man. I have done both you and Gerald a terrible wrong. I am greatly changed, Rachel, greatly changed. I am no more the man that walked out into the misty darkness – when was it – three nights ago? No – the reckoning has fallen upon me. The images that haunted me have fled. I have reconciled my wife to heaven and my son to – wherever the lost souls cry out and gnash their teeth in agony! O God be merciful to Hardy! I have known that agony and it has blinded me to the goodness that dwelt around me. So, why do you not look at me with angry eyes? Why do you not say, "I could have loved you as a father, Heaton, aye, in the beginning I could but your evil has hardened my heart and your sufferings now are nothing to me. Your death will scarcely be mourned."

"I will never leave you," wept I, amazed at the change in him.

At this he grew strangely agitated and this caused a severe coughing fit that racked his weak frame so strongly that he appeared to swoon. In vain did I protest about his wet clothing; he would not remove it and at length I made up the fire as it was the only way to dry him. I begged leave to send for a doctor but he would not permit it. He was, he affirmed, very happy and that no medicine in the world could produce the effects he felt now. By and by it grew lighter and I beseeched him to eat which he agreed to do, partaking of a little food with great relish. The spasms of coughing were becoming more frequent and though I maintained he would be better moved to his bed he affirmed he could not be any more comfortable.

"No blankets on earth could bring me the softness or warmth I presently feel in my soul," he murmured. He seemed to smile and rambled on when his breath allowed of all the things he meant to do in the spring.

"We shall buy a fine carriage," whispered he. "With a pair of grey horses to pull it and you shall choose a new gown – the finest I can afford. As for Gerald and Errin – they must..." but I bid him think no more of my brother or his daughter but try to sleep while I perform my duties.

"No, don't leave me," begged he, so earnestly that I could not but comply and I readily agreed to stay until he was asleep whereupon I tiptoed quietly away.

NOVEMBER 29TH.

I wish I could record that Mr Grimshaw is better today but, alas, he is not. His fever is still very high and his cough takes every bit of his breath away. I hope if he maintains his food intake for another day he will quite overcome this chill and, having plenty now to live for, will fight to survive. Last night he wished to talk to me of something that troubled him and though I begged him to save his breath he persisted in conversation.

"Rachel," affirmed he. "I have been a very wicked man and have hurt everyone that crossed my path. Both my wife and son are dead, my daughter lost to me and you are the only thing left - sent by providence to ease my pains. My wickedness is now at an end and if I should be spared my remaining years shall be devoted to good works. I would like to meet your brother, to have my Errin step across the threshold of Westerdale with a light heart."

"You shall be spared," affirmed I, for I truly believed it. "But I will listen to no more talk tonight and if you start conversing again I will leave you entirely."

He smiled at this and I, certain now of his slow but complete recovery, lulled him to sleep with a song Mama sang to me – O so many years ago. I fear he slumbered badly for I woke many times to his racking cough and the tragic groans of his dreams.

Today, however, he seems passably quiet – a blessing not lightly bestowed after his distress of the past weeks. In his present mood he is a gentle and endearing patient. I have just made some porridge and toast which will be his third meal after God knows how many days of fasting and I fear his stomach will be so shrunken I must take great care not to overfill it. Already I can perceive the good effects this welcome food is having upon his constitution; his eye is brighter and his cheeks have a vague colour.

This morning passed away pleasantly enough; I kneaded the bread and swept the hearth but in all my duties scarcely left the kitchen so my nurse's eye was always upon him. He said very little and though he never expressed gratitude I felt that emotion was always present and I had only to stoke the fire or refold his blankets and some of it would come tumbling over me.

In the evening I enquired if I should read to him in order to help the long winter darkness dispel a little. Another bitter shower of snow defiled the moorland and a weary wind blew down the chimney and danced among the flames. Heaton affirmed that he would enjoy that and left the choice of book to me, whereupon I reached down a volume of verse and choosing several that I deemed suitable I began to read. At first he seemed engrossed in my words, but after half an hour or so of reading I realised he was not listening. His whole attention was on the window behind me, one pane of which I had boarded up to prevent the plaintive howl of wind. The other pane, though, was naked and at this he stared, transfixed, his eyes widening, the flare of his nostrils portraying horror and shock.

"What is it?" cried I, putting down my book and raising my eyes. "Father – what do you see?"

"A blurred face," whispered he, attempting to rise and becoming furious when he could not.

I bade him remain where he was and rising myself went over to the window. Outside I could see the whitened moorland and the bleak landscape melting into a colourless sky which was a whirl of snow and sleet. My eyes searched the scenery but apart from the grim outline of the gravestone, rising dark and erect in a sea of pallor, I could make out nothing at all. I turned back.

"You are mistaken," cried I. "There is no one there, Father. Your eyes deceive you. It is the fever that weakens you and makes you susceptible to visual images. Your imagination is sorely out of joint and your nerves must be affected likewise."

"No," gasped he, shaking his head. "I saw a face – one which is known to me although I thought it was back in the grave. Why has it suddenly risen? Was it really dead? O God – that cannot be! I killed it – I shot it! Why are its eyes like HERS! I thought her torture was over!"

He gabbled on in such a way for several minutes and perceiving he still fixed his wild eyes on the window I brought down the shutter in order to end his panic.

He would not be quiet, however, and affirmed it was out there still.

"But I have drawn the blinds, Father, " soothed I. "And it has gone away and will haunt you no more."

"It will come into the room!" screamed he, falling forward onto his knees, beseechingly. "If it does not see me it'll come looking and I can't stand that."

I bade him compose himself. He was acting ridiculously and sobbing hysterically. I guided him back to his chair and threw the dislodged rugs over his quaking form.

I resumed my reading but even that failed to pacify him and ere long I ceased and murmured since he was so inattentive I would leave him and retire to bed.

"Don't go!" cried he as I rose to carry out my plan. "Please don't go. When you are gone it may come in and I shall be all alone."

But I was tired of his feverish ramblings and told him that unless he remained silent and tried to sleep I would leave him. At this his face grew dark, but he conquered his emotional fears and at length closed his eyes.

It is now past ten o'clock and I have watched over him this past hour whilst writing this. Occasionally he groans in his sleep and several times he has coughed but otherwise he seems peaceful and so much better that I shall leave him now with hopes of a full recovery.

NOVEMBER 30TH.

At last I am enjoying the comfort of a contented heart and an easy mind which manifest themselves in a full night of uninterrupted sleep. This morning I feel so refreshed that I shall ask Heaton for permission to take a walk upon the moorland to breathe the cold, clear air. He is certainly well enough to be left now and has just consumed a light yet nourishing breakfast.

The day is delightful! The snow ceased in the night and a watery sun graced the firmament, already powerful enough to melt the frozen water so, from my window, vague patches of green swell appear in between drifts of white.

When asked my father-in-law gave permission to my walking out on Heldon as long as I did not leave him for too long. He hoped it would put new colour into cheeks that were ghastly pale and he feared that I was sickening for something. I eased his mind immediately – I had no feelings of illness and, indeed I had never felt happier.

"It is entirely due to your homecoming, Heaton!" breathed I, throwing on my cloak. "Before I seemed certain to lose you but your change has invigorated me. You were steadily sliding into death but now how swiftly you turn away from it and pace the road to recovery! That, alone, gives me joy!"

He said nothing to this but only shook his head as though mistrustful of my words. I kissed him fondly, donned my bonnet and quit the house. I went in a carefree way and looked upon everything with a loving and approving eye. Climbing the tiny hillocks the air was so pure and cold it revived my stagnant lungs. How I wished Heaton could consume this sweetness!

Two miles of fast walking only strengthened my resolution for exercise and the sky gleamed as blue as in summer. No wind broke the calm surface of the heath and it seemed winter had fled, temporarily, and November had turned into May. A few strange birds, doubtless visitors from other lands, graced the stunted bushes or fed on the thawed greenery.

Ere long it began to grow darker and a violet light defiled the west, announcing the approach of dusk. At this omen I turned back and was beginning to retrace my steps when a small brown horse came into view. I recognised its rider at once and she called out that I might stop and spare her a moment's conversation. I paused, let the horse draw closer and after assisting its rider to dismount I gave her a big hug, giving earnest enquiries for her health.

"I am well," replied Errin. "And your brother likewise though your letters have saddened and troubled him. Is is really likely Father will die?"

"Until today I would have said so," murmured I. "But he is much improved and taking nourishment three times a day. His hunger is increasing and I am led to believe he will make a full recovery. His mind still wanders but he is calmer and his fever diminished."

"And his cough?" she enquired, evidently having read the details of my letters.

"It still troubles him a great deal," I replied, frankly. "But it is no worse – oh no – of that I am sure and with increasing vigour from a plentiful diet it will recede."

She professed herself glad to hear that.

"For although I cannot love him," she murmured. "He is my father and for that I am concerned for him."

I thought she seemed taller than last time I saw her and plumper too, her frame doubtlessly filling out with her comfortable style of living. Her hair was longer and thicker but her brown eyes were as soft as ever.

"You seem pale and listless," she affirmed. "How wan your cheeks are and how thin your frame. Have you had a very hard time?"

"It has, upon occasions, been difficult," I replied. "But I am certain that the worst of my problems are over and Heaton has changed so radically you would not recognise him. His evil ways are past and a new found gentleness pervades his being. He smiles and laughs and has plans for the spring that include you and Gerald. But he does not like me to be long from his side and as I have been gone for over an hour I must return to him."

"Your words amaze me," she replied, rather mistrustfully. "And I would certainly like to hear more. Come – get up behind me and Lucinda will take us to Garstang."

In vain I protested and reaffirmed my intentions to return home.

"No," said she. "I will not take second place to Heaton! If he has spared you for one hour he can surely spare you for another and, besides, if he has improved, you will have days, months and years to be together. I am very weary, too, for Gerald has gone to Laxingham on business and will not return till tomorrow." I was persuaded and mounting her horse enjoyed a gentle canter over the moor until we descended the decline that led to the stable yards of Garstang.

How vividly did its outline bring back my dream to haunt me! I yearned to be inside, too. And yet some part of me felt repelled. Here I had spent all my happiest childhood hours and from its dour protection had I been whisked away by an imprudent marriage. How familiar did every nook and cranny seem now!

We dismounted in the stable yard and despatched the horse to Gerald's osier, then mounted the steps and entered the back door. The kitchen and scullery had seen only slight alterations, remaining largely as I remembered them in my girlhood. I would have stayed longer and lingered over familiar haunts but Errin, eager to return to the fireside, coaxed me into the hallway and on into the parlour.

An immense blaze lit the hearth and dispelled the dark shadows. Errin called to her maid to light the candles and bring two chairs close to the fire.

"And, Prudence," affirmed she. "Bring us some cake and tea. Plenty, too, as we've been riding on the moors and Mrs Grimshaw has walked far."

I protested at this and said I could stay but a few minutes but Errin brushed my words aside and went on to question me about the change in Heaton. This I answered gladly as I enjoyed illuminating a pleasant side of his character. I became completely engrossed in my words and whilst outwardly consuming tea and cake, inwardly I was desperately trying to destroy the old image of Heaton and place a fresh one in my heart.

Time ticked by, the twilight deepened into darkness and a heavy wind arose bringing with it squally showers that rattled against the window panes. Realisation hit me and I was moved to look at the time. It was past seven o'clock and I jumped up in horror at my delay in setting out for home. I bade Errin call the maid to fetch my cloak.

The maid was called but she affirmed it was pouring profusely and thundering too. In vain hope that she was mistaken I approached the window. The night was so black that, at first, I could see nothing, but after a moment or two I saw the heavens split in golden sulphur and then a heart rending crash hit my ears. The window was blurred with heavy rain.

Errin bade me to calm down – the storm would soon blow over but in case the tempest kept me marooned here I noticed she ordered her maid to lay another place for dinner. When I heard this I became distressed.

"Is there no way I can get home?" wailed I, as the thunder rumbled loudly and lightening split the heavens. "Mr Grimshaw will be out of his head with worry and think me drowned in a bog hole."

"Indeed, so you will be if you venture out on such a night," said my hostess, not unkindly.

"What am I to do then?" I cried. "For I must get home tonight! Is there no carriage I can borrow?"

"Alas, no. Gerald has taken the phaeton to Laxingham."

"Then can I not take a horse?"

"But they would be uncontrollable in such weather. There is no other way, Rachel. You must remain till it blows over."

At this I sank despairingly into my seat and repeated my comments on Heaton's frenzy at my absence.

"He will know you have taken shelter," replied Errin. "Never fear, Rachel, I will tell the maid to serve dinner early so that you may be ready to go if a lull occurs."

But I could eat little dinner and my mind wandered constantly to the kitchen at Westerdale. After the meal Errin sat reading by the fire and I stood by the window watching for a lull, whereupon I should be off at once. Errin watched me anxiously but made no comments and as I seemed preoccupied with my inner reflections she took solace in her book and left me in peace.

NOVEMBER 31ST.

It was after midnight before Errin, evidently having finished her book, shut it up and laying it down yawned wearily and remarked how late it was. Only then did I turn from my silent vigil and throwing up my hands in despair, prayed for help.

The storm showed no signs of easing; in fact it seemed to get stronger as the night wore on. My cousin ignored my pleas to return home on foot, which I was now prepared to do. In vain did I entreat; she stood firm and pronounced the walk would be my death.

"Dearest Rachel!" cried she, in mock horror at my proposed journey. "By no means will I allow any such thing. Were your brother here he would forbid it too. I shall get the spare room prepared for you so you can retire there for the rest of the night.